DEMON FLYER

JOHN RUST

SEVERED PRESS

HOBART TASMANIA

DEMON FLYER

This book is dedicated to my father, John George Rust (1941-2019). I cannot thank you enough for all the love and support you have given me my whole life. I am blessed to have had a Dad like you.

ONE

"Pathetic. Just fucking pathetic."

Asnawi Adsit scowled and shook his head at the pile of fish flopping around the deck of his boat. Little scads and fringscale sardines. Not even a hundred pounds worth. Worst of all, not a snapper among them, one of the most sought-after fish in the Java Sea.

But it had been nearly two weeks since he caught any. No snappers meant less money to bring home to his family.

Adsit grunted and looked up at his two crewmen, Slamet and Bagas, who stretched out a tarp to cover the catch. "Put out the nets again. This time we'll head northeast."

"But it's almost dark." The young, lanky Bagas nodded toward the distance. The sun just skimmed the horizon, creating orange and blue hues in the dusk sky.

Face scrunched, Adsit stomped toward Bagas. The teen swallowed, his gaze dropping to the tarp. "Is that the excuse you will take back to your family? That you could not help support them because it got dark? We need every rupiah we can get. So we keep fishing."

"Things would not be so bad if it was not for that oil spill," grumbled the muscular Slamet as he lay the tarp on top of the fish.

"Yes, but complaining about it will not change anything. We must do what we can. Now store these fish, then put out the nets again."

After putting the fish on ice below deck, Adsit took the wheel and pointed his boat northeast. His hands flexed on the wheel, his compact body tensing as he stared out at the rolling waves. Like Slamet, he also worried about the large portion of the Java Sea affected by the oil spill. Unlike him, he did not voice those concerns.

Idiots! Stupid, careless shits. Even two months after the accident, he still couldn't believe an oil tanker and a container ship could collide. It didn't matter that it happened at night. Those ships had all manner of instruments to prevent accidents. It came down to the competence – or lack thereof – of the crews.

And because of it, all fishermen in this part of Indonesia suffered.

Yes, the oil spill had been cleaned up, mostly. But how many fish died because of it? How many fled to other parts of the sea? The company that owned the tanker said it would help those affected by the disaster. Well, Adsit had yet to see any help from them. He doubted he ever would.

He looked out the open door of the pilothouse. Bagas and Slamet watched the net trailing behind the boat. Adsit always made sure to keep an eye on those two. Neither were the most skilled fishermen he'd ever worked with. Then again, finding good people had grown difficult over the years. Too many of the young had no desire to do this job. Why work on a smelly, bobbing boat when they could live in a big city like Jakarta or Semarang?

They will think differently when there is no one left to catch the fish they eat.

Those who did want to fish sought out the larger fisheries, like his two eldest sons. Adsit scowled at the thought. How many fish, how many rupiah had those companies cost him and his family? And now they built that damn harbor and processing plant south of his village.

Have they not taken enough fish and enough crew from us?

Darkness fell over the Java Sea. Adsit ordered Bagas to turn on the boat's sole spotlight to alert any nearby boats of their presence. He ate a sandwich and drank tea from his thermos, trolling one part of the sea, then another.

He'd just finished his sandwich when the boat slowed. He straightened, aware of the ever-increasing drag. His chest heaved with excitement. A big catch.

Adsit hurried out of the pilothouse, then stopped. Something in the night sky caught his eye. A green light.

He cranked an eyebrow. An airplane? No, too low and too small.

The light faded into nothingness.

Adsit continued aft. He'd seen his share of weird lights in the sky during his more than twenty years at sea. So long as they didn't interfere with his fishing, he didn't care what they were.

He helped Bagas and Slamet reel in the net. A wave of fish spilled out from it, covering the deck.

"Wow," blurted Bagas. "Look at them all."

Adsit indeed looked at them. Snappers. Lots and lots of them. Fish the big companies would not get their hands on.

He spun around to his two crewmen, arms outstretched. "You see. If we had gone back home because it was dark, we would not have had such a catch."

Both men nodded.

Adsit smiled wide, catching sight of the small green light again. He ignored it. They needed to get these fish on ice quickly.

Adsit slid down the hatch below deck, the storage area with its piles of ice next to him. Bagas handed fish to Slamet, who handed them down to Adsit, who tossed them onto the ice.

"Come on! Faster!" he urged them on. Fish began to rot the moment they died. They needed to get them in storage and keep them cool to maintain their freshness and fetch a higher price at market.

Just from the feel of them, Adsit could tell they were fully grown. Between 20 to 25 pounds each. This would help –

Something thumped the boat, knocking it to starboard. Adsit slipped and fell. A bolt of pain shot through his ass and leg.

"What the hell was that?"

He barely finished his last word when screams erupted from the deck.

Concern flashed through Adsit. Had there been a shark hidden among the catch? Surely they would have found it before now.

The screams grew louder. Not screams of surprise, but of terror.

Heart pounding, Adsit scrambled to his feet. Another thump rippled through the deck. Someone had fallen.

He took a couple of steps up the ladder and peeked through the open hatch. Fear paralyzed him.

Something large crouched on the deck. Something with wings, and a huge beak that tore into Bagas.

Slamet thrust a boat hook at the creature. It jerked, rearing back its beak. No, not a beak. More like a snout, like that of a crocodile. It let out a throaty, warbling cry. Pieces of flesh and intestine fell from its slender jaws. Pieces of Bagas.

Adsit shivered. He took a shaky breath as Slamet stabbed the beast again. He tried to suppress his fright. This was his boat, and he was captain. He had to help Slamet kill this . . . thing.

Adsit took another step up the ladder.

Something *whooshed* overhead. Another large, winged creature knocked Slamet to the deck. With wide eyes, Adsit watched its jaws rip open the man's chest. His scream turned into a blood-choked gurgle.

Eyes shut, Adsit slid down the ladder and scrambled through the narrow, wooden passage. His stomach twisted into a painful, fiery knot. Bagas's and Slamet's screams still echoed in his ears. He imagined those snouts tearing into him, killing him.

A whimper nearly escaped his throat. Terror threatened to wash over him. He had to fight it off, be a captain. And when a captain's boat was in trouble, he had to call for help.

Adsit climbed the ladder to the pilothouse. He checked aft. The bird monsters continued to tear into the corpses of his crew. He tried to swallow through his tightened throat, but couldn't.

Allah have mercy on them.

He snatched the mike from his old radio set.

"Mayday. Mayday. This is the *Gita*. We are . . ." He scrunched his face and gripped the mike tighter, trying to figure out his position and not think about being eaten. "We are one hundred miles northeast of Pulau Madura. Our boat is being attacked --"

Something slammed into his shoulder. Bones snapped. Adsit cried out as blades of pain raced up and down his arm. He fell to the deck, clutching his left shoulder, screaming. Through the slits of his eyes, he saw an enormous snout plunge through the entry of the pilothouse.

No!

Jaws clamped down on his leg. Adsit screamed louder as the creature dragged him outside.

TWO

Jack Rastun drummed his fingers against his knee as the SUV pulled into the parking lot. *Keep your anger in check*, he told himself. Try to keep emotion out of it.

It would be a miracle if he could follow his own advice.

The vehicle jerked to a halt. Karen Thatcher sat in the driver's seat, staring straight ahead, flexing her hands on the wheel.

"You ready?" he asked.

She turned to him, her smooth, round face stiff. She exhaled, her lean body relaxing, somewhat. "Yeah."

Karen shoved open the door and slid out. "Remember," she said over her shoulder. "Keep your wiseass comments to yourself, and for God's sake, don't insult anyone."

"I got the message the last four times you told me."

"Well I don't want to make this worse than it already is," Karen snapped.

Rastun was about to respond, but kept his mouth shut. He didn't want to start an argument with Karen, not in the parking lot of her daughter's school. They needed to present a united front.

He walked with purpose toward the two-story red brick building. The sign mounted on the overhang above the front entrance read ROSE HILL MIDDLE SCHOOL.

Karen strode a few steps ahead of him, unsmiling, her gaze locked on the double doors. Rastun wondered if his fiancée could keep from going off on anyone. He couldn't blame her if she did. After what Emily had told them . . .

They walked down the tiled hallway to the main office. A round-faced girl with dark brown hair sat in one of the chairs in the waiting area. She smiled when Rastun and Karen entered. Not the brightest of smiles, he noted.

"Hey, Mom. Jack."

"Hey, sweetie." Karen rubbed her daughter's shoulder. "You okay?"

"Mm-hmm." She nodded. The smile faded. Emily's gaze fell to the floor.

"It's gonna be okay, kiddo," Rastun reassured her. "We'll straighten this out."

"I hope so," she replied without looking at him.

The sight made him madder, invoking memories from two days ago when Emily told him and Karen everything her social studies teacher had said and done.

The receptionist led them to the principal's office. Behind the desk sat a smartly dressed, portly woman with cocoa skin and coiffed hair. Seated in one of the chairs to Rastun's left was a woman with short brown hair and glasses. Her face scrunched, her eyes forming into angry slits. Rastun suppressed a grunt of bemusement. Did this woman think she could intimidate them with a glare?

"Miss Thatcher. Mister Rastun. Emily." Principal Debra Theobald stood and shook their hands. "Thank you for coming."

"Considering what my daughter told us, I don't think we had much choice."

Rastun glanced at Karen. Apparently, there wasn't much room for typical pleasantries in this meeting.

Fine by me.

"Uh-huh," Theobald muttered.

Once everyone took their seats, the principal smoothed out her suit jacket. "So you know, I was talking with Miss Popovich," she nodded at the other woman. "She feels Emily is exaggerating the situation in order to get out of her detention."

"But I'm not," Emily blurted.

"Emily." Karen put a gentle hand on her daughter's shoulder, then looked back at Theobald. "I really have a hard time believing that Emily is exaggerating one of her teachers calling us murderers and claiming she'll grow up to be a horrible person." She said the last few words with a sharpened tone.

"Well . . ." Theobald held up her palms. "Perhaps Miss Popovich should have chosen her words better. But I sympathize with her concern that Emily is in a household with an atmosphere of violence."

Rastun's eyes widened. Shock overwhelmed his anger. What the hell? Did she think they were beating Emily?

He started to open his mouth, but Karen beat him to it. "Excuse me? An 'atmosphere of violence.'? I do not abuse my daughter, and neither does Jack."

"I'm not talking about physical abuse," Popovich chimed in. "I'm talking about your jobs. You go around the country claiming to protect cryptids, but wind up shooting them and anyone who gets in your way."

"We only shoot cryptids that pose a clear and present danger to ourselves or others." Rastun managed to keep his tone even. "As for the people who got in our way, they were psychopaths who tried to kill us."

Popovich snorted, crossing her arms.

Yup. One of those who won't let facts stand in the way of their version of reality.

"Our school has a zero-tolerance policy when it comes to violence," said Theobald. "That's probably where Miss Popovich's concern comes from."

"Name one time Emily has ever been violent in school." Rastun stabbed his index finger at the ceiling.

"She could become violent the longer she's around you two," Popovich said curtly.

"That's ridiculous," Karen snapped. "Where do you get off even suggesting that?"

The teacher let out a gasp of disbelief. "Where? Really? You commit genocide in South Carolina and you ask me that question?"

Lines dug into Rastun's face. There it was. The crux of their problem with Popovich. The lizard men expedition last summer. Popovich didn't like the fact the FUBI had killed most of the creatures and felt justified taking her anger out on Emily.

His phone vibrated against his hip. Rastun ignored it. He had more important matters to deal with.

"That's bullcrap," Karen shot back. "The lizard men killed several people and threatened everyone in Lee County. We had no choice but to do what we did."

"Please." Popovich practically spat out the word. "Your fiancé was in the Army. He just likes killing things, and apparently, he's gotten you to think the same way. I'm not going to stand by and let Emily or any other student be taught that murdering endangered species is fun."

Rastun tilted his head, brow furrowed. How the hell did a whackjob like this become a teacher? "If you really think I enjoyed anything that happened in South Carolina, you are deluded."

His jaw tightened, remembering his promise to Karen not to throw out insults. He glanced back at her. She aimed a harsh glare at Popovich. Either the jab hadn't registered with her – which he doubted – or she was so mad at this dumbass teacher she didn't care.

Principal Theobald, however, didn't let it pass. "Mister Rastun, there is no need to make disparaging remarks about one of my teachers."

"But you're fine with one of your teachers making disparaging remarks about us to Emily." Karen's voice shot up. "And you're fine with her giving my daughter a bad grade just because she doesn't like us."

"If this is about Emily's report on the structure of government," said Popovich, "I gave her a fair grade."

"You can really say that?" Karen pulled a few pieces of paper from her purse and slapped them down on the principal's desk. "Jack and I read it over. It's a good report and deserves a lot better than a D."

The skin around Popovich's nose crinkled. "That's what any parent would say. And how many years of experience in the education field do you have, Miss Thatcher?"

Karen's face reddened. Emily's mouth fell open. Rastun's hands practically crushed the armrests of his chair, his rage reaching Krakatoa proportions. The arrogance of this woman astounded him.

He was about to say something, but again, Karen beat him to it.

"This is how you let your teachers speak to people?" She leaned forward in her chair, her burning gaze directed at Theobald. "You let them intimidate twelve-year-old girls and punish them because they don't like what we do for a living?"

"Miss Thatcher, please lower your voice." Theobald's tone was calm yet firm. "I try not to interfere with my teachers when it comes to grades and discipline. I have faith in them to make the right decisions. If Miss Popovich felt your daughter's assignment deserved a D, then I stand by her. As for punishment, Emily did tell Miss Popovich to shut up."

"Only because she was constantly running us down in front of her." Karen threw up her arms. "How long was Emily supposed to take that?"

"Regardless of the circumstances, we cannot allow that sort of disrespect to go unpunished," said Theobald.

"Then how about put Emily in a different social studies class so that 'disrespect' doesn't happen again?"

Theobald frowned, not a sincere one, Rastun thought.

"I'm sorry, Miss Thatcher, but due to scheduling and class sizes, that won't be possible."

Rastun shook his head. He'd had enough of this damn principal. She just found ways to spin this, maybe because she thought having a crazy hag like Popovich in her school would reflect poorly on her. Or maybe Theobald agreed with the teacher's opinion of him and Karen.

He turned to Karen. "I don't think we're going to get anywhere here. Looks like it's time to kick this upstairs. Take it to the school board. Heck, maybe just go right to the superintendent."

"It will be your word against that of a teacher with twenty-plus years of experience," said Theobald. "Plus, there's the matter of Emily's detention for disrespecting Miss Popovich, and all the media attention you've had in the past."

"What does that have to do with anything?" asked Rastun.

"The sea raptor, the lizard men. They've made you both celebrities. The school board and the superintendent may feel you're only doing this to seek attention and keep your names in the news."

Rastun gritted his teeth. Theobald wasn't just siding with her teacher. She was trying to sweep this whole issue under the rug. Make sure her school didn't look bad.

Make sure *she* didn't look bad.

"You're right," said Karen. "We are celebrities, which means we've been interviewed plenty of times. And some of the people who've interviewed us like us a lot. I think they'd be interested to hear how one of your teachers has been treating my daughter."

Rastun turned to her. Karen gave him a sideways glance, a glint in her eye. He grinned, knowing where she was going with this.

"Yeah," he said. "Some of those interviewers, they love doing stories about teachers bullying students who have a different point of view. Or in this case, who don't approve of the profession of a family member. A story like that could be fodder for them for days."

"Jack is also a decorated Army veteran," Karen added. "The public doesn't like to see veterans disrespected."

Rastun leaned back, his smile growing. "I think Rose Hill Middle School is about to become famous, for all the wrong reasons."

Theobald clenched her fingers, staring down at her desk. Miss Popovich shifted in her seat, her expression sourer than before.

The principal's shoulders sagged. She raised her head, gazing at Rastun, Karen, and Emily. "Could you give Miss Popovich and I a few minutes?"

Rastun looked at Karen, who nodded. They left Theobald's office with Emily in tow, sitting in the lime green plastic chairs in the small waiting area.

Reaching for his phone, Rastun checked the screen to see it was Randy Ehrenberg who had called. He considered calling him back, but didn't want to be in the middle of talking to the cryptozoologist when Theobald and Popovich broke up their meeting. He'd wait until the situation with Emily and her teacher had been resolved.

He gazed at the door, thinking about Popovich's issues with him and Karen. Would he have liked it if the lizard men expedition ended with most of the creatures alive and tagged for further research? Of course. The job of the Foundation for Undocumented Biological Investigation was to protect and study cryptids. But the numerous attacks by the lizard men didn't give him much choice. Had he and his team not killed those beasts, more people would have died, probably him, Karen, and Ehrenberg included.

Hopefully there are more out there. But in the nine months since the expedition, no more lizard men had been sighted in Lee County.

The door to Principal Theobald's office opened. She and Miss Popovich walked over to them, a sneer marring the teacher's compact face.

"Miss Thatcher, Mister Rastun, Emily." Theobald forced a smile. "Miss Popovich has something to say."

Popovich's mouth slowly, almost reluctantly opened. "I would like to apologize to all of you for any defamatory comments I made. It was unprofessional of me to let my personal opinions influence the way I treat Emily. I'm sorry if she took offense to anything I said about you two."

Rastun gave a perfunctory nod, though given Popovich's deliberate tone, he doubted the woman meant the apology.

"That's all well and good." Karen folded her arms. "But can you assure us this won't happen again?"

Popovich's jaw stiffened for a moment. "It won't happen again."

"And the grade on her report?" asked Karen.

The teacher stared at the floor for a moment. "A B-minus is a fair grade." She spoke just above a whisper, clearly not happy.

"I've also reduced the number of days Emily will have to serve detention from five to two," said Theobald.

"What?" Emily blurted. "But she was saying all kinds of bad stuff about Mom and Jack."

"Perhaps." Theobald held up a hand, then turned her attention to Karen. "But we cannot have students yelling at teachers, regardless of the situation. That would undermine the authority of our faculty."

Karen let out a sharp breath, gazing to the side for a few seconds. She then looked at Emily. "Sorry, Em, but your principal is right."

"What? But --"

"Emily," Karen said in a stern tone.

Emily frowned and snapped her head to the left, deliberately not looking at her mother.

A minute later, Rastun, Karen, and Emily left the office.

"Well, score a win for the good guys," said Rastun.

"Yeah, but I still have to do detention. That sucks." Emily frowned.

"Hey." Karen looked down at her daughter, eyes narrowed. "We got your teacher to stop picking on you, *and* we got the grade on your report changed. Sometimes we don't get everything we want. That's life. And I'm still waiting for a 'thank you.'"

"Thank you." Emily sighed. "Jack, don't you think doing detention is unfair?"

"Sorry, kiddo. I gotta go with your principal on this one."

Emily let out an exasperated breath. "But Miss Popovich is a jerk."

"No argument there, but I dealt with a lot of officers in the Army who were jerks, and I certainly couldn't yell back at them. It comes down to the old adage, 'Respect the rank, not the person.'"

Emily's face scrunched, obviously unhappy he had not taken her side on this.

They piled into Karen's SUV. She started the engine as Rastun got out his phone and called back Ehrenberg. The cryptozoologist picked up on the third ring.

"Hey, Jack."

"Hey, Doc. I saw you called. Sorry I couldn't get back with you sooner. We were in a meeting with Emily's principal and one of her teachers."

"Well, I hope everything went well."

"Actually, it did. So what's up?"

"Question? Have you ever been to Indonesia?" Ehrenberg asked.

"Nope," answered Rastun. "That wasn't part of the Jack Rastun World Tour when I was in the Army."

"Well, that's about to change."

"What's in Indonesia that suddenly makes it interesting to us?"

"Pterosaurs." Ehrenberg paused for a beat. "Pterosaurs that have eaten some fishermen."

THREE

Rastun spotted two familiar figures as he pulled into the parking lot of FUBI headquarters. One of them, a mountain of a man with short dark hair and black horn-rimmed glasses, waved as Rastun pulled up next to the pair's SUV. The square-shaped logo on the vehicle's door read ASTER TECHNOLOGIES.

"Ready for an all-expense paid trip to Indonesia?" asked Rastun as he got out of his car.

A huge smile lit up the face of Wendell "Geek" Hewitt, Rastun's former NCO in the Army Rangers. "Exotic jungles, exotic food, killer prehistoric monsters. What's not to love?"

The two exchanged handshakes and slaps on the shoulder, with Geek's slap nearly knocking Rastun's arm out of his socket.

"I'm glad Aster's letting you go with us again." Karen gave Geek a hug.

"Are you kidding? The Foundation's turning into a gold mine for us. The way our Aster Seven dart guns and those poison darts worked in South Carolina, we got a big order from the Pentagon. Some of the NATO countries and South Korea are also interested in them, along with our Flapjack drones. Field testing with you guys is putting money in our pockets as well as yours." Geek referred to the deal worked out by Roland Parker, the FUBI's billionaire benefactor. The Foundation received a bonus if any hardware Aster field-tested with them got picked up by the military or law enforcement.

The Golden Poison Frog darts, however, worked too well. Their sale to various special ops units sparked loud, hysterical claims from politicians, the press, and the social media outrage mob that the FUBI was a para-military group. Boycotts had been threatened against Aster, forcing its CEO to issue a new policy that the FUBI could only have the darts in the most dire of situations.

Rastun wondered how many people had to die before a situation was deemed "dire."

"I had to look up this Ropen thing on Wikipedia," said the dark-haired, stocky woman next to Geek. "So now we've got flying dinosaurs out there?"

"Technically," Rastun raised a finger, "pterosaurs, if that's what the Ropen are, are not dinosaurs. They're just reptiles. At least, that's what Randy told me."

Alana Kurowski, Geek's assistant, shrugged. "Well, they look like dinosaurs to me."

"Yeah," Geek said as the group started toward the six-story, glass office building that housed FUBI headquarters. "I've never heard of these Ropens either until last night. How many different cryptids are there?"

"Lots," Karen answered. "Randy does a cryptid recognition class each week. He's been doing it for nearly two years and we still haven't covered every cryptid out there."

Alana huffed. "I never knew there was so much weird shit in the world."

"No." Rastun stepped onto the walkway. "Weird shit would be investigating UFOs and ghosts. These are simply animals that haven't been officially documented."

"Yeah, and they all want to kill us."

Rastun found it hard to argue with Alana. While Sasquatch tended to shy away from people, sea raptors and lizard men did not. Far from it. And creatures like the Chupacabra, Mothman, and the Beast of Bray Road – if they existed – did not seem the sort to enjoy belly rubs.

The four passed the decorative wood carvings of Sasquatch and lake monsters that lined the concrete path leading to the glass doors. They went inside and walked by the horseshoe-shaped reception desk in the spacious lobby and took the stairs to the fourth floor.

They entered the conference room, set up like a smaller version of a college lecture hall. A lean, bearded man in a Hawaiian shirt stood near the stage, along with a thick man with bronze skin and dark hair tied in a ponytail. Dr. Randy Ehrenberg and FUBI Director Edward Lynch. They spoke to a middle-aged Asian man who wore a bland dark suit and plain red tie. Rastun didn't recognize him, but he had the air of a bureaucrat.

Ehrenberg and Lynch greeted them, with the director aiming a hand at the Asian man.

"This is Dian Purnomo, Indonesia's Ambassador to the United States. Mister Ambassador, Jack Rastun, Karen Thatcher, Wendell Hewitt, and Alana Kurowski."

Rastun stiffened, about to come to attention, then stopped. Three years a civilian and he still sometimes had trouble suppressing all the discipline and protocol drilled into him by the Army.

Purnomo extended his hand. Rastun figured the Indonesians were serious about the Ropen if they sent their ambassador and not some dime-a-dozen embassy flunky.

"Mister Rastun. It is a pleasure."

"Thank you, sir." He shook hands with the ambassador, noting that they were both around the same height, five-foot-ten. Purnomo, however, had a paunchy frame and a double chin, a sharp contrast to Rastun's lean, firm build.

"You have gained quite the reputation in the monster hunting world."

"Thank you, sir, but I'm just doing my job."

Another brief smile from Purnomo. "And quite a job you have done with the sea raptor and the lizard men, which is the reason my government specifically asked for you and your team."

Rastun just nodded. The man did like to throw around platitudes, just like any diplomat worth his salt.

Purnomo shook hands with the others before more people trickled into the room. Wildlife Biologist Petal Garland, Director of Field Security Salvatore Lipeli, and field security specialists Alfonso Herrera, Pete McClure, and Norgay.

"All right." Lynch clasped his hands together. "If everyone could take a seat, we can begin."

Rastun and the others sat in the first row.

"As Doctor Ehrenberg told you," said Lynch, "we had another deadly incident involving a cryptid. The Indonesian government has requested the FUBI's help in finding the creatures responsible. That's the reason for Ambassador Purnomo's presence. Ambassador, I turn it over to you."

"Thank you, Director Lynch." Purnomo smoothed out his suit before taking the stage.

"Three days ago, one of our Maritime Security vessels in the Java Sea picked up a distress call from a small fishing boat. When they came across it, they found it under attack. One of the sailors videoed the incident. Doctor, if you please."

Ehrenberg, sitting at a desk off to the side, tapped on a laptop. Moments later, the large wall monitor flickered to life.

A darkened sea appeared. Rastun leaned forward, forehead wrinkled, trying to pick out specific details. Luckily, the fishing boat had a running light on the bow. It cast just enough illumination to show . . .

"My God," Karen spoke in a hushed tone.

Rastun straightened, his gaze locked on the large, streamlined creature with long wings and a pointy crest on its head. It appeared there were three in all, each one taller than the boat's pilothouse. He knew of no bird even close to being that big.

Something thumped off camera, jarring Rastun out of his reminiscing. Tracers zipped across the blackened water and past the fishing boat. The Maritime Security vessel's machine gun. The creatures leapt away from the vessel, one of them showing off a long, whip-like tail.

"They don't look like pterodactyls," said Karen as the video ended. "At least not like the ones I've seen in movies."

"According to witness descriptions over the years," replied Ehrenberg, "they appear similar to the rhamphorhymnchus or the dimorphodon. But both of those creatures were much smaller compared to the Ropen."

"The crew of the maritime security ship estimated their size at roughly fifteen feet tall," said Purnomo.

"The largest known pterosaur is the Quetzalcoatlus." Petal crossed her legs as she spoke. "But it stood at around ten feet tall, and its neck was much longer than those creatures. It's possible this could be some undiscovered species of pterosaur."

"They certainly are taller than the pilothouse." Ehrenberg looked at the ambassador. "It'd help if we could get the dimensions of the boat and properly determine the size of those Ropen."

"That will not be a problem, Doctor Ehrenberg. I can even arrange for you and your team to inspect the boat. Maritime Security towed it back to their base in Jakarta."

"That would be great."

"I'd also like to see the original video and examine it," said Karen.

"If you are worried about this being a fake, I assure you it is not," Purnomo spoke in a soothing tone. "Nearly everyone on the Maritime Security ship witnessed these creatures, and the crew and their captain are highly regarded within the service."

"I have no doubt. But our equipment here might be able to pick out more details about these creatures and help us learn more about them."

Rastun suppressed the grin that began to form. He had to hand it to Karen. He certainly couldn't have come up with a more diplomatic way of saying, "I don't care if the Dali Lama himself shot that video. We're going to make sure it's not a hoax."

"I'll see it is made available to you." Purnomo nodded.

"What about the bodies of the crew members?" asked Lipeli.

Purnomo's shoulders sagged a bit. "They found one, the captain, Asnawi Adsit. He was partially devoured. The other two crewmen were not located. Maritime Security believes the creatures flew off with them."

"I can certainly enhance the video to see if that's the case," said Karen.

"Good. Good."

"So where the heck are these things coming from?" asked McClure, a former 82nd Airborne officer.

"Most sightings and folklore are concentrated on Papua and New Guinea," Ehrenberg answered.

"Which is two thousand miles from where Captain Adsit's boat was attacked," Purnomo noted.

Rastun shrugged. "That really doesn't mean much, Mister Ambassador. There are a lot of birds that will migrate thousands of miles. Heck, the Arctic Tern migrates from the Arctic to the Antarctic. That's a round trip of over forty-nine thousand miles every year."

"Ha!" Ehrenberg let out a laugh. "Once again, all those summers working at the Philadelphia Zoo pay off."

Rastun softly chuckled as Petal spoke. "There is a lot of evidence to suggest that large pterosaurs could fly as far as ten thousand miles at a stretch. So two thousand miles is nothing to them."

Norgay held up a hand. "Then for all we know, these creatures could have been passing over Indonesia when they attacked the fishing boat. They could be anywhere in the Pacific by now."

Ehrenberg bobbed his head from side-to-side in thought before responding to the former Gurkha. "That is a possibility. Still, those creatures are a ringer for most descriptions of the Ropen, and like I said, Indonesia is their territory."

"Can I assume these Ropen are like regular birds and build nests?" asked Geek.

"There is some evidence to suggest pterosaurs had nesting habits similar to many modern-day birds," Ehrenberg answered.

"Sweet. We can bring along our Flapjacks to try and find them."

"I don't know how effective your drones will be." Ehrenberg's face scrunched in a doubtful expression. "Along with a thick jungle canopy, there are some theories that Ropen may nest in caves."

"Not a problem." Geek grinned. "Aster developed a drone called the Alley Cat. Looks like an RC car, but a lot quieter. Its main job is locating terrorists holed up in caves, but it could be handy finding flying dinosaurs . . ." He glanced over to Rastun. "'Scuse me, flying reptiles."

"Ambassador." Rastun turned to Purnomo. "Do you know if there have been any missing boats in the Java Sea recently?"

He nodded slowly. "There are two other boats that have been reported missing since these attacks. We fear they may have also been attacked by the Ropen."

Ehrenberg slid forward in his seat. "What were their last known positions?"

"They were within a one hundred-fifty-kilometer radius of this boat." Purnomo nodded to the screen. "Our fishing industry has already been harmed by the oil spill. Attacks by prehistoric monsters will only compound the problem."

"And what'll happen if we find any Ropen?" asked Ehrenberg.

"They must be killed."

Ehrenberg flexed his jaw, shifting in his seat. "You mean the ones that attacked the fishing boat, right?"

"No." Purnomo shook his head. "All of them."

"What?" Karen blurted, her mouth hanging open in shock. "You want us to wipe out an entire species? A species everyone thought extinct for millions of years?"

"With all due respect, Mister Ambassador," said Director Lynch. "The purpose of the FUBI is to protect cryptids, not kill them."

Purnomo's forehead wrinkled, seeming to regard Lynch with disbelief. "Your Mister Rastun has killed such creatures before." He pointed at him.

"I had no choice in those situations," Rastun told him. "Lives were at stake."

"Lives are at stake here as well. So are livelihoods. Thirty percent of all fish in my country come from the Java Sea. If more Ropen attacks disrupt fishing in that area, it will have a serious impact on our economy. The cost of fish will go up. Thousands could be out of work. Not only fishermen, but drivers who transport fish, those who work in markets or restaurants."

Rastun leaned back, tapping a finger on the armrest. He sympathized with Purnomo's concerns. He did not want to see lots of people lose their jobs, but he also did not want to see a species as unique as the Ropen exterminated.

"It's SOP . . ."

Purnomo's brow furrowed in a confused look.

"Sorry. It's standard operating procedure to destroy any animal that kills a human. Those are the ones we need to target, not the entire species."

"How will you be able to tell the difference between the ones who killed the fishermen and the ones who didn't?" Purnomo held out his hands.

"Most animals are territorial," answered Ehrenberg. "If we see them, or hear reports of them, in the same general area of this attack, if they fly close to other boats, then it's likely those are the Ropen we're looking for. Though an autopsy would need to be done to examine the contents of their stomachs to confirm it."

"They could also be vital to the environment," Petal chimed in.

Purnomo tilted his head. "Vital how? They are monsters."

"No. They're predators, large ones. They probably help control the local marine population. If you kill all of them, that means too many fish and other animals in the sea."

"Then that is good. There will be more fish for us to catch."

"No." Petal shook her head. "It'll mean not enough food to go around. A lot of animals will starve to death, and many of the fish you do catch won't be as big as before."

Purnomo bit his lower lip, his gaze dropping to the floor in thought. "But these Ropen, they are dangerous."

"So are tigers," said Rastun. "But your country has laws and programs to protect them. You also have conservation efforts in place for Komodo Dragons, rhinoceroses, and orangutans. Indonesia has a solid reputation for protecting endangered species. How will it look if you didn't do that for an animal I imagine is rarer than the Javan Rhino?"

The Ambassador stared at him, letting out a slow breath, mulling it over. "I am sure my government and your organization can reach an agreement beneficial to all involved . . . even the Ropen." He flashed a brief smile.

The briefing broke up a few minutes later, with Lynch and Purnomo staying behind, probably to hammer out any other details in the deal between the FUBI and the Indonesian government.

Rastun caught Karen glancing over her shoulder a couple of times, a concerned look on her face.

"Problem, hon?"

"Just a feeling about the ambassador," she replied as they exited the auditorium. "I'm worried he wasn't sincere about not killing all the Ropen."

Rastun locked eyes with Karen and nodded. "You and me both."

FOUR

Salsa music blared from the cell phone on the dresser, snapping Cesar Marques out of his sleep. Groaning, he reached out and slapped the device until the alarm fell silent.

Letting out a breath, he stared up at the ceiling with its faded, beige paint. Part of him wanted to remain in bed. His new job wasn't what he expected. Too many meetings. Too much paperwork and going over budgets and organizational goals. And the sensitivity training sessions. He used to be all for such things until he began attending those classes. Hours and hours of them, which kept him from doing the job he'd been hired to do.

Frowning, Marques threw off the covers and slid his lean frame out of bed. He stretched, staring down at the mattress. Three weeks he'd been in New York, a city overflowing with gorgeous women from diverse backgrounds, and he still hadn't gotten laid.

Too much work. Too much damn work, and all of it indoors.

This is not what I wanted. He padded to the bathroom, running a hand through his thick hair.

Be patient. You'll be out in the field soon. He told himself that countless times a day. Eventually, it would come true.

Hopefully, soon.

He showered, shaved, and put on the damn suit and tie that he hated so much. But his boss told him he needed to look presentable when at the office.

Another reason he needed to get back into the field as soon as possible.

Marques checked his phone and discovered forty texts, all coming within the last few hours. Many contained attachments of photos, videos, or links to news stories.

Look at this . . . Check this out . . . These things are real . . . guess who they're sending after them?

"What's got everyone excited?" Brow crinkled, he tapped the link to one of the videos.

He gaped at his phone, eyes wide.

Even though it was night, he could still make out the silhouettes of three huge birds perched on a boat. He studied the long beaks and the angular wings . . . and the tails. Whip-like, reptilian. Shock and excitement rippled through him.

Pterosaurs! Someone had taken a video of living, breathing pterosaurs.

Marques read the news stories that went with the footage. The video had been shot by the crew of an Indonesian Maritime Security Agency boat a few days ago. The creatures had been identified as Ropen. He'd been on an expedition to try and find them years ago, but with no success.

They really do exist. Creatures from the age of dinosaurs, alive today. He'd always felt some had to have survived K-pg Extinction Event.

Now he just hoped the Indonesian government would work to protect them like they had so many other endangered animals.

Marques grimaced when he read that the three-man crew of the fishing boat had been killed. Unfortunate, but pterosaurs were predators. They only followed their natural instincts. He hoped the Indonesians wouldn't use those deaths as an excuse to wipe out what had to be one of the most unique species on the planet.

He read further down the article, stopping at one paragraph.

"Shit." He scowled, clenching the phone tighter.

The fucking FUBI was headed to Indonesia to search for the Ropen.

Marques thumped the phone against his side. Why the hell did those butchers have to get involved?

He shook his head, thinking about the interviews he'd seen with Jack Rastun, Karen Thatcher, Randy Ehrenberg, and FUBI Director Edward Lynch. They all said the purpose of their organization was to protect cryptids. Liars. If they really wanted to protect cryptids, they wouldn't hire ex-soldiers like Rastun.

Marques called his boss. There was no way he could stand by and let this genocide happen.

"Good morning, Cesar."

"Did you see the news?" He had no time for pleasantries, even with his boss.

"I assume you are referring to the Ropen video. Yes. Very interesting. Astounding, even."

"You heard who they are sending to look for them?"

"Yes. The FUBI. Jack Rastun, Randy Ehrenberg, Karen Thatcher and the rest of their team."

Marques paced across his bedroom, jaw flexing. "We cannot let them kill the Ropen."

"But what can we do?"

"We stop them." Marques threw out his free hand. "Isn't that why you hired me?"

"Your group has barely gotten on its feet. In fact, other than your administrative assistant, you do not have a group."

Marques snorted. If only they'd have let him spend more time looking over resumes instead of shuffling him from one stupid bullshit meeting to another. "How will it look if we stand by and do nothing while the FUBI slaughters more cryptids?"

His boss sighed. "We might be able to apply some pressure on the Indonesian government to keep the FUBI from killing the Ropen."

"And what if the Indonesians ignore us? No, the only way to stop them is with direct action."

"And do you plan on doing that all by yourself?"

Marques let out a slow, frustrated breath. He thought about doing it himself. One man taking on the system. Maybe . . .

His shoulders sagged. For something like this, he needed more people. People not afraid to protect rare creatures by any means necessary.

But he didn't have people yet. Maybe he could speed read through the resumes, pick a dozen or so. But could they drop everything and get to Indonesia? How long would it take for all of them to arrive?

Dammit, he needed people he could trust, people who . . .

Marques' head snapped up. "I think there might be a group that can help me, and they're already in Indonesia."

He made his case to his boss, who approved. Next, Marques got on his satellite phone. After three rings, a woman answered.

"Cesar? Oh my gosh, it's been too long."

"That it has, my sweet."

"How are you?" asked Paulette Thompson.

"I'm doing well. Still settling into my new job."

"Yeah, I saw that on your Instagram. Congratulations."

"Thank you. Actually, that's the reason I'm calling. Your boat is still in Indonesia, right?"

"Yeah. Mine and lots of others. We're not letting any more fucking oil tankers through here."

"Good. Well, with so many other boats there, perhaps you can pull yourself away for a while."

"Why?"

"I have a proposition for you."

"Is this proposition business or pleasure?" Paulette asked coyly.

"There's no reason it can't be both."

Paulette giggled. It made Marques' heart speed up. He also got hard, remembering the last time he and the lovely blond from California were together.

"So what do you have in mind?" she asked.

"How would you like to take on the FUBI?"

FIVE

"Finally, we're here."

Rastun turned to Karen, who sat next to him. She let out a relieved breath after speaking and gazed out the plane's window as it rolled down the runway of Jakarta's Soekarno-Hatta International Airport.

"Not the first really long-ass flight I've ever had," he said. "But certainly the most comfortable." Unlike the C-17 or C-130 transports he'd flown on during his Army days, Roland Parker's Gulfstream jet had plush seats, plenty of leg room, and pretty good food.

"They could serve margaritas all day and have a personal masseuse on board, but a day-and-a-half stuck in a plane is way too long."

Rastun tilted his head. "What do you need a masseuse for when you have me?"

"Because they're professionals who know what they're doing." Karen gave him a wry grin.

"Fine." Rastun scoffed. "Maybe you should marry one of them instead."

"Hmm." Karen pinched her chin between her thumb and index finger. "I'll take it under consideration."

Rastun gave her a faux scowl.

Karen giggled. "I love you." She kissed him on the cheek.

"Yeah, right." Rastun flashed her a smile as the jet crept up to the terminal.

After deplaning and collecting their luggage, the group made its way through the spacious terminal. Rastun took point, eyes darting left to right, looking for any potential trouble. All he saw were people streaming by, hauling bags, looking at their phones, or going in and out of shops, restaurants, and bathrooms.

An uneven line of people stood ahead of them, most holding placards in various languages. Rastun's gaze settled on three men in beige uniforms, one of them standing out in front with a placard that read, "FUBI."

"I guess that's our welcoming committee." Ehrenberg picked up his pace.

One of the uniformed men, slender with an angular face, stepped forward. Rastun took note of the man's shoulder boards, each one with three gold stripes. He had to be an officer.

"Dr. Ehrenberg?" the man asked.

"At your service." Ehrenberg smiled wide and gave a slight bow.

"I am Lieutenant Bahar, Maritime Security Agency." He extended a hand, which Ehrenberg shook. "Welcome to Indonesia."

"Happy to be here, Lieutenant." He introduced Bahar and the other two MSA members – Seamen Haryadi and Tama -- to the rest of the expedition.

"We have been assigned to take you to our base," Bahar said as he started walking. "Our cars are parked just outside, but I urge you to be aware. There is a protest in front of the terminal."

"What are they protesting?" Petal's forehead wrinkled in concern.

Bahar gazed around at the group. "You."

Herrera snorted, throwing out his arms. "We've barely been in this country five minutes. What the hell did we do to piss 'em off?"

"It's probably what we've *done,*" said Petal. "I imagine they're mad about how we killed the lizard men. They must think we'll do the same to the Ropen."

"Would they rather we get eaten like those fishermen?" asked Alana, an edge to her voice.

"I'm sure there are some who'd like that," replied Rastun. His muscles coiled as he stared through the glass doors of the airport's exit. There had to be a hundred civilians across the street, many holding signs or raising their fists. A line of police in riot gear stood in front of them. The protesters were angry, but not violent. He hoped they remained that way.

The doors slid open. Heat and suffocating humidity greeted them. So did the enraged bellowing of the protestors. Rastun couldn't make out what anyone in the crowd said, but some of the signs they held were in English.

MURDERERS GO HOME!

CRYPTID KILLERS!

"'Justice for Lizard People?'" Geek read one of the signs aloud. He turned to Rastun, face scrunched. "Seriously?"

Rastun shrugged. "There's about two hundred-sixty million people in this country. A certain percentage of them have to be whackjobs."

Geek looked back at the protesters. "Yeah, and I think all of 'em came out to greet us."

Another group mobbed the sidewalk, most holding either cameras or microphones. The press, a mix of local and international. They hollered out questions, their words merging into a loud, unintelligible babble.

Rastun ignored them and studied the protestors. Their shouting got louder. Many gestured emphatically at them.

"Let's get our stuff loaded ASAP."

Bahar regarded the crowd, face tightening in concern. "I agree with you, Mister Rastun."

They shoved their luggage and gear into the cargo holds of the three white Suburbans, the Maritime Security Agency logo displayed on their doors. Every few seconds, Rastun glanced at the protestors. Their screaming intensified. He swore he heard a few people yell, "Fuck you!" and "Die!"

A couple of protestors stomped up to the police line. Two cops held up their hands, warning them to get back. Other protestors got within a foot of the police, yelling at them or at the FUBI.

Karen shoved her last bag into the back of the Suburban, slammed the door, and scanned the crowd. Her shoulders stiffened. "This is getting kind of ugly."

"There's no 'kind of' about it." Rastun checked around. Everything had been loaded onto the MSA vehicles. Good. Now they could –

Something whipped through the air.

"Down!" He grabbed Karen's shoulder and pulled her to the ground.

"What the hell?"

The words barely left her mouth when a plastic water bottle bounced across the asphalt a few feet away.

A second water bottle struck the door of another Suburban, just missing Herrera's head.

"Shit!" he blurted.

A rock thudded against the Suburban to Rastun's right.

"Everyone in the cars. Go! Go! Go!"

He and Karen sprinted around their Suburban, Rastun shielding her. Something thumped next to him. A soda can ricocheted off the taillight.

Karen scrambled inside, followed by Geek. Rastun poked his head up a couple of inches over the roof. The riot police pressed up against the crowd, trying to push them back. Protesters banged against the plastic shields. More debris arced through the air. Bottles, cans, rocks, even a couple of shoes, one of which struck Seaman Haryadi in the back.

"Let's go, Doc." Rastun waved Ehrenberg into the passenger seat. Bahar threw open the driver's side door when a can thudded off the roof.

The engine revved. Rastun leapt into the backseat and slammed the door shut. He checked out the windows. No one else from the expedition remained outside.

He opened his mouth, ready to tell Bahar to get the hell out of Dodge. The MSA officer was way ahead of him. He revved the engine and raced away from the curb. The other two Suburbans roared after them. The protestors pointed at their vehicles. Several started to charge, only to get blasted in the face by streams of pepper spray.

"Well damn." Geek watched the police and protesters battle it out. "We're popular in this country, aren't we?"

"My apologies for what happened," Bahar said as he approached the entrance to the highway.

"Not your fault, Lieutenant," said Rastun. "You weren't throwing shit at us."

"The protestors were already here when we arrived," Bahar explained. "They doubled about an hour before your plane landed, and became more vocal."

"I'm sure they got wind of our arrival time somehow." Rastun faced forward. "It's not like our trip here is a state secret."

Irritation churned inside him. He should have anticipated a reception like that, given the backlash they'd received after the lizard men expedition. But what could he do to keep their trip a secret?

Not much, unfortunately. The FUBI was a civilian organization, not a military one. Director Lynch and Roland Parker wanted them to be as transparent as possible. So did the representatives and senators on Capitol Hill who decided how much of the Department of Agriculture's budget should be allocated to the Foundation as part of its public/private partnership. Trying to do anything on the sly might reinforce the belief among some in the public, and some politicians, that the FUBI was a quasi-paramilitary outfit.

The Suburbans motored up the ramp and joined the mass of vehicles on the highway. Traffic was stop-start. When it did start, it rarely went above 20 mph.

About ten minutes into their trip, the only vehicles making any decent progress were the scooters zipping between cars and trucks.

"Is traffic always this bad?" Karen asked Bahar.

"Actually, it is not bad right now. It will be worse later in the day."

Rastun drew his head back and looked out the windows as the traffic slowed to a snail's pace. "Lieutenant, if the traffic gets any worse, this place'll be a parking lot."

Bahar shrugged. "This is life in Jakarta, sir."

Karen let out a short, incredulous breath and turned to Rastun. "Remind me never to complain about rush hour traffic back in Alexandria."

The Suburban slowed more, crawling along the highway at five miles per hour.

"So I understand it was your boat that came across the Ropen," Ehrenberg said to Bahar.

"That is correct, sir. I was on the bridge at the time." Bahar shook his head. "Part of me still cannot believe what I saw. I have heard stories of the Ropen. Some of the older maritime sergeants told me they have seen the Ropen lights. I thought they were myths, until a few nights ago."

"We heard there were a couple of other boats that went missing since that fishing boat was attacked," said Karen. "Have they been found yet?"

"No. We also learned of another boat reported overdue last night. It's part of the Mainaky Fisheries fleet out of Pulau Kangean. That is the second boat of theirs that has gone missing."

"I bet that's making their fishermen have second thoughts of going out to sea again," said Rastun.

"Their CEO was on TV this morning," Bahar glanced over his shoulder at him, "demanding the government stop the attacks."

"How? Get a plane to fly around the Java Sea with a banner that says, 'Ropen, please stop eating our fishermen.'"

Bahar chuckled briefly.

The Maritime Security Agency base in Jakarta was nine miles from the airport. It took nearly an hour to get there, and they had another welcoming committee near the main gate.

Rastun counted more than two dozen protestors. Just like back at the airport, they held up signs and shook their fists. A group of riot police in front of them.

The guard at the gate waved the little convoy through. The Suburbans drove up to the docks, where Rastun spotted a wooden fishing boat with a battered pilothouse. That had to be the *Gita,* the boat attacked by the Ropen.

"What's the deal with the suit parade?" asked Geek.

Five people stood near the fishing boat's dock. Four wore dark suits, while the fifth had on a beige MSA uniform.

"Smells like bureaucrats." Rastun eyed the group.

"Here to help or to fuck things up?"

Rastun glanced at Geek. "You ever met a helpful bureaucrat?"

"Right. Stupid question."

Bahar chuckled softly. Rastun gave him a slight nod. His opinion of the MSA officer rose a few notches.

They exited the Suburbans and walked over to the Indonesians. A medium-built man with receding hair and glasses stepped forward.

"Greetings." He nodded to them. "I am Wikana Fariz, Ministry of Foreign Affairs. I have been assigned as your interpreter."

He introduced them to the others. The uniformed man, a lieutenant, was an aide to the base commander. The men in the suits came from various government agencies; Ministry of Agriculture, Ministry of Maritime Affairs and Fisheries, and Ministry of Environment and Forestry. Their titles seemed to run together for Rastun. "Special Assistant

Deputy Under Secretary for Some Such Thing." Basically, pencil pushers with fancy names.

"We are to observe your investigation of the *Gita*," said the Maritime Affairs rep, with Wikana translating, "and report your findings back to our respective agencies. We also wish to know where you will be searching for the Ropen."

"Of course." Ehrenberg bounced a little on the balls of his feet. "We just need to get our equipment, then we can get started."

He powerwalked back to the lead Suburban, threw open the back door, and yanked out a duffle bag.

Karen gazed at him for a bit, then looked at Rastun. "I don't think I've ever seen Randy this anxious to start an investigation."

"A day-and-a-half cooped up in a plane, another hour stuck in a car, I'd be anxious to do anything that didn't involve traveling from Point A to Point B."

Once the equipment was unloaded, every member of the expedition slipped on latex gloves and plastic shoe covers, similar to what crime scene investigators wore to reduce evidence contamination. Rastun thought it might be a moot point, figuring the crew from Bahar's ship tramped all over the fishing boat.

Still, it was SOP.

"We've got plenty more for you, gentlemen." Ehrenberg raised his covered foot.

Wikana translated. The ministers scrunched their faces, stared at one another, and shook their heads. The Environment rep relayed his response through Wikana.

"Thank you, but you have many people in your group, and the boat is rather small. We shall observe from the dock."

Rastun bit off a grunt. He leaned close to Karen's ear and whispered. "Translation, I don't want to get my nice suit dirty."

"Behave," Karen warned out the side of her mouth.

Not even the aide to the base commander volunteered. Staff weenie all the way.

"I will take a pair." Bahar stepped forward.

Ehrenberg handed the man some "booties," which he slipped over his boots. That earned him a few more notches of respect from Rastun. Just like when he served, he preferred officers who didn't shy away from getting their hands dirty.

They boarded the *Gita*, a stale, foul odor hovering in the air around it.

"Damn." Herrera waved a hand in front of his face. "Imagine having to work on this thing every day."

"After a while, you probably get used to it." Rastun shrugged, examining the deck. Behind him, he heard the clicks of Karen's camera. Patches of dried blood, looking more black than red, covered much of the aft section.

"Looks like the Ropen really worked over those poor guys," said Geek as he stared at the large dark stains.

"Mm," Rastun grunted. Most of the blood patches had the imprints of boots. As he suspected, the MSA had stomped all over the deck, heedless of preserving evidence. Though in their defense, finding any survivors of the attack had likely been first and foremost in their minds.

They located a few slender outlines in the blood, which could have been a clawed footprint. But boot marks overlapped them, making accurate measurements impossible.

"Look," Norgay called out near the stern. The ex-Gurkha picked up a boat hook and pointed to the tip, covered in dried blood.

"I'm guessing the crew didn't go down without a fight," commented Geek.

Rastun stared at the hook, recalling the MSA's video of the attack he and Karen had watched back at FUBI headquarters. Along with his fiancée determining it had not been faked, she had enlarged the images enough to show one man being hauled into the air in a Ropen's talons. The poor guy's arms had been moving. He had still been alive.

Rastun clenched his teeth. He couldn't imagine how terrified the fisherman must have been. In the claws of a prehistoric monster, being flown to God only knew where. Had he resigned himself to his fate? Screamed the entire time? Maybe he had bled out from his injuries and died before the Ropen got him back to its nest. He hoped for the last one. Guilt accompanied the thought, but he had watched people mauled and eaten by cryptids. It was a horrific way to go.

"Let's get some samples." Ehrenberg pulled out a scalpel and a test tube from his pack. Norgay held the hook steady while he scraped flecks of blood into the tube. Karen then took several shots of the tip of the boat hook.

They proceeded below decks, everyone grimacing from the stench of rotten fish. With the engines shut down, that meant the refrigeration unit had been turned off. So no ice to keep the fish from spoiling.

Rastun and the others splashed through water from the melted ice to the pile of fish in the rear of the cargo hold. None of them had been disturbed.

"I don't like this," Ehrenberg spoke through his sleeve, trying to keep out the foul odor.

"You talking about the smell or something else, Doc?" asked McClure.

"Well, both. But my big concern is most theories suggest the Ropen's diet is mainly comprised of fish. If they attacked the crew but left the fish intact, it may indicate they prefer human flesh."

"Or the Maritime Security boat chased them off before they could slurp down some tuna," said Geek, "or whatever these things are."

"Snapper, actually," Petal corrected him.

"Either way, it looks like the Ropen have a taste for humans now." Ehrenberg frowned. "Definitely not good."

The team climbed out of the *Gita*. The bureaucrats no longer stood along the dock. The engine of one of the Suburbans hummed, and the silhouettes of people sat inside. One appeared to drink from a water bottle. Doors opened, and the men climbed out of the air-conditioned vehicle and back into the hot, humid air.

"Did you find anything useful?" asked the chubby Maritime Affairs rep.

"We found what look like Ropen footprints." Ehrenberg glanced back at the fishing boat. "The problem is many of them were trampled on by the Maritime people who boarded the ship, so we can't get any accurate measurements. It looks like none of the fish were eaten, which means the Ropen only went after the crew. Also, it appears one of the crew stabbed a Ropen with a boat hook."

"Do you think he killed it?" The Agriculture rep, Novanto, straightened as he spoke, the words spilling out his mouth.

"No idea." Ehrenberg shook his head.

"None of the monsters seemed badly wounded when we chased them off the boat," Bahar added.

"Will they attack more fishing boats?" asked the Maritime Affairs rep, Sofwan.

"Again . . ." Ehrenberg held out his hands. "I can't say with absolute certainty. These Ropen could have been migrating and just happened to come across the boat. Or they could be establishing a new territory, which means any boat in the Java Sea is in danger."

Sofwan shifted his weight, grimacing and staring from side to side. Wikana translated for him, "If there are more attacks, fishermen will not go out to sea. The young may also be less inclined to pursue fishing as an occupation. This could ruin the entire industry."

"Now, Mister Sofwan." Ehrenberg raised his hands. "We're going to do everything we can to find these Ropen and prevent any further harm to the local fishing industry."

"How will you do that?" asked the Environment rep.

"Well, your government has allowed us onboard Lieutenant Bahar's boat. We plan on patrolling the area where the *Gita* was attacked. Also, I want to send some of my people to Captain Adsit's village to interview the residents and see if any of them have seen Ropen in the Java Sea. It might help us narrow down our search. Our hope is to tranquilize one of them and fit it with a GPS collar to track it back to its nest. We might luck out and find more of them."

Ehrenberg turned to the staff weenie. "We're going to need a helicopter to fly our people to the village, if that's not a problem."

"No, sir. We have been told to accommodate all your requests in your search for the Ropen."

"Our boat is also equipped with a helicopter pad," Bahar added.

"Great. Thank you." He nodded to the two MSA officers, then turned to the expedition. "Jack, Karen, Geek, Petal, Norgay. I want you guys to do the interviews in the villages."

"You got it, Doc," Rastun replied, the others nodding.

"Just find these creatures before they attack any more fishing boats," Sofwan told them.

"That's the plan, sir." Rastun looked over his shoulder at the *Gita*, thinking of all the blood on the deck, imagining the final moments for Adsit and his men.

He prayed they could find the Ropen before anyone else suffered the same, horrifying fate.

SIX

Marques' eyes flickered from the mass of traffic in front of him to the van's speedometer. Just fifteen kilometers per hour.

He sighed, shifting in his seat. He'd been stuck in the terrible traffic of Rio and Los Angeles, but this? Neither of those cities compared to the snail's pace of Jakarta. The harbor where Paulette docked her yacht was five or six kilometers away. It'd probably take a half-hour to get there, if they were lucky.

Marques shifted in the passenger seat again, clenching his legs together. Of course, he had to take a piss.

"Man, this is bullshit," said a voice from behind.

Marques turned to the backseat. A slender man with hair past his neck and a thick beard pressed a shoulder against the side of the van. "How long is it gonna take to get back to the boat?"

"Little bit," said Kiswanto, the compact Indonesian driver. "Traffic not bad bad."

The man likely meant to say, "not too bad," Marques figured, but he only had a limited grasp of English.

I can't believe it could be worse. Actually, he could. They could be stopped completely. For a long time.

"'Not bad bad'?" The bearded man, Thomas Griffin, threw his hands up. "Seriously? This is worse than LA. How the fuck can anyone put up with this?"

"Will you shut the hell up," barked a round woman with short blue hair. "You think whining about it will make everyone go faster?"

"What, you having fun taking forever to get back to the damn boat?"

"No," snapped the woman, Lenna. "But I'm not gonna throw a tantrum over it, like a typical man when you don't get your way."

"I'm not throwing a tantrum," Griffin's tone rose with each word. "I'm just saying. Shit, why don't they do something about the traffic here?"

"Yes, maybe you and the other men who run this city can all whip out your magic dicks and make the traffic disappear."

Griffin screwed up his face and shook his head. "Man, whatever."

"Don't say, 'man' to me." Lenna jabbed a finger at him.

Griffin scowled and folded his arms.

The thin Asian woman with short hair sitting between them huffed and looked up at the ceiling. "Okay, enough of this," she muttered, pulling out a pair of earbuds from her pocket.

"Oh, so sorry to disturb you, your highness," snapped Lenna.

Kory Hyo rolled her eyes, shoved the buds into her ears, and leaned back, listening to music on her phone.

Marques moaned and turned around, starting to have second thoughts on recruiting Paulette and her crew for this job. Griffin, a one-time famous TV star, acted like a spoiled brat, despite being in his mid-twenties. Lenna possessed a quick temper, which she displayed at the slightest perceived insult.

Marques wished he could have left them, and their bickering, behind. But he had needed help loading all those boxes into the van. He glanced past the three activists to the cargo hold, packed with cardboard boxes. He thought of the contents inside them, figuring he had more than enough to do what needed to be done.

His eyes shifted to Kory, who leaned her head back, absorbed in whatever song played on her phone. At least she was a quiet sort, and far more attractive than Lenna. If Paulette hadn't been on the yacht, he'd be trying to bed Kory.

Marques faced forward again, the rows and rows of vehicles still crawling along the highway. He glanced at Kiswanto, the man's face relaxed, near expressionless. The slow traffic and the argument between Griffin and Lenna did not seem to bother him.

Marques' gaze lingered on the Indonesian. Kiswanto headed up a local environmental group here in Jakarta and had helped Paulette with several protests following the oil spill. She vouched for him, but Marques had his doubts.

Kiswanto had served in the Indonesian navy for six years. Marques did not like military people. They were murderers, their crimes rewarded and celebrated by their governments. Maybe Kiswanto did see the error of his ways and now worked for the betterment of the Earth, but could whatever blood he had on his hands ever be completely washed away?

Marques pressed his back into his seat. He did not have much choice when it came to who he worked with here. Until he could staff his group with the people he wanted, he had to use Paulette's friends.

His phone chirped, alerting him to a text. Marques checked the screen and straightened. He'd been waiting for this message from his contact in the government.

FUBI will sail on MSA vessel Grantin around five today. I have attached their planned course and photos of the ship.

Marques nodded. Even with this damn traffic, they should make it back to the yacht and unload the boxes with plenty of time to spare before the *Grantin* sailed.

Another text came from his contact.

Four FUBI members will take a helicopter to Pulau Kangean to interview villagers about Ropen sightings.

Marques grunted. A shame that Paulette's rich family hadn't bought her a helicopter to go along with her yacht. Then they could keep an eye on both FUBI groups.

Forget the one going to Pulau Kangean. They were going there to talk to people. The rest of them on the Maritime Security boat would be actively searching for the Ropen in the Java Sea. He needed to concentrate on them and do whatever it took to keep them from harming those creatures.

SEVEN

Manda van Giersbergen's eyes darted from her companions on the jungle trail to the canopy of trees above her. She tensed as she saw the partially blocked sun sinking toward the west. *Are we going to get to the village before it gets dark?*

Their guide had warned them the jungle was no place to be at night. Not only did the darkness make it easy to get lost, but one also had to worry about animals like crocodiles and snakes.

Snakes. The thought of them made Manda shiver and made her check the ground around her. Thankfully, she saw no slithering, slimy reptiles.

She looked ahead, where Willem leaned against Mr. Bauer. The round, blond boy hobbled on his one good foot while their teacher had an arm around his shoulder.

Stupid Willem. Why did the clumsy ass have to slip and fall and sprain his ankle? That slowed everyone down.

Manda glimpsed through the trees at the jagged rays of the sun. She hugged her thin body, teeth clenched. *Please get to the village before dark.*

Sweat soaked her brow, soaked her whole body. She took a gulp from her water bottle. The heat was unbearable, worse than when she and her parents went to the Grand Canyon a couple of years ago. At least there she did not have to deal with humidity. Here, it felt like being wrapped in wet, hot towels.

Why did I put my name in for this trip? Because she would be finished with high school next year and her parents thought such a trip would look good when applying for university, especially since she wanted to study environmental science.

The trees around them thinned, then vanished. Beyond them stretched a field of stumps. The ground dropped off into a ravine to Manda's right. Another tree line sat over a kilometer away.

"What happened here?" asked a lean girl with flawless features.

Their guide, Mr. Saputra, turned to Ella. "Logging. Probably illegal. Most of it is in this country."

"Another example of deforestation," Mr. Bauer said to the students. Even while propping up Willem, he couldn't pass up an opportunity to teach. "Logging, fires, and farming are responsible for the loss of nearly half of Indonesia's forested areas. Not only does it shrink the habitat of already endangered species, the loss of so many trees can impact the global climate."

Manda swung her head left to right as they continued walking, taking in the devastation. Anger sparked within her at the people who had done this. Did they not know the damage they were causing not just to their own country, but the entire planet?

Did they not care?

"Mister Bauer?" Willem spoke through clenched teeth. "Can we rest for a bit?"

The teacher stared at him for a couple of seconds. "All right."

Manda swallowed and glanced at the sun, not far from the horizon. "B-But, Mister Bauer. It will be dark soon."

The teacher looked at her, then Willem, then the sky. "We can afford a couple of minutes rest, especially for Willem. We should reach the village before sundown."

"Mm," was Manda's soft reply. She had her doubts.

Mr. Bauer helped Willem down on a tree stump. Ella sat next to the fourth student in their group, Derek, a tall boy with wavy black hair and a trim yet solid frame from years of competitive swimming. She started flirting immediately, laughing loudly at something he said.

Manda lowered her head. She had no chance with a boy like Derek. She was beanpole thin with barely noticeable breasts, the opposite of Ella.

Derek had practically ignored her ever since they flew out of Amsterdam. And Willem. He was okay, but awkward.

Manda sighed. She would have been better off staying home. She missed her parents, her friends, the cooler weather . . . and peeing in an actual bathroom.

Speaking of which . . .

"Mister Bauer, I need to go to the bathroom."

"Okay, Manda. Just stay close."

She nodded and looked to the tree line. She had no desire to be by herself in the thick jungle where snakes could be.

Manda peered over the small incline. A dirty stream flowed about three meters below. Too shallow for a crocodile to hide in. At least, she hoped so. There were a few bushes along the banks. Good enough for some privacy.

Manda started down the ravine, angling her body so she wouldn't slip and fall. She reached the bush and squatted behind it. Three more days, she thought. Three more days and she could use real bathrooms all the time again.

She pulled up her pants and started up the ravine, crawling more than walking. It was pretty steep, but she took her time and reached the lip.

Ella screamed.

Manda gasped, jerking her head up. Something moved to her right, something big.

An enormous winged creature dove at the clearing. Manda trembled, eyeing the jagged teeth in its long snout, the pointy crest on its head, and the whip-like tail with a diamond tip.

Her eyes widened. My God, it was that monster she heard about on the news when they arrived in Jakarta. The Ropen.

Ella screamed again and ran. Derek leapt up and followed her.

The Ropen knocked him down with its snout. It flapped its huge wings, hovering over Derek.

Frozen by fear, Manda watched as the monster brought down a clawed foot. A wet, ripping sound followed. Blood poured from the huge gashes in Derek's back. Manda couldn't close her eyes, trembling at the horrific sight.

Ella let out another scream and tripped over a stump. She scrambled back to her feet.

The Ropen brought its wings forward, planting its forward talons into the ground. The monster bounded after Ella. It caught her in two jumps, clamping its jaws down on her shoulder. She let out a gurgling cry as the monster shook her. Manda's mouth fell open as the Ropen ripped off Ella's right arm. Blood flew from the wound. Ella stumbled and fell.

A throaty cry burst from the creature's mouth. It sank its talons into Ella's back, sending up a shower of blood.

Someone else screamed. Trembling, Manda turned away from the Ropen tearing apart Ella.

A second creature stalked Willem as he crawled across the ground. Tears blurred Manda's vision.

The other Ropen opened its jaws and bit down on Willem's legs, yanking him off the ground. The sweat on Manda's body turned ice cold. Her shivering grew more violent, thinking of those monsters ripping her to pieces.

She looked around for Mr. Bauer. The teacher lay in a heap, unmoving, red staining his shoulders and head.

A third Ropen lifted its snout from the ground, something stringy hanging out its mouth, dripping dark liquid. Was that Mr. Saputra? Or part of him?

The Ropen that had grabbed Willem turned toward her.

Manda ducked, looking at the bush she'd just used as a bathroom. She could hide behind that.

She twisted and slid toward it on her rear, using her hands and the balls of her feet to push her down the ravine as fast as she could. She angled to the left, too fast. Manda kicked and clawed furiously to right herself.

She flipped over and tumbled into the stream.

EIGHT

Dawn had not yet broken when the MSA helicopter carrying Rastun, Karen, and their team touched down in a field on Pulau Kangean, just outside the village of Kalisangka. A pickup sat on the nearby road, a pear-shaped man leaning against it. A bright orange dot hovered by his face. He was smoking.

They climbed out of the chopper and jogged away from it bent at the waist, straightening as they left behind the rotor wash.

"You are the monster hunters?" Wikana translated the man's question.

"We are. Jack Rastun. Field Security Specialist."

"Chief Brigadier Mohede, National Police. I've been assigned as your escort."

"Thank you for taking the time to do this." Rastun shook his hand, suppressing the urge to grimace at the stale odor of smoke that surrounded the cop. "We appreciate it."

"Ha!" Mohede barked, the cigarette dangling from his lips. "Not much happens around here. I'm grateful for anything to relieve the boredom."

Rastun chuckled, then introduced the rest of the team. He noticed Karen's face straining, as if trying to hold back a yawn.

"If we could," Petal began, "we'd like to start by talking to the fishermen here, see if any of them have had Ropen sightings."

"Then you are just in time. Most of them will be putting out to sea in another hour." Mohede blew a cloud of smoke toward them. Petal's nose wrinkled in disgust. So did Karen's. Rastun knew his fiancée despised cigarette smoke. It appeared Petal was in the same boat.

She spoke through her grimace. "Do you know of anyone in the village who may have seen the Ropen recently?"

"We have gotten a few calls about strange lights in the sky."

"Strange how?" Petal cocked her head.

"They would glow for a few seconds, then disappear."

"Did they say what color they were?"

"Yellow, orange, blue. No one can keep their stories straight."

Rastun stared at the darkened ground in thought. That did match past descriptions of the Ropen lights.

Mohede shrugged and blew out more smoke, again, toward them. "Who knows if it's really the Ropen or not? It could be planes, shooting stars, anything. People around here are scared after Adsit and his men got eaten. Any light they see in the sky they'll think it's a Ropen."

"Still, if we could talk to the people who reported them, that would be great," said Petal.

"I know a couple of them personally. But the rest, we didn't get their names."

Petal frowned.

"We should get going to the docks," Rastun suggested. He wanted to start the interviews in Kalisangka as soon as possible. The director of the Mainaky Fisheries facility south of the village had demanded a meeting with the FUBI for two o'clock this afternoon. Not asked for, according to Ehrenberg, *demanded.*

"His exact words," the cryptozoologist had told him, "were, 'I want them in my office to tell me how they will stop these demons from attacking my other boats.'"

Rastun looked forward to that meeting as much as he looked forward to getting the flu.

The group followed Mohede to his pickup, rust spots marring its faded brown paint.

Karen and Petal climbed into the bed. Rastun figured neither of them desired to ride shotgun next to a man who stank of smoke.

Norgay sat up front. If the odor bothered him, the unflappable Gurkha did not show the slightest hint of it.

Once Rastun and Wikana settled into the bed, the engine of the old Toyota pickup sputtered once, twice, three times, then finally turned over.

Karen leaned close to Rastun. "I think it might be time for the police department here to invest in a new vehicle. Even a used one . . . less used than this one."

"This far out in the boondocks, these guys are probably on the bottom of the list when it comes to a new vehicle."

The first rays of orange cut through the darkness as they drove into Kalisangka proper. Clusters of wooden houses lay among the trees, the lights on in many of them. Several people walked along the streets, looking as though they were returning home instead of leaving for work. With Indonesia being a Muslim country, Rastun figured morning prayer had come to an end.

Karen yawned as the darkened sea came into view.

"You should've tried to sleep on the flight over," said Rastun.

Karen's face scrunched. "Seriously? You think I could sleep with all the noise that damn helicopter makes?" She "tsked" and waved a hand. "Like it would matter. It's barely five o'clock. Who can even function at this hour?"

"I can."

Karen let out an exasperated sigh. "Well, you like being up when *normal* people are asleep."

"I didn't say I like it. I just know how to deal with it."

"Goodie for you." Karen yawned again.

Grinning, Rastun nudged Karen's shoulder. She was *so* not a morning person.

A couple of fishing boats had just gotten underway by the time they reached the docks. Most remained, their crews storing supplies, topping off fuel tanks, and performing last-minute maintenance. Mohede led them to the nearest boat, captained by a thick, unsmiling man.

"We'd like to ask you some questions about the Ropen," Petal told him.

The captain scowled at her and grunted. "I don't have time." Wikana translated the words, even added the inflection of annoyance. "My crew and I have work to do, so leave us to it."

He turned his back on them.

"Friendly," Karen muttered, shaking her head.

Petal let out a slow breath. "Let's hope we have better luck with the next one."

They approached another fishing boat named *Asrul*, where a firmly built, bare-chested young man worked on some of the gear lines. He stopped his task when he saw them, his eyes widening. Rastun followed the man's gaze, right to Karen.

"Good morning." Petal greeted him.

The young man's head whipped toward her. He gave her a not very subtle once-over with his eyes.

"I'm Doctor Petal Garland with the FUBI." Wikana translated for her.

The young man gave a quick shake of the head as if snapping out of his lustful trance. "Oh. Sorry. Actually, I speak English. My name is Ismed." He shook all their hands. "Yes. Yes. I read in the news you were coming here to find the Ropen." His eyes lingered on Petal, then darted over to Karen.

A spark of jealousy rose in Rastun, which he quickly snuffed out. The kid couldn't be more than twenty, maybe lived in this village all his life. Probably didn't do a lot of traveling aside from being out on a fishing boat and likely saw the same people day in and day out. He couldn't imagine the pool of single young women here being that big. So when two attractive American women suddenly dropped in on him, the hormones went into overdrive.

So long as he looked and didn't touch, or didn't say anything derogatory, everything would be fine.

"We'd like to talk to you and the rest of the crew about the Ropen," said Petal. "If you have some time."

"Yes. Of course." Ismed's smile faded. "I knew Mister Adsit since I was little. He lived down the road from me. He was a good man. I'd like to help you."

Ismed went to the pilothouse and returned with the captain and another mate. Unlike the first fishing boat, this crew was willing to talk to them.

"So long as it does not take too long," said Captain Chudori. "We cannot afford to waste daylight."

Rastun nodded. "I guess after what happened to Captain Adsit, you don't want to do any fishing at night."

"Of course not," Wikana translated for Chudori. "That's when the damn Ropen come out. They are all over the place now."

"So you've seen them?" Petal took a step forward, the anxiousness in her voice evident. "You and others?"

"Not the demons themselves. But we've seen the lights." Chudori pointed to the sky.

"When? How many times?" Petal held out her phone, its recorder running.

"Everyone sees the lights from time to time. But ever since they attacked Ansawi's boat, we've seen them more."

"How often?" Petal asked while Karen took pictures. Ismed stared at the camera, smiling wide.

Actually, he probably stared more at Karen than the camera.

"Probably a dozen times the night after Ansawi and his men were killed. Then maybe seven or eight times the next night. Right, Omar?" He looked to the mate.

Omar nodded. "Yes, I saw them, too. A lot."

"After the other boats went missing, that's when we decided to stop fishing at night." Chudori shook his head. "Less time at sea, less fish, less money. And our hauls were small before all this. That damn fishing company." He scowled.

"Maybe Allah will smile on us and the Ropen will eat all of Mainaky's crews." Omar laughed.

"Where did you see the lights?" Petal tried to get the crew back on track.

Chudori looked toward the sea. "Probably a hundred thirty kilometers north of here."

"Have other fishermen seen Ropen lights multiple times over, say, the past week?"

All three nodded at Petal's question and mentioned the stories they'd heard from other fishermen. Karen slung her camera strap over her shoulder and got out her iPad. She brought up a map of the Java Sea and asked them to point out the sightings.

Well, Chudori and Omar did. Ismed just stared at Karen with a dopey grin.

Rastun rolled his eyes, the young man's ogling annoying him. *You're ten seconds away from getting a bucket of cold water dumped on you.*

He stepped over to her, shooting a glare at Ismed. The young man caught his eye. His smile evaporated and his gaze fell to the boat's deck.

Karen marked the Ropen light sightings with red dots. There were a lot of them between 50 to 200 miles north and east of Pulau Kangean.

"I've also seen them from the village." Ismed looked up at Karen.

"You have? Where?" She zoomed in so a map of the village filled her iPad.

"It was here." He pointed to a road about two miles from the docks. "I was walking home two nights ago and saw it in the distance. It lit up, then disappeared."

"Did you notice which direction it was going?" asked Rastun.

Ismed shook his head. "No. I only saw it for a second or two."

"Azwar at the market also said he saw the lights the past few nights," Omar noted.

"Did he say exactly where?" Karen's finger hovered over the screen.

"No, he did not. He just said he saw them."

Rastun stepped over to Karen, who stared at the red dots on the screen before turning to him. "So what do you think?" she asked. "Could this island be where they're nesting, or are they just passing through from somewhere else?"

Rastun's lips pressed together for a few moments in thought. "Don't know. But whatever the case, it looks like we can declare Pulau Kangean a Ropen hot spot."

Omar's eyes bulged. "The Ropen are living here? On our island?"

"We don't know that for sure." Rastun held up a calming hand. "We need to do more investigation to determine that."

"And when you find them, you will kill them?" Omar leaned forward, anxiousness radiating from him.

Rastun's jaw stiffened, gazing at the dark water lapping against the boat's stern. He did not want to lie, but he felt that Omar, and maybe the rest of the crew, would not like his answer.

Petal beat him to it. "We will, unfortunately, have to put down the creatures that killed Captain Adsit and his crew. The rest we will work with the government to preserve."

Chudori snapped a hand through the air. "Preserve them for what? To kill more of us? Eat more fish that we should be catching?"

"They are rare animals," said Ismed. "We should protect them. Not the ones that ate Mister Adsit. Only the ones that have not killed anyone."

Chudori snorted. "You sound like the foreign animal lovers that come here. They care about the lives of dangerous animals more than us poor fishermen trying to feed our families." He looked toward the horizon. "The sun is rising. We need to cast off."

"May I get my picture taken with them?" Ismed reached into his pocket, probably for a cell phone. His eyes darted between Karen and Petal.

"The American women are not interested in you," Chudori snapped. "Now come. We have work to do."

Ismed frowned and resumed checking the gear line.

"Thank you for your time," said Petal.

Chudori gave a short grunt and stalked toward the pilot house. Ismed and Omar both replied, "You're welcome," the younger fisherman with great enthusiasm.

Rastun started back to Mohede's pickup when Karen sidled up to him.

"Watch where you step," she whispered in his ear.

"Why?"

Karen glanced over her shoulder at Ismed. "I don't want you slipping on all the drool that kid left behind."

NINE

Most of the other fishing boats had set out to sea during their interview with Chudori's crew. Others were about to depart and did not have time to talk to the FUBI. Instead, Rastun and his team interviewed several dock workers. All had heard stories of the Ropen lights from fishermen. A handful even spotted them over the village as recently as two days ago.

The group then went to the homes of the wives of some of the fishermen. The first one they visited, the woman insisted they share breakfast with her and her teenage son before any interviews. Bread with crushed peanuts, a bean porridge, and tea were on the menu. Rastun thought it was pretty good, certainly better than an MRE or an energy bar.

The FUBI team also had food and drink offered at the second house they went to, and the third. By the time they came to their fourth house, Rastun was stuffed.

"I hope the people here don't give us any more food," Karen said to him as they started up the dirt path. "I'm gonna have to run an extra ten miles just to burn off everything I've eaten this morning."

Rastun shrugged. "Some Muslims are big on hospitality. There's a lot of stuff in the Koran about going all-out to make guests feel welcome, whether they're Muslim or not."

"Well, I hope they won't take offense when I turn down any more food. Otherwise, you'll have to roll me out of there."

They chuckled as they neared the porch. The wife did indeed offer them food, which everyone politely declined. Though they did take more tea.

And all of them had to use the bathroom before leaving.

Four homes, four interviews, pretty much the same story. Reports of the Ropen and Ropen lights went back generations. All the wives said their husbands, as well as their sons, fathers, and other relatives who fished, mentioned seeing the lights at one time or another.

"But if you are out on the sea long enough, you will see them," one wife told them. "It is not unusual." Her jaw had stiffened for a moment. "Until now, it was not of any concern."

Another wife thought she'd seen Ropen lights a couple of nights ago, but could not be sure. The nine-year-old child of another woman said he had seen the lights when playing outside three days ago.

"Are there any caves on this island?" Petal, through Wikana, asked Mohede as their pickup bounced along a rutted road, passing a café and an electronics store.

"There are some in the interior."

Petal nodded and turned back to the others in the bed. "We'll have to check them out. All those Ropen light sightings make me think they weren't migrating and just happened upon Adsit's boat. This island could be their nest."

"Or another nearby island," Karen offered. "And there are a lot of nearby islands around here."

Rastun groaned. That was probably the main reason why the Ropen had stayed hidden for so long. More than 13,000 islands made up the country of Indonesia. Some big, some medium-sized, some small, and less than half of them populated. Sure they narrowed down the creatures' location. Still, how many islands were within a 500-mile radius of Pulau Kangean? Hundreds? A thousand? More? The Ropen could be on any one of them. He could get every person from his old Ranger Battalion to search this region of Indonesia for a full year and they still may not find any Ropen nests.

And we don't have a battalion of people. Just nine of us, plus a boatload of Indonesian coasties.

The task seemed daunting, but he'd faced daunting odds before, both in the Army and the FUBI, and succeeded in spite of them.

Most of the time.

They pulled up to a simple one-story wooden house, where a short, squat woman swept the porch.

Mohede's shoulders sagged while he held the steering wheel.

"Something wrong?" asked Karen.

The cop stared at the home in silence for a couple of moments. "This is where Surati lives. Asnawi Adsit's wife."

Karen closed her eyes and lowered her head.

Rastun also stared at the woman sweeping, his sympathy rising. He'd been around his fair share of widows, saw the grief in their eyes, and felt helpless to do anything to comfort them.

They exited the pickup and walked up to the porch. The woman stopped sweeping.

"Excuse me, Surati?" Petal put a foot on the wooden porch.

"Surati is my sister. I am Soehaemi. I am here to help her. Her husband died at sea last week."

"Yes, we know," Petal replied after Wikana finished translating. "Please accept our condolences. We're with the Foundation for Undocumented Biological Investigation from America."

After introductions were made, Petal said, "We're here to try and find the Ropen."

Soehaemi huffed. "Those demons. I hope when you do find them, you kill them all. They have visited this grief on my sister."

Rastun glanced at Petal, hoping she would not talk about their plan to protect the prehistoric creatures. He didn't think Soehaemi was in the mood to hear that.

Thankfully, Petal said nothing.

"Would it be okay if we talk to your sister?" asked Karen.

Soehaemi's hand flexed on her broom handle. "If you talk to her, will it help you find the monsters that killed Asnawi?"

"It might."

The woman eyed Karen, looked away in thought, then back to her. "I will ask. Wait here."

Soehaemi went inside. A minute passed, then two. Rastun rocked back on his heels, part of him grateful for the delay, but another part wanting to get the unpleasant job done with as quickly as possible. All the while, he prayed no one said anything to upset Adsit's widow.

Soehaemi emerged from the house. "She says she will speak to you. Come." She waved them inside.

They entered to find a reedy woman dressed in simple black clothing sitting in an old wooden chair, head down, hands clenched together and resting on her lap. Behind the chair stood a slender boy in his teens, arms folded, glaring at Rastun and his group. A son, he guessed. One who appeared very protective of his mother. In another chair in the corner of the living room sat a wrinkly old man clutching a cane. Soehaemi introduced him as her father, Fuganto. The son was Hamdan.

"Sit." Soehaemi waved them to a couch and a couple of chairs.

Rastun, Karen, and Petal took the couch. Wikana and Mohede sat in the chairs. Norgay stood by the door in a bodyguard posture. Rastun did not expect any trouble, though since joining the FUBI two years ago, trouble seemed to pop up when least expected. He had no problem with Norgay standing sentry.

"Breadfruit? Yams? Tea?" Soehaemi asked matter-of-factly.

They all politely declined.

She gave a curt nod, as though satisfied with her bare minimum effort of hospitality.

Petal activated the recorder on her phone. "First, Mrs. Adsit, we all want to extend our condolences for the loss of your husband."

"Thank you," Surati replied, then sniffled.

"Do you know if your husband ever saw the Ropen or Ropen lights before he . . . before that night?"

"Yes. He saw the lights. Most fishermen do. But they never . . . they never attacked any boats." She lifted her head, jaw quivering. "Why did they do so now?"

"I'm sorry, we don't know yet," Petal answered. "What about lights over the village? Have you or your family seen them?"

"No." Surati shook her head. "But I have heard others say they have seen them."

"So have I," her sister added.

"Did they say when?" Karen asked, iPad at the ready. "The direction?"

Neither had any specifics. But that's how things usually went with civilians, Rastun thought. They did not converse like they were giving an after-action report. *At 2205 hours, I was walking west on Something-Something Road half-a-klick from the intersection with This-and-That Road when I spotted an orange light moving northwest.* Instead, they just said, "I was out walking a couple of nights ago and saw this weird light in the sky."

"And you, Hamdan?" Petal asked the son. "Has anyone you know seen Ropen lights?"

"No, but my one brother, Agung, did a couple of years ago."

"Is he around?"

"No, I'm sorry. He and my other brother came home for a few days after my father died, but they are back at work for Mainaky."

Fuganto growled. "They go help the big fishing company, instead of helping their family."

Hamdan sighed and shook his head. Rastun wondered if the boy had heard this complaint before from his grandfather.

"Why are there so many lights now?" Wikana translated Hamdan's question. "Are the Ropen going to attack more boats? Will they attack the village?"

Petal chewed on her bottom lip, as though searching for the right answer.

"We don't have enough intel . . . I mean, information to determine that," Rastun replied.

"They will," Fuganto declared in a deep, aged voice. "They were going to come after us one day."

Surati's face strained. Her shoulders shook as a tear slid down her cheek.

"Father, please," urged Soehaemi. "You're upsetting Su-"

"Hush!" He snapped a withered hand at his daughter. "There are not as many fish in the seas as there were when I was young. The Ropen eat fish. When fish are scarce, they must eat something else. They eat us."

Surati shuddered. More tears spilled from her eyes.

"Stop it, Grandfather." Hamdan glared at the old man.

"Mind your tongue when I'm talking." Fuganto shook his cane at his grandson. "They need to know this if they want to find and kill the demon flyers." He redirected his gaze to the couch. "They've attacked boats before."

Karen hovered a finger over her iPad. "Where and when was --"

"Bah!" Fuganto waved her to be quiet.

Karen's face hardened as the old man went on. "Boats always go missing. It is not only because of storms or because they are poorly built. A friend of mine was out fishing one day and came across another boat. No crew. Blood all over the deck."

Surati let out a sob. Hamdan put a hand on his mother's shoulder.

"Ropen did it," said Fuganto. "I'm sure of it."

Or pirates. Or one of the crew went crazy. Rastun thought it, but didn't say it.

Karen stared at Fuganto, as though waiting for him to start talking again. When he did not, she asked, "When did this happen?"

He looked up at the ceiling, contemplating. "Forty, fifty years ago."

"And where?"

"The Java Sea." Fuganto squinted. "Or was it the Flores Sea?"

Rastun turned to Karen, who gave the briefest of frowns. He could sense his fiancée's thoughts. *Scant details, poor memory, no actual eyewitnesses. Unreliable account.*

"They'll keep attacking boats, I tell you," said Fuganto. "The Ropen, they're hungry. They're going to eat more people, like they did Asnawi."

Surati broke down.

"Dammit, Grandfather!" Hamdan shouted.

"Don't you raise your voice at me!" Fuganto shook his cane, first at his grandson, then at Rastun and Karen. "You find them. You find them and kill them."

"Father, please." Soehaemi knelt in front of her crying sister, clutching her hands. "That's enough."

"Shut up." Fuganto nearly lunged forward in his chair.

Karen leaned closer to Rastun. "I think we better go."

"Yeah, no argument from me."

He stood, clearing his throat. "Um, thank you for your time. Again, we're sorry for your loss."

The others stood and started to leave.

Fuganto slammed his cane into the floor. "The caves. Check the caves. That's where they live."

"We will," replied Rastun.

"And graveyards. Watch around the graveyards."

"Yes, thank you, sir." Petal spoke softly, hoping to calm down the old man. "We've heard stories that the Ropen may have dug up corpses in the past."

"They are not stories. They have done it, and not far from here."

Petal halted. "Where?"

"Near Torjek. Years ago. They dug up the graves. Tore up the bodies. Ropen did it. You go kill them. All of them."

The FUBI team said nothing and saw themselves out.

"Torjek . . . Torjek." Karen checked the map on her iPad as they walked back to the pickup. "Okay, here it is. Looks like it's about twenty-five miles east of here."

"It could be worth checking out," said Petal. "I doubt there's any physical evidence at the site after all these years, but the locals may know something useful."

"It's more likely those graverobbers were human and not Ropen," Rastun countered. "Besides, most of the stories he told were second-hand, maybe even third-hand."

"Probably. Still, it's another lead we should follow up on."

Everyone got back into Mohede's pickup. The engine coughed twice before it turned over. The vehicle rattled down the road to their next destination.

When Mohede pulled up in front of the house, a voice crackled over his radio. The cop answered, listened to the person on the other end, then gave a short response.

"What's going on?" asked Rastun.

Mohede turned to face the group. Wikana translated, "My apologies. I cannot escort you anymore today."

"Why not?" Distress tinged Petal's voice.

"I have been ordered to take part in a search for a group of Dutch students who have gone missing."

TEN

The beeping alarm from Wendall "Geek" Hewitt's cell phone bore through his sleep. His eyes snapped open and he rose off his thin pillow . . . then stopped before his head banged against the bottom of the bunk above him. The beds in the *Grantin's* crew quarters had been set up like a bookshelf, stacked three high. With no guest quarters, the FUBI team had to "hot bunk" with the MSA personnel, taking the bed of a crew member on duty at the time. Space came at a premium on the ship the size of *Grantin.*

It took an effort for his eyes to fully open. His body was still on East Coast time. Looking at his cell, it would be early morning back home. Here in the Java Sea, it was early afternoon.

The Ropen also complicated his battle against jet lag. Since it hunted at night, the FUBI would be up and about well before and well after oh-dark-thirty.

So much for getting back to a normal sleep schedule.

Just gotta deal with it.

After a trip to the head, Geek slipped on his boots and checked his weapons and equipment. All in good shape. He wolfed down a couple of energy bars and proceeded topside. While the *Grantin* had lookouts posted, Captain Rastun and Dr. Ehrenberg wanted one FUBI member on watch, just in case a Ropen decided on an afternoon stroll . . . or soar, he guessed.

"It's not that unusual for a nocturnal animal to be up and active during the day," Ehrenberg had told him.

He put on his Oakley Fuel Cell polarized sunglasses just before he stepped onto the deck. Brilliant blue skies greeted him. Geek swung his head left, then right, and spotted Captain McClure near the stern. The former paratrooper had his back toward him, apparently staring into the horizon.

"Here to relieve you, sir."

McClure turned to him, lowering his binoculars. "Thanks, Geek."

"Anything going on I should be aware of?"

The side of McClure's mouth curled. "Maybe, maybe not. Take a look out there." He pointed past the stern.

Geek raised his binoculars. He zoomed in on an angular, triple-decker yacht, roughly two miles behind the *Grantin.*

"Nice boat. Checking out girls in bikinis?"

McClure grunted out a laugh. "Sorry to disappoint you, but I haven't seen any."

"So why the interest?"

"Because it's been shadowing us since I came on watch."

Geek lowered the binoculars, shifting his gaze between McClure and the speck of the yacht. The FUBI had set up a three-hour watch rotation. Why would a bunch of rich people be trailing an MSA boat that long?

"They done anything suspicious?" he asked. "I mean, other than tailing us?"

"Nope." McClure shook his head. "They've kept their distance."

Lips pressed together, Geek peered through the binoculars again, running scenarios through his head. Could it be a coincidence? Maybe the yacht happened to be on the same course as the *Grantin*.

But we're searching in a grid pattern, making turns all the time. Why would that yacht be turning with us?

"Pirates" crossed Geek's mind. They were fairly active throughout Indonesia. But he knew of no pirates that used a yacht that cost millions of dollars. And what pirates would be dumb enough to attack an armed patrol boat?

"Does Captain Teguh know?" Geek referred to *Grantin's* skipper.

"Affirmative, though he thinks it's rich foreign tourists out for a thrill, following us to see if we rescue someone or fight some pirates."

"You'd think they'd get bored after watching us do nothing for three hours."

"Yeah, well, your guess is as good as mine," said McClure. "Keep an eye on them, just in case."

"Will do, sir."

McClure slapped him on the shoulder and departed.

Geek watched the yacht, which did nothing interesting. He then scanned the sky. No sign of the Ropen. Back to the yacht again. No cannons or Jolly Roger flags sprouted from the vessel. This watch was shaping up to be like most . . . uneventful.

Most times, that was a good thing. Besides, three hours standing watch in the middle of the Java Sea was better than three hours in an office. Dangerous as these monster hunts could be, he was glad to be a part of them. While Aster Technologies employed him as a field tester, he seemed to spend more time indoors than actually in the field testing cool weapons and gadgets. Too many damn meetings, too many damn reports to deal with, and God help him if he had to attend one more sensitivity training session. Like his parents hadn't taught him growing up to not act like a jerkoff. He didn't need some Social Justice Warrior wannabe telling him he was a bad person because he happened to have a shlong.

Yeah, he would much rather be out here. The downside was being away from Angela and their three children. He'd had to leave them far too many times while in the Army. But these short excursions with Captain Rastun and the FUBI were a lot easier on his family than a deployment that could last months, even a full year.

"Geek."

He spun around to find Ehrenberg standing a few feet away.

"What is it, Doc?"

"Meeting time. We're all getting together in the wardroom."

Geek let out a soft sigh. Even in the middle of the fucking ocean, he still had to go to a damn meeting.

Even though the captain and ship's officers dined in the wardroom, the place couldn't be any bigger than the typical college dorm room. Again, space was at a premium on this vessel. Captain Teguh sat at the head of the table, with Lieutenant Bahar to his left. Ehrenberg sat to the skipper's immediate right, and Geek settled into the chair next to him.

Teguh, an unsmiling, officious-looking man with glasses, knitted his eyebrows together as he stared at Geek. The captain slid a few inches to the right, trying to put as much distance between them as possible.

Really? Since coming aboard the *Grantin,* every time he and Teguh found themselves in the same room, the Indonesian went out of his way to not stand or sit next to him. Geek figured he knew Teguh's issue with him. The captain measured in at only 5'5 and probably 160 pounds. Geek had eight inches and seventy pounds over him, making him a giant compared to Teguh, along with most of *Grantin's* crew. He'd encountered a few officers like that in the Army, so embarrassed by their short stature they resented being around much bigger men like him.

His problem, not mine.

Alana, Herrera, and McClure took their seats, everyone nearly shoulder-to-shoulder around the small table.

So glad I didn't join the Navy or Coast Guard. He'd go nuts if he had to be stuck on a small ship like this for months on end.

"So what's all the excitement, Doc?" asked Herrera.

"I just got a call from Jack. He, Karen, and Petal have gotten numerous eyewitness reports on Pulau Kangean of Ropen lights over the past week."

"Could that be the island where they are coming from?" asked Bahar.

Ehrenberg shrugged. "It might be. It certainly is a good lead. Plus, Jack informed me the local police are searching for a group of Dutch students who are overdue from an eco-education trip."

"You thinking the Ropen may have gotten them?" Geek settled his arms on the table.

"It's a possibility."

"So you want me to take my boat to Pulau Kangean?" From Teguh's tone, he made it sound like a major inconvenience.

"No," Ehrenberg answered. "I still want us to keep searching this area for any Ropen. But we should send some more people there to help Jack and Petal and the others. With your permission, Captain, I'd like your helicopter to return to *Grantin* so it can fly Geek, Alana, and Alfonso to Pulau Kangean."

"We should also add some of our men to the team, sir," Bahar added. "We have seen ourselves how deadly the Ropen are. Mister Rastun will need all the help we can provide."

A sour expression formed on Teguh's face. He let out a slow breath. "Very well," he spoke in heavily accented English. "Recall the helicopter. Pick four crew to accompany the Americans. That should suffice."

"Yes, Captain," replied Bahar.

"Thank you, Captain." Ehrenberg smiled.

Teguh gave him a curt nod. Geek figured the skipper did not like a civilian – a foreign one, no less – telling him what to do on his ship. But Teguh had his marching orders from his government. Accommodate all requests by the FUBI in its search for the Ropen.

The meeting broke up. Geek ordered Alana and Herrera to gather their gear and get it ready to load in the chopper when it returned. He would have helped them, but he had his watch to finish.

The yacht still shadowed them. It continued to do so for the next hour, and the next hour after that.

Twenty minutes before his shift ended, *Grantin* turned to port.

The yacht did *not* follow.

Geek watched it sail north, and eventually out of sight.

While gone from view, the yacht was not gone from his thoughts. Geek gazed in the direction the vessel had vanished, unable to shake the nagging concern.

Why were those people following the *Grantin* in the first place?

ELEVEN

"Hello! Anyone out there?"

Rastun winced at Petal's shouting, then forced himself to relax. A by-product of his Ranger days, where stealth had been drilled into him.

But this wasn't the Rangers and this Indonesian jungle was not enemy territory. They didn't have to worry about tipping off any bad guys. They could shout out for the missing Dutch students, who could also shout back.

If they're still alive.

He clenched his jaw, trying to think positive.

"Anyone out there?" Rastun called out. So did Karen, Norgay, Wikana, and their guide from Kalisangka, a whipcord thin man named Pinurbo.

No one called back.

They continued east on the main jungle trail the students would have taken to get to the village. Rastun's eyes swept over the ground, taking stock of branches, brush, fallen leaves and twigs, and the dirt, alert for indentations, bends, or any other unnatural disturbances. Anything to indicate the students had moved through this area.

He found no such signs.

The group came upon another trail that branched off to the north. Pinurbo pointed and said something in his native tongue.

"We should look down this trail," Wikana translated. "It is not unusual for tourists to wander along another trail by mistake."

Rastun nodded. Even the most experienced outdoorsmen could get lost in a jungle.

They trekked down the path, several branches in their way. Rastun checked for any breaks or bends before shoving them aside. He saw no sign the students had come this way.

"Look." Karen, who walked next to him, pointed to the muddy bank of a small lake.

A wavy line traced through the darkened ground with round indentations on either side. Rastun held his breath, looking at the tracks, then the water.

Pinurbo spoke, followed by Wikana's translation. "We must back up, carefully." He turned to the guide, saying one word. Rastun figured it was, "Why?"

Pinurbo answered, though Rastun did not need any translation. He had a very good idea what made those tracks.

He heard Wikana swallow before he translated, a tremor in his voice. "He-He says there is a crocodile in the lake."

"Not just any crocodile." Petal eyed the lake. "In this part of the world, it's likely a saltwater crocodile."

Rastun's hand hovered near his holster. Salties were the most aggressive crocodilian species toward humans, and could grow up to twenty feet in length.

His cheek twitched, thinking of the Glock 17 he carried, wishing he had something with more stopping power, like his Steyr AUG. But the rifle was back on the *Grantin.* They'd come to Pulau Kangean to interview the locals. He didn't need a rifle for that. Aside from his knife, he'd left most of his gear back on the boat. How could he have known he'd be asked to take part in a search and rescue mission?

Note to self. Next time, bring more stuff. Just in case.

They continued backing up. Rastun saw no disturbances in the water. A scan of the bank turned up no sign of shredded clothing or gear or body parts, anything to indicate the Dutch students ran afoul of the croc.

The group made it back to the main path, with Pinurbo warning them to stay alert. Rastun knew salties usually stuck close to water, but usually did not mean always.

They hiked another three miles, finding no trace of the Dutch students. Pinurbo then pointed ahead of them. Wikana translated, "There's a clearing just ahead. Loggers cut down that part of the jungle."

The group came upon a swath of tree stumps broken up by patches of dirt and grass. The air around Rastun heated up immediately with no canopy to block the sun. He took a long pull from his water bottle and moved forward, checking the ground around him. There was no sign of any recent human activity.

Rastun lifted his gaze to the blue sky. All clear. The position of the sun indicated mid-afternoon. They'd long since missed their appointed meeting at Mainaky Fisheries. Unavoidable. Finding the missing students took precedence.

Not that the director's assistant seemed to comprehend that.

"Mister Pistaka set up this meeting for two o'clock," the man had told him over the phone. "He is very busy. You must be here at two o'clock."

"Like I said," Rastun had replied. "There are six people missing in the jungle and they may have been attacked by Ropen. We have to help find them."

The assistant had paused. "The police can search. You must be here at two o'clock for the meeting."

"Yeah, well that ain't happening."

The assistant had again insisted they be at Mainaky Fisheries at two. Rastun just hung up without a word.

"Hello!" Karen's yell brought him back to the present. "Anybody here?"

She was answered by silence.

"Let's spread out," ordered Rastun. "Five yards abreast."

They lined up and marched forward, Rastun walking near the edge of a ravine. Several bushes lined the banks of a dirty stream running along the bottom. They called out to the students. No one answered.

Rastun exhaled in frustration and worry. The students were high school age, just a few years older than Emily. He thought of their parents back in The Netherlands. They had to be out of their minds with worry. He could only imagine how scared he and Karen would be if it had been Emily lost out here. Too many things in the jungle could kill you besides the Ropen. Crocodiles, snakes, disease-carrying mosquitos, the elements.

He hoped the students just took a wrong path and . . .

Rastun halted. Something lay on the ground ahead of him, slender and wrapped in beige cloth.

"I got something." He walked toward the object. His shoulders sagged as he halted a couple of feet from it.

"What is it?" Petal jogged up to him, then stopped, letting out a short gasp. "Oh my God."

They stared at a severed arm. Female, judging by the small hand and thin fingers. Bits of flesh were missing and parts of the sleeve had been torn away. Probably birds or small mammals scavenging for food. Patches of dried blood stained the ground around it. A coppery smell tinged the air.

"I found something, too," announced Karen.

Both Rastun and Petal turned to her. Karen held up a shredded backpack coated with a dark substance.

"There is a large patch of blood here, too." Norgay, standing about twenty yards away, pointed to the ground.

Pinurbo found another blood patch, along with a torn piece of clothing. Wikana stood a few feet from the guide, grimacing, his head turned as though trying not to see the blood.

They surveyed the area and identified five separate places where blood stained the ground and the stumps.

"Those poor people." Karen shook her head.

Rastun placed a gentle hand on her shoulder. The veins in his neck stuck out as he thought of the families of these people breaking down when they received the horrible news.

He stared at one of the blood patches, brow furrowed. "There should be six."

"What?" Wikana muttered.

"Mohede said there were six missing. Four students, their instructor, and a local guide. There are only five areas of concentrated blood spatter. One of them got away."

"Maybe they made it into the jungle," suggested Petal.

"No," said Norgay. "It is quite a distance from where the attack took place to the tree line. The person would likely be terrified, running for all he or she was worth. Look at all the stumps. I doubt they could have made it to the jungle without tripping over one."

"And then the Ropen would have been on them," added Rastun.

"The ravine." Karen headed toward it. "They could have gone down there."

She stood at the edge, moving her head left to right. Rastun approached just as she pointed. "Jack, there."

He spotted groove marks in the dirt, then a few sections of flattened and scuffed earth going toward the stream. Someone had slipped and fallen here.

"Hello?" Rastun shouted. "Anyone there? Hello?"

No one answered.

"C'mon." He glanced at Karen before starting down the ravine. She followed, joined by the others. Wikana slipped and fell, but was helped up by Pinurbo.

They neared the bank of the brownish stream, calling out for the survivor. Rastun and Karen checked the nearest bush. No one behind it. Same with the second bush.

The third had a pair of hiking boots sticking out of it.

The group hurried along the bank. Rastun focused on those boots, looking for the slightest hint of movement. *Please be alive.*

He dropped to his knees when he reached the bush. A thin girl with brown hair lay curled up in a fetal position. Her wide eyes stared right at him, but she didn't notice him. Sympathy swelled within him. The girl was in shock. Had she witnessed the attack on her friends?

"Hey," Rastun said in a soft voice as the others gathered around. "Hey. We're here to help you."

The girl said nothing, just remained oblivious to the rest of the world.

"You're okay, honey." Rastun reached out to her. "We're gonna get you home."

58

He gave her shoulder a light touch.

The girl let out a raspy scream. She sat up and thrashed about.

"It's okay." Karen came up behind the girl and wrapped her arms around her. "You're okay. You're okay." She repeated the words in a soothing tone.

The girl settled down, emitting gasping sobs. Karen held on to her. The girl's eyes fluttered and her head lolled from side-to-side.

"I think she might be dehydrated." Petal pulled a water bottle from her pack. "Here, sweetie."

She gave the bottle to the girl. Karen eased up on her hug so the girl could take it. She pressed it to her mouth. Most of the water went down her throat, the rest dribbled down her chin and onto her shirt. The girl was about to take another gulp when Karen took hold of the bottle.

"Not so fast. We don't want you getting sick."

The girl took some shaky breaths and looked at the others. She said something in Dutch.

"Who are you?" Wikana translated.

"I'm Jack Rastun." He introduced the others. "We're with the FUBI."

After Wikana translated, Rastun asked, "What's your name?"

The girl took a couple of slow breaths before responding. "M-Manda. Manda van Giersbergen." She blinked, her gaze on Rastun. "FUBI? You're . . . You're the monster hunters." This time she spoke in accented English.

"That's right."

Manda shivered, drawing her knees up. "They . . . They killed them. All of them."

"Do you mean the Ropen?" asked Petal.

Manda nodded, shutting her eyes. Karen gently clutched the girl's shoulders as she spoke. "We . . . We stopped for a rest. Willem sprained his ankle. We had to stop. Why did we stop?"

She let out a choked sob.

"It's okay, honey." Karen stroked Manda's matted hair. "You're safe now."

Manda released a staggered breath. "I came down here to pee, when I came back . . ." She shuddered, face tightening. "They came and . . . and . . . they killed everyone."

"How many Ropen?" asked Rastun.

"Three. They killed them. They killed them."

She burst into tears. Karen wrapped Manda in a tight hug, rocking her back and forth.

Rastun lowered his head, his heart going out to the traumatized teen.

Petal knelt beside him. "They might have accidentally stumbled into the Ropen's territory."

"If that's the case, we should get back to the jungle." Rastun looked to the sky. "We're too exposed here."

"Manda," Karen said to her. "Are you hurt in any way?"

She sniffled. "N-No. I don't think so."

Karen helped the girl to her feet. They headed back up the slope, their progress slowed by Manda walking on shaky legs. Rastun reached the lip of the ravine and checked over his shoulder, mentally urging the girl to hurry. The sooner they got back in the jungle, the better he'd –

"Inbound," blurted Norgay.

Rastun looked to where Norgay pointed. A dark, winged shape with a whip-like tail soared over the clearing.

TWELVE

Manda screamed as the Ropen dove at them.

Rastun looked back at the jungle. He doubted they could cover the open ground to the tree line before the creature started picking them off.

"Back down the ravine." He pulled out his Glock. "Go! Go! Go!"

They hurried down the slope, Rastun and Norgay bringing up the rear to cover them. Pinurbo drew his machete.

Rastun glanced from one side of the ravine to the other. It wasn't all that narrow, but it should be narrow enough to keep the Ropen, with its large wingspan, from flying down after them.

Wikana half-ran, half-slid along the stream. He checked behind him once, twice . . . then tripped and fell. Brown water splashed up around him. He pushed himself to his knees and spat out a mouthful of filthy water.

"Wikana! Are you okay?" Petal rushed over to help him.

"Okay or not, you need to move your ass," barked Rastun.

Wikana scrambled to his feet, stumbling at first, then running through the water.

Manda screamed again, holding on to Karen tightly, her eyes aimed above them. Both Rastun and Norgay followed her gaze.

The Ropen perched on the edge of the ravine on all fours, resembling a giant lizard with long triangular wings attached to its forearms. Rastun stared down the length of the stream. Ahead of them lay a pile of branches and other debris, probably left over from the logging operation. Beyond it, the stream ran all the way into the jungle.

He looked back at the creature. It remained on the edge, its inky black eyes staring at them. As he thought, its wingspan was too long to swoop down the ravine.

The Ropen croaked and leaped down the slope. It jumped again, nearly slipping. The creature righted itself and sprang forward.

"Keep going!" Rastun spun around, feet apart, pistol raised. Norgay did the same.

The Ropen's next jump put it alongside the stream. It let out a throaty cry and pushed itself up on two feet. Rastun held his breath as he stared down the Glock's sights. Damn, but the thing was big. Fifteen, maybe sixteen feet tall. The Ropen let out another cry, showing off rows of sharp teeth.

Rastun focused on his pistol for a second. It seemed a piss poor weapon against an animal that large. But it was all he had, and he needed to keep this monster busy so Karen and the others could get away.

He fired. So did Norgay. The Ropen wailed and stomped its talons. Little bloody holes formed on the snout and its torso, but it did not go down.

The pair squeezed off another volley of 9mm rounds, backing up as they did. Rastun raised his pistol, going for a headshot. He pulled the trigger three times. Two rounds missed. The third grazed the center of its snout.

The reptile bellowed and leapt toward them.

"Fuck," Rastun hissed as he and Norgay dashed through the stream, kicking up curtains of water. He reloaded his Glock, scowling. The damn thing just didn't have enough stopping power against a beast that size.

The Ropen wailed again. Rastun twisted around and fired three times. Little streams of blood ran down the Ropen's side.

It still didn't look close to going down.

The Ropen cried out and jumped. It flapped its wings once, twice, brushing them against the slopes on either side. The Ropen barely gained any altitude.

It jumped again, splashing down in the stream a few feet from Rastun and Norgay. Rastun got off a shot at point-blank range. The round burrowed into the Ropen's side. It wailed, stood on its hind legs, and swept its wings forward. Rastun turned to throw himself on the ground.

Too late. Stinging pain exploded across his back. He fell, toppling into the stream, face and shoulders splashing down in the water.

He pushed himself to all fours in time to see the Ropen's tail whipping at Norgay. He dove for the ground. The tail just missed him, but his gunhand sank into the mud along the bank.

Rastun glanced at his right hand, all his muscles clenching. His Glock was gone.

He scanned the ground around him. No sign of it. Had it fallen into the murky water?

Rastun looked up. The Ropen stared at him, mouth opening.

Norgay's arm flashed out. Rastun caught sight of the curved blade in his hand. The Kukri, the traditional knife of the Gurkhas. It sliced into the Ropen's left wing once, twice, three times.

The monster screeched, twisting around toward Norgay. The Nepalese held up the Kukri, ready for another slash.

The Ropen snapped at him. Norgay dove to the right, just avoiding it. The creature stepped toward him.

Rastun drew his own knife and jammed it into the creature's right wing. It wailed. Rastun stabbed it again.

The Ropen leapt away from them. Rastun figured, like most animals, it had no desire to get in a protracted fight and risk further injury. Badly wounded animals did not survive long in the wild.

The winged reptile jumped further down the stream. Fear stabbed Rastun's gut as it went after Karen and the others.

***

Karen heard Jack yell her name. She twisted around.

The Ropen charged toward them.

Manda unleashed a prolonged, terrified scream.

"C'mon! Keep going!" Karen shoved the Dutch girl forward. She tried to ignore the hammering of her heart and her fear of being torn apart and eaten. The fear of Jack, Petal, Manda, and the others being killed. All that mattered was getting to the cover of the jungle.

The debris pile blocked their path. They ran up the bank to avoid it. Karen looked over her shoulder. The Ropen jumped again. Several small trails of red ran down its body. How many times had Jack and Norgay shot it?

Wikana's foot caught on a pile of branches. He cried out and fell.

Karen turned, ready to help the fallen translator, when Pinurbo rushed past, gripping his machete.

Wikana clawed at the ground, gasping in fear, trying to push himself up.

The Ropen jumped again, landing barely ten feet from the translator. He screamed.

Pinurbo grabbed Wikana's shoulder and hauled him to his feet. He waved for him to run, which he did, as fast as he could.

Pinurbo turned just as the Ropen jumped.

"Look out!" Karen yelled.

The monster landed right behind their guide. Pinurbo swung around and raised his machete.

The Ropen caught Pinurbo's arm in its jaws. He cried out in agony.

The monster whipped its snout around, throwing Pinurbo to the ground. His right arm dangled uselessly, connected by just a few strands of bloody flesh.

The Ropen sank the talons of its left forearm into Pinurbo and ripped down his waist. Blood gushed from the gaping wound. Pieces of intestine hung out his torn gut.

Karen grimaced and turned away. Pinurbo was beyond help. She fought to put his death out of her mind and concentrate on keeping the others safe.

The Ropen jumped toward them. The thing was roughly twenty feet away.

Karen glanced at the debris pile, looking for a big enough branch to use as a weapon. Maybe she could hold off the Ropen for a bit, give Manda and the others time to get away and time for Jack and Norgay to get closer to shoot it.

She spotted something yellow and metal among the branches. Was it . . .

She reached down and yanked it through the debris. Just as she thought; a chainsaw, rusted with much of the paint chipped off. Probably thrown away by some logger.

Karen didn't have much experience with power tools, but she'd seen people use chainsaws on TV and movies. Shouldn't there be some sort of rope . . .

There. On the right side. She pulled it.

Nothing happened.

"Shit."

The Ropen jumped again, landing barely six feet from her. She shivered when its maw opened, revealing its teeth. So many sharp teeth.

The monster lunged at her.

Karen grunted and swung the chainsaw. Her arms shook as it struck the Ropen's jaw. It blared in pain, its head snapping backwards. Blood trickled from its jaw as it raised up on its haunches.

She backed away, keeping the chainsaw in front of her. The Ropen stepped toward her. Gritting her teeth, she got ready for another swing.

"Down!" Jack called out from behind the Ropen.

Karen dropped to her stomach. Gunfire cracked a split-second later.

***

Norgay's Glock fired three times, then stopped. Rastun glanced over at him. The Gurkha racked the pistol to clear the jam, then fired two more times.

It jammed again.

Rastun scowled. His Glock was somewhere at the bottom of the creek and Norgay's pistol probably had too much mud in it to work properly.

The Ropen screeched and swung around. Norgay cleared his Glock and fired. He pulled the trigger again.

Nothing.

Snorting, he holstered the mud-caked pistol and drew his Kukri.

Rastun gripped his knife, clenching his teeth. Two knives against a fifteen-foot prehistoric monster. Great odds.

The Ropen jumped toward them. He and Norgay retreated, blades out. Rastun's mind raced through tactics. How many stabs to the torso would it take to bring that creature down? Probably a lot, and sure as hell it wouldn't stand still and let them stab it repeatedly.

The Ropen leapt again. Both Rastun and Norgay rolled away just as it landed, throwing up a curtain of muddy water.

Rastun focused on its legs.

"Legs!" he shouted to Norgay. "Go for the legs!"

Rastun sprang to his feet. He ran toward the Ropen, blaring out a war cry. The monster turned to him, mouth open, ready to lunge.

Just what he wanted.

Norgay charged the beast and drove his Kukri into the right leg. The Ropen threw back its head and screeched.

Rastun dove, rolled, and came up next to the left leg. He plunged the blade into it twice.

The Ropen kicked out. Razor-sharp talons flashed right past Rastun's face. The creature wobbled backwards.

Rastun and Norgay stabbed the legs again. The monster squealed and stumbled. It flapped its wings, forcing them to retreat. The beast could not generate enough lift and fell on its back.

The pair moved toward the head. The Ropen snapped at them, whipping its wings, driving them back. Rastun caught sight of Pinurbo's shredded and bloody body lying on the bank. Beside him lay his machete.

Rastun dashed over and snatched up the blade. He bounded back to the Ropen, still thrashing and snapping. Norgay circled the monster, trying to find an opening to deliver the killing blow. He couldn't. The former Gurkha let out a few shouts, thrusting his Kukri at the creature, distracting it. Rastun gave the flapping wings a wide berth, coming around till he lined up with the Ropen's head. He sprinted forward.

The Ropen twisted around and snapped at him. Rastun jumped back. The monster lunged its jaws toward him.

Karen ran past, a chainsaw over her head. She swung down, catching the Ropen on the side of the head. The rusted, dull teeth slid over its right eye.

The Ropen cried out, its head thrusting toward Karen. She fell back, the chainsaw flying out of her hand.

Rastun ran forward, raising the machete. He plunged it into the Ropen's throat. Blood cascaded from the wound. Rastun lifted the machete and brought it down again. More blood gushed out the Ropen's neck. It trembled, then lay still.

Exhaling, Rastun backed away, then saw Karen sitting in the stream. He helped her to her feet and hugged her, their clothing damp with water and sweat.

"You okay?" asked Karen.

"Fine. You?"

She nodded against his chest. He looked down the stream. No sign of Petal, Manda, or Wikana. It appeared they made it to the jungle.

Releasing Karen, Rastun stared down at the bloodied and dead Ropen.

"Well, that's one down, and who knows how many more to go."

THIRTEEN

Marques had the fork almost to his mouth when Lenna shrieked. He jerked, sending the scoop of vegan mac and cheese flying off his fork and plopping onto the table in *Earth Warrior's* dining area.

"What the fuck?" Griffin glared at the beer he had spilled down his shirt.

The phone slipped from Lenna's hand onto the table. She gaped at it, drawing loud breaths.

"What is it?" Paulette leaned forward in her seat. "Are you okay?"

Lenna gasped twice. "Those fucking bastards! They murdered one!"

"What the hell are you talking about?" Griffin snatched a napkin and wiped at the wet stain on his shirt.

"The fucking FUBI. They killed a Ropen. Look." Lenna shoved her phone to the middle of the table.

Marques and the others stared at the screen. It showed an article on Lenna's Twitter page. The headline read, "One Dead in Another Ropen Attack."

The FUBI expedition in Indonesia was attacked today by a Ropen, leaving one of its members dead, according to a spokesperson for the monster-hunting organization. Two of the expedition's field security specialists fought off the flying dinosaur – It's not a dinosaur, Marques thought -- *shooting it numerous times before it was killed.*

"Dammit." He thumped his fist on the table. Paulette reached over and clutched his hand.

He read on. *The FUBI had been helping in the search for some missing tourists on Pulau Kangean when the Ropen appeared. Their local guide was killed before they shot and stabbed the animal to death.* The article did not name the field security specialists, but Marques knew one of them had to be Jack Rastun. His contact told him the son-of-a-bitch was part of the FUBI team sent to that island.

A hot breath flowed from his nose, his anger building, along with a sense of failure. He'd been sent here to keep Rastun and his group from killing any more cryptids. But one of these magnificent creatures lay dead, with Rastun and his sick friends celebrating their latest kill.

Yeah. More interviews. More book deals. More people thinking you're a hero for slaughtering one of the most endangered species on the planet.

Griffin looked at the phone, then to Marques, then to Lenna. He slammed his hand on the table. "Man, those fucking Nazi murdering scumbags. This is . . . it's a crime against nature. But they're not gonna get away with it. Right, guys?"

"I'm not a guy, asshole!" Lenna snapped.

"Okay." Griffin threw up his arms. "I mean everyone, okay?"

Marques got up and stormed away from the table. He was not in the mood for Lenna being offended at everything or the washed-up actor pretending he gave a damn about the Ropen.

"We'll be at the island soon," Paulette told him.

He spun around to face her. "And how many more Ropen will die before we get there? Maybe there won't be any left to save."

"Seriously, Cesar?" Paulette tilted her head. "We'll be at Pulau Kangean before dawn. I doubt the FUBI can kill every single Ropen before then."

"They wiped out an entire colony of lizard people in one night. Maybe they'll do it to the Ropen." His face scrunched. "Can't this damn boat go any faster?"

"It's going as fast as it can." An edge crept into Paulette's voice. "It's a big-ass yacht, not a race car."

Marques snorted. He finally had a job where he could truly make a difference, and he was stuck in the middle of the ocean while one of the world's rarest species became even rarer thanks to a gang of murderers.

"Well, I'll tell you what I'm gonna do," Lenna grabbed her phone, "I'm gonna blow this motherfucker up on Twitter."

"Yes, that will be productive," Marques grumbled.

Lenna swung around in her chair. "You'll see when this starts trending. Everyone's gonna gang up on these shit-bastards."

Scowling, Marques stalked out of the dining area. Did Lenna really think a lot of Tweets would make a difference? He'd been quite the keyboard warrior years ago. But no matter how many of his causes got liked or retweeted or trended, endangered animals still died, forests still got cut down, and the air still got polluted. Only direct action would make any real difference.

If only they could get to Pulau Kangean in time.

He took the steps up to the bridge, where Kory was at the helm. She glanced over her shoulder. "I heard Lenna shouting down there. What pissed her off this time?"

Marques told her about the FUBI killing the Ropen.

Kory scowled. "What is wrong with those people?"

"They're bloodthirsty maniacs, and we can't do anything to stop them." Marques pressed his hands against the window, glaring out at the darkened sea.

Kory did a double-take. "What are you talking about? That's why we're here, isn't it?"

Marques opened his mouth, ready to snap at her, but stopped himself. He exhaled slowly.

She's right. Stopping the FUBI was the reason he was here, the reason his organization existed. He'd scolded Lenna about how tweeting would do no good. Well, so would being mad about a setback. A tragic setback, no doubt, but he couldn't let it consume him. The other Ropen depended on him. All the other cryptids out there the FUBI wanted to hunt depended on him.

Marques put more pressure on the windows, trying to expel all his rage and guilt. He needed to clear his head, think, come up with a plan to deal with Rastun's team.

He got his satellite phone and called his contact. "I need to know what Jack Rastun's team is up to on Pulau Kangean. Do we know what parts of the island they are going to search?"

"I do not know, but I will find out. I will get back to you in an hour."

Marques clipped the sat phone to his belt, loosened his muscles, and headed back to the dining area. He found Paulette, Lenna, and Griffin all on their phones.

"Yo," the actor said. "Jack Rastun's parents run the Philadelphia Zoo, right? Why don't I call for a boycott of it?"

"Good idea, Thomas." Paulette nodded to him.

"Will wonders never cease," Lenna muttered.

Griffin ignored her and typed away on his phone.

Marques sat down and finished the rest of his vegan mac and cheese.

"Looks like you've calmed down." Paulette rubbed his back.

"Yes. I probably shouldn't have overreacted. I was just pissed about the FUBI killing that Ropen."

"I know. We're all mad about it."

"Maybe we'll get lucky and some other Ropen will eat fucking Jack Rastun and his shitbag friends," said Lenna.

Marques chuckled, as did Paulette. Griffin let out a very loud, very forced laugh.

An hour later, Marques was in his and Paulette's cabin, stretched out on their bed and listening to music on his laptop, when his sat phone rang. It was his contact.

"Rastun and his team are scheduled to meet with officials from Mainaky Fisheries tomorrow morning, then plan to investigate the graveyards in Torjek in the afternoon."

Marques nodded. He'd heard stories that the Ropen dug up graves to eat dead bodies.

A smile grew on his face. They could reach Torjek well ahead of the FUBI and he'd make certain they never killed another Ropen.

FOURTEEN

Karen's eyes snapped open. She clenched the sheets so tight her fingers got sore. Her heart slammed against her chest. For a second, she swore the jaws of the Ropen were snapping down on her.

Just a dream. Just a dream, she kept repeating in her mind, inhaling deeply to calm herself. She forced her fingers to loosen on the sheets.

Another close call. Karen rolled on her back, gazing around the small space above the coffee shop that served as a hotel room. Actually, hotel room was too generous. There was a bed, a window, and a nightstand and table that had both seen better days. She figured the shop owner saw no need to upgrade. Tourists didn't exactly flock to Kalisangka.

She glanced at Jack, lying beside her, fast asleep. Was he having nightmares about the Ropen attack? It wouldn't surprise her. He was prone to them, from both his time in the Army and the FUBI.

And now I'm racking up a good number of them myself. Karen forced her eyes shut, trying to get back to sleep and forget about the fear of the Ropen mere feet away from her, the dread she would never see Emily again, the shredded body of their guide, Pinurbo.

She managed to nod off a couple of times before a blend of operatic vocals and metal music blared from Jack's phone. Epica's "Beyond the Matrix." She groaned at the alarm song, wishing it would stop, wishing she could get more sleep. Wondering if she could without thinking of Ropen and dead guides.

Jack mercifully shut off the alarm. "Morning," he said before kissing her cheek.

"Mmm yeah," she grumbled.

He rolled out of bed and hit the floor, rattling off one hundred pushups and one hundred sit-ups before heading off to the communal bathroom. Karen had forced herself to sit on the edge of the bed by the time Jack returned.

"Bathroom's all yours," he said.

"Mm-hmm." She stared at her bare feet, gripping the edges of the mattress.

Jack sat beside her and put an arm around her. Some of her tension melted away. "You okay?" he asked.

"Yeah." She turned to face him. "I'm fine."

His face stiffened in concern. "Nightmare?"

She avoided eye contact. "That obvious, huh?"

Jack put a gentle hand on her leg. "Just part of the coping process. Just remember, we made it out okay." His shoulders sagged. "Most of us."

Karen's heart ached as she stared at Jack's face. He always took it hard when he lost people under his charge.

"You did everything you could." She ran her fingers over his stubbly cheek.

"Yeah, maybe." He let out a sharp breath. "Well, we better get rolling. Got another busy day ahead of us."

He pushed himself off the bed.

Karen sighed. That was that. Maybe later he'd talk about Pinurbo's death. Maybe she'd have to get him to talk about it, or maybe he'd just keep it bottled up and deal with it on his own. Or try to. It was always a crapshoot with Jack in that respect.

She went through her own morning routine of stretches, crunches, and planks before heading to the bathroom. Not the dirtiest she'd ever been in, yet not the cleanest, either. She didn't linger and took care of business, coming out in fresh clothes.

Karen took a few steps and stopped at the room two doors down from hers and Jack's. Manda's room. Concern grew within her. Yes, the Ropen attack had haunted Karen's sleep, but that was not the first life or death situation she'd been in. She couldn't imagine how terrifying the Dutch girl's dreams had been, if she even managed to sleep.

She knocked on the door. "Manda, it's Karen. Are you up?"

The door opened seconds later. Karen fought to keep from biting her lip when she saw the girl. Her face looked drawn and her eyes were red. Manda had definitely gotten little, if any, sleep.

"I just wanted to see if you're okay, honey."

"I'm fine, thank you," she mumbled, then padded to her bed. She plopped down on the edge, picking up her phone, flexing her fingers around it.

"Can you get a signal?" Karen entered the small room and sat beside her. "Reception here is spotty."

Manda nodded. "My parents called an hour ago. They were boarding their plane to fly here."

Karen smiled. In a couple of hours, the Maritime Security Agency would fly Manda to Bali, where a representative from the Dutch embassy would wait with her until her parents arrived.

"I'm sure your mom and dad will be happy to see you."

"Uh-huh." Manda ran a thumb up and down the side of her phone.

"Hey." Karen put an arm around the girl's shoulders. "I know what happened yesterday has to be the scariest thing in the world for you. It's going to take time for you to process it. Same with me. I was scared, too."

"No, that can't be true." Manda looked at Karen. "You were brave. You fought that monster. I . . . I . . ."

Tears spilled from the girl's eyes. "I was mad at Willem because he got hurt and slowed us down, and jealous of Ella because she was better looking than me, and I saw them . . . they're dead, and I thought . . ."

Manda broke down. Karen wrapped her in a hug, stroking her hair. "It's okay, sweetie. It's okay."

She held the Dutch girl for several minutes until she cried herself out.

"I'm sorry." Manda rubbed her hands under her damp eyes.

"Don't be. It's okay."

Manda gave her a shaky smile. "Thank you. You're very nice. The people on Twitter, they're idiots. They don't know anything about you."

"What do you mean?" Karen tilted her head.

Manda held up her phone. Karen looked at the trending section.

#Ropen . . . #FUBI . . . #StopRopenKillers. All had well over 100,000 tweets.

Oh shit.

She asked Manda to click on #StopRopenKillers.

"Fucking Murderers . . . Throw all #FUBI Nazis in jail and let them get raped . . . Hope #Ropen eats all #FUBI assholes and shits them out into a volcano #StopRopenKillers #RopenLivesMatter."

Those were some of the tamer tweets.

"They are stupid." Manda scowled. "They didn't see what those monsters did. They can all go to hell."

"Don't let them get to you." Karen rubbed Manda's arm. "They're just venting."

She left the room, telling the girl they would be heading down to breakfast soon. Worry surged through Karen as she returned to her room.

"I checked on Manda," she told Jack. "She seems to be doing okay, all things considered."

"Good. Poor kid, musta been hell for her." His brow furrowed. "You okay?"

Karen sighed. Apparently, she hadn't kept the worry off her face. "Manda told me yesterday's attack is trending on Twitter."

"No surprise."

"There's a lot of people calling us murderers and Nazis and all that stupid crap."

Jack shrugged. "And how's that different from any other day? Except maybe there are more crazies because the attack just happened."

"What about Emily?" Karen threw out an arm. "What if that teacher decides to start giving her crap again because of this?"

"I think she got the message the first time that we aren't going to put up with that."

"She might think differently now that we're ten thousand miles away. Or what if some of her classmates give her a hard time? What if some random wacko does something to her?" Jack crossed the room and grasped her shoulders. "Hey, hey. Give Emily a call and tell her to be on guard, and tell the same thing to the Bradfords." They were the parents of Emily's best friend from youth soccer she was staying with. "And for good measure, I'll call Colonel Lipeli and get him to have one of our field security specialists swing by from time to time to keep an eye on her."

Karen exhaled, her shoulders relaxed. "Okay. Okay. I just wish I was back home to make sure she's safe."

"So do I. But we'll have people keeping an eye on her. She'll be fine." Jack kissed her forehead.

"Thanks." She hugged him.

After making their calls, they headed for Manda's room. "It'd be nice if things could be different," said Karen.

Jack looked over his shoulder at her. "What do you mean?"

"That we had more expeditions where we didn't have to kill cryptids or deal with all this hate."

"I wouldn't mind that, either. I mean, our mission statement is to protect cryptids. But let's face it, we're the FUBI's A-Team. When those things turn dangerous, we're the ones they send in to deal with them. We can't let a bunch of dipshits on Twitter dictate what we do in the field. We just have to ride it out."

Karen reluctantly nodded, hoping they could ride it out without any consequences for Emily, or anyone else.

They fetched Manda, then went to Wikana's room. The translator had a stiff air about him. The man's eyes were red, the skin beneath them creased, as though he hadn't gotten much sleep. It appeared he, too, suffered from nightmares.

"Are you okay?" she asked.

"I am fine," he muttered, turning away. He probably did not want to admit his fears, especially to a woman.

The little group headed downstairs to the café. Half the tables were occupied, mostly by women, their husbands probably out to sea already. Two of the women Karen recognized.

Upon making eye contact, Soehaemi, Adsit's sister-in-law, nodded to them and stood, along with her sister, Surati. Adsit's widow carried a bamboo basket with what appeared to be bowls wrapped in cloth.

After greeting one another, Wikana translated for Surati.

"We heard how you killed the demon flyer that killed my husband." Though her voice was animated, Karen noticed moisture in the woman's eyes. "I wanted to come thank you."

Several other women sitting in the café nodded or gave a quick voice of approval.

"You're welcome," Karen said. She had no idea if the Ropen that attacked them was indeed the one that devoured Adsit, but she wasn't about to say that to the poor woman.

"You're welcome, ma'am." Jack nodded. "We're just doing our job."

"This is for you." Surati held out the basket. "I wish it was more, but I had to do something to show our gratitude."

"We appreciate it. Thank you." Jack took the basket.

Soehaemi placed a hand on Surati's shoulder. "Knowing the monster is dead will help my sister, our whole family."

Karen nodded and gave them a brief smile, not telling them there were more Ropen out there.

After another round of thank yous, Surati and Soehaemi exited the café. Karen watched them go when something across the rutted, dirt road caught her attention. Or rather, someone. A compact Indonesian man sat against a tree, slowly tapping a cell phone against his knee. His gaze was aimed directly at the coffee shop.

The back of Karen's neck tingled. Something about the man seemed out of place.

The four sat at a table in the center of the café and ordered breakfast. Karen gave the basket of rice, salted fish, and *krupuk* crackers to Manda so she'd have something to eat on her trip to Bali. A couple of times as Karen ate, she glanced out the open front entrance. The man still sat against the tree, staring at the coffee shop.

Karen popped a forkful of yellow rice and eggs from her plate of Nasi Kuning in her mouth when a large man entered the coffee shop.

"Hey, Geek," Karen greeted him. Geek, Alana, Herrera, and four MSA crewmembers arrived from the *Grantin* last night by chopper and stayed at a couple of other cafés nearby.

"Morning, Sergeant," said Jack. "You eat yet?"

"No, sir, but that can wait. We may have a problem."

Both Karen and Jack sat up straighter. "What is it?" she asked.

"Unwanted company, maybe. Let me show you."

Jack told Wikana and Manda to stay put while he and Karen followed Geek outside.

The man by the tree watched them walk down the road, then got up and trailed them, thumbing the screen of his phone.

"Guys, I think we're being followed," Karen alerted Jack and Geek.

The pair glanced over their shoulders. So did Karen. The man stayed about twenty-five yards away, looking from one side of the road to the other, never directly at them.

What the hell's up with that guy? Karen became more conscious of the pepper spray and collapsible baton clipped to her belt.

They approached the harbor, where a small crowd of about a dozen people had gathered, mostly old women and pre-teens.

"Right there." Geek pointed to where the crowd stared.

A large, gleaming white boat with three decks sat at anchor about half-a-mile away.

"Nice yacht." Jack stared at it.

"A *really* nice yacht," Karen added. It had to be a 75-footer. Bigger than many of the yachts she encountered while sailing or jet skiing around Tampa Bay in her youth. No wonder these people turned out. She doubted a boat like that showed up in Kalisangka every day.

Geek turned to her. "That really nice yacht was shadowing the *Grantin* yesterday."

"Why?" asked Karen.

"No idea." Geek shrugged. "But first it's following us, and now it's here, a day after you guys off that Ropen. And on top of that, we've got this dicklick on our six." He nodded behind them.

The man was still there, still about twenty-five yards away. His gaze shifted between them and his phone as he apparently texted.

Karen looked back at the yacht. She dug into her camera bag, pulled out her Nikon, and attached a 500mm lens to it.

After adjusting the zoom, she started snapping pictures. Thankfully, the yacht was anchored in such a way she clearly saw the name on the side. *Earth Warrior.* She even had a good view of the boat registration, noting the first two letters. CA.

Karen moved to the deck, spotting a fit blond with her hair tied in a ponytail. Unfortunately, she had her back toward Karen.

C'mon, turn around.

Her finger hovered over the button, waiting for the woman to –

"Stop! No pictures!"

Karen jumped and spun around, lowering her camera. Jack and Geek whirled toward the compact Indonesian man stomping toward them, jabbing his phone in their direction.

"No pictures!"

"What the fuck's your problem?" demanded Geek.

Jack tensed, like a snake in human form, coiled and ready to strike.

The man stopped a few yards away. He glanced between Jack and Geek, hesitant. Licking his lips, he pointed toward the yacht. "That celebrity. Want privacy. No pictures."

"Celebrity my ass," barked Geek. "What celebrity would vacation here?" He stepped closer to the man. "Are you from that yacht? Why are you following us?"

The man held his ground. Karen took the opportunity to angle her camera up, aiming it at the man, and surreptitiously snapped a few pictures.

"Not know." The man shook his head. "No follow."

"Bullshit, pal."

The crowd had all its attention on the confrontation. Karen looked back at Geek, lines of anger creasing his face.

"Geek." Karen put a hand on his arm, nodding toward the crowd.

He stared at them, then back to the man, and growled.

"Let's go, people," said Jack. "We're done here."

He raised two fingers in a V, pointed to his eyes, then at the Indonesian. Geek glared at the man as they passed him. He glared back.

"Sorry," Karen said as they headed back to the coffee shop. This time, the man did not follow. "I didn't think it would look good on the FUBI if you went all Guantanamo Bay on him."

"I wasn't gonna pound on the asshole," said Geek. "Just yell at him until he wet his pants and spilled his guts."

"Still wouldn't look good with a crowd around."

Geek grunted. "Mm, yeah."

"Besides." Karen held out her camera, pointing it to the ground. "I got more than enough pics to identify that yacht."

Jack and Geek looked at the camera's screen as Karen scrolled through her pictures. She was pleased that she managed to get a decent headshot of the Indonesian man. Too bad the woman on the yacht wouldn't turn around.

"Not only did I get the yacht's name, I also got its registration. First two letters are CA. It's registered in California."

Geek turned back toward the harbor. "Maybe our fuckhead friend was right. Maybe it does belong to some celebrity. They do love taking up causes. I guess now their cause is, 'Save the Ropen.'"

"Whoever it is," said Jack, "they've got a crap-ton of money if they can afford a yacht like that, and they seem to have some kind of interest in us."

"I can send these pics to our favorite deputy marshal," Karen suggested. "I'm sure he can find out who they are."

Jack smiled and snaked an arm around her shoulders. "You read my mind, babe."

FIFTEEN

Rastun bounced in the bed as Mohede's pickup struck a hole in the road . . . again. They couldn't seem to drive more than fifty feet without hitting some rut that shook the old truck.

He took a long pull from his water bottle. Everyone else had also pounded down water since recovering the dead Ropen earlier this morning. They'd had to haul it out of the ravine the old-fashioned way, with ropes and muscle. The effort left them soaked with sweat, and with the jungle heat and humidity climbing by the hour, they had to stave off dehydration.

The dead Ropen had been loaded into an Indonesian Air Force helicopter for transport to the Maritime Security Agency base in Bali. There, researchers from the Bogor Zoology Museum would study it and check its stomach contents to see if it had eaten the Dutch students and/or Adsit's crew.

The jungle thinned out. Rastun leaned past the cab, taking in the sight in the distance. Karen slid beside him.

"Fish processing plant?" she said. "Looks like they built a small city."

Rastun nodded, eyeing the collection of wooden huts. A couple of cell phone towers rose from the edge of the village. Just beyond it lay an asphalt airstrip with an orange windsock at the southern end of the runway. Near the water's edge was the Mainaky Fisheries processing plant, a series of square-shaped buildings surrounded by a chain-link fence. Fishing boats sat in the small harbor, more modern-looking than the ones he'd seen in Kalisangka.

Rastun's brow furrowed. He checked his watch. It was after eleven in the morning. Shouldn't those boats be out to sea?

"Hey, something's going on over there." Herrera pointed to the plant's entrance. A large group of people stood near the gate, many shaking their fists in the air.

Mohede's pickup stopped about forty feet from the crowd. Behind them, a second pickup with Norgay, Alana, and the MSA squad halted.

"Some kind of protest?" Rastun asked Mohede when the cop opened the door.

"Looks like it," Wikana translated for him. "Some of the local fishermen have held protests against Mainaky, even vandalized their facility."

The FUBI followed Mohede toward the protest. Rastun estimated the crowd's size at a few dozen. Their separate voices merged into a sustained, angry shout.

"Any idea what they're saying?" He turned to Wikana.

The translator scrunched his face, as if straining to hear. "Not going out . . . do something . . . not going to die for you."

A voice blared through a megaphone. Rastun spotted the man holding it. Short and thin with glasses and wearing a white dress shirt and tie. He stood on the other side of the fence. Some kind of executive type. Two other men flanked him. Definitely not executive types. They wore slate gray fatigues and ballcaps with sunglasses, shotguns slung over their shoulders. Even from this distance, Rastun picked up on their military bearing. The uniforms, however, did not look like standard issue for the Indonesian Armed Forces. Private security?

Wikana translated the executive's words as they drew closer. "The CEO is sympathetic to your concerns about the Ropen attacks and wants to resolve this problem." The executive gazed at one of the fishermen at the head of the crowd. "Joko. Come meet with me and hear my ideas."

The stout man with weathered skin and short gray-black hair looked at the other fishermen. Many nodded, and Joko headed for the gate. One of the gray-clad guards let him inside.

"So I guess this wasn't out of work fishermen protesting," said Geek. "Looks like Mainaky's guys don't want to go out to sea with the Ropen flying around."

"I can't say I blame them." Karen snapped a picture of the crowd. "Mainaky's already lost two boats."

The executive and Joko headed toward one of the buildings. The other fishermen quieted down, talking amongst themselves. The two security guards watched them with stiff, serious expressions.

"C'mon." Petal quickened her step. "Let's get some interviews."

She pulled out her phone and started recording before she reached the crowd. Wikana walked next to her, translating her greeting.

"We're with the FUBI and want to talk to anyone who has seen the Ropen or the Ropen lights."

"FUBI?" blurted one of the fishermen. "You killed the demon flyer yesterday."

"Yes." Petal's shoulders sagged a bit. "We had no choice. It was --"

"These are the people that killed the demon flyer!" The fisherman swung out his arm in Petal's direction.

Rastun tensed, ready for trouble. Instead, the crowd broke out in applause and cheers. Several stepped forward to shake their hands. Wikana translated the volley of words best he could.

"Thank you . . . You are heroes . . . Kill more of the demons."

Two rather short men in their twenties with well-toned physiques nearly pushed their way through the crowd.

"Thank you. Thank you." One of them clasped Rastun's hands, shaking them like he wanted to rip his arms out of their sockets. "Those fucking demon flyers killed our father. I hope you kill more." Wikana translated for him.

Karen's eyes widened. "Wait. Is Asnawi Adsit your father?"

"Yes. Yes. I'm Agung. This is my brother, Sitor."

"We talked to your family the other day," said Karen.

"Are they doing well?" asked Sitor.

Karen tilted her head to one side. "As well as they could be. Your mother is still pretty upset. Understandably so."

Agung lowered his head. "We wished we could have stayed longer, but our boss would not give us more time off. He wants us out to sea."

Rastun gazed around the crowd. "Looks to me like you don't want to go."

The older fisherman Petal initially greeted let out a snort. "We already lost Irman and Fadini's boats. Everyone says it has to be the demon flyers. And Mister Pistaka still wants us to go out and fish?" The man stabbed a hand toward the facility. "To hell with that. I will not get eaten."

Agung, Sitor, and many other fishermen nodded or blurted, "Yeah."

Petal asked again if she could interview them. The fishermen eagerly agreed.

"I saw the lights twice, two nights ago," stated the older fisherman, whose name was Habib. "Many of us have seen the lights, especially over the last few weeks."

Rastun heard the creak of the gate opening. One of the guards marched toward them. The man said something sharply in Indonesian, then switched to English. "Stop. No more interviews."

"Please," said Petal. "I'm just getting --"

"I said no interviews. You will embarrass this company."

"I'm not," Petal pleaded. "I'm just --"

"Put your phone down now!" The guard's hand came up like he was going to snatch the phone away from Petal.

Rastun and Norgay formed a human wall in front of him.

"You lay a hand on her, I'm gonna lay a hand on you." Rastun kept his tone even. "A very painful hand."

He stared right into the guard's sunglasses, having to dip his chin to do so. The other man stood three inches shorter than Rastun, but had a thick build. The patch on his left breast read ZAINA.

Zaina did not back down. "You must have permission before speaking to any employees of Mainaky Fisheries."

"Fuck off, Zaina," said Habib, inciting laughter from other fishermen. "You're not our boss. You don't even work for Mainaky."

"I am sure Mister Pistaka would not want you speaking to these foreigners."

"Then let him say that himself." Habib turned back to Petal. "Are you still recording? Come on. I will tell you my story."

"You will not." Zaina stepped forward.

Rastun blocked him.

"Out of my way!" Zaina demanded. "This is Mainaky Fisheries property, which means I have authority."

"Bullshit. This is a public road."

"Unfortunately, he is correct." Mohede ambled over. "Mainaky owns all the land around here." He swept an arm in front of him, frowning as he did. Maybe he and the fishermen in Kalisangka were on the same page when it came to not liking the fishing company.

The barest hint of a smug smile flashed over Zaina's face. "So, as a representative of Mainaky Fisheries, you will stop talking to our employees." His head snapped toward the fishermen. "And none of you are allowed to speak to them without Mister Pistaka's permission."

The fishermen groused in their native language. Even though Rastun did not speak a lick of Indonesian, his gut told him some of the words uttered at Zaina were "fuck" and "you."

The security guard looked back at Rastun. "Now you must leave. I do not want you causing more trouble."

"Not happening, pal."

Lines etched into Zaina's face. His shoulders rose, trying to appear intimidating. Rastun met his gaze, not moving a muscle.

"I am ordering you to leave or you will be arrested for trespassing." He glanced at Mohede. The cop grunted and took a drag on his cigarette.

"Your boss invited us here," said Rastun. "So I think he's the only one who can tell us to take a hike."

Zaina glared at him, then looked at Mohede.

"What?" The cop shrugged. "Mister Rastun's right. If your boss invited the Americans here, he's the one who needs to tell them to leave."

Zaina snorted, then stomped away, yanking out his cell phone. He spoke in rapid, angry Indonesian for a minute or so. He then shoved the phone in his pocket.

"You may stay." The words sounded like he had to force them out of his mouth. "Mister Pistaka will meet with you when he has resolved this situation." He glanced at the fishermen. "But do not speak to any Mainaky employees, and that comes from Mister Pistaka himself."

"Now was that so hard?" Rastun beamed.

Zaina scowled.

Rastun kept smiling and walked back to the others.

"I think we should hire this guy as a field security specialist," he said once out of Zaina's earshot.

Herrera scoffed. "I'd rather work with the Taliban."

A half-hour passed before Pistaka and the apparent leader of the fishermen, Joko, returned to the gate. Joko gathered his co-workers around him. Whatever he said could not be heard by Rastun, Wikana, or the others. Some of the fishermen nodded in agreement. A few had angry retorts, including Sitor. Joko seemed to mollify them.

Another few minutes passed, and the vast majority of fishermen nodded. Joko headed over to Pistaka and the two shook hands.

"I guess the strike's over," said Karen.

The fishermen dispersed. Pistaka turned toward the FUBI, his face pinched in an annoyed expression.

"Well, let's get this over with." Rastun started over to the man, the others following.

After the introductions, Pistaka looked them over with a sour expression. "Our meeting was supposed to take place yesterday," he said in English. "I had to make several changes to my schedule, and then this happened." He aimed a hand at the patch of earth where the fishermen had protested.

Rastun responded, "Like I said yesterday, Mister Pistaka, we were helping with a search and rescue operation."

"Does your organization normally look for missing people?"

"No."

"Then you should have left it to the police." Pistaka turned to Chief Brigadier Mohede.

Rastun shrugged. "What can I say? We like helping people."

"By the way," Karen chimed in. "We did find one of those students and saved her from being eaten by a Ropen, if that means anything to you."

Pistaka glared at her. Karen didn't blink.

"Come." Pistaka set off toward one of the buildings. "I am behind enough on my work as it is."

Rastun and his team followed. So did Zaina. Rastun stared at the patch on the man's upper right sleeve. A roaring tiger, claws extended. Three Indonesian words were written above it, with the English translation below the animal's image. Tiger Force Security.

Pistaka led them to a conference room with swivel chairs and a couple of landscape paintings that could have come from some bargain store. They all sat, except Zaina, who stood in a corner behind Pistaka, seated at the head of the table.

"So I take it your labor problems have been resolved?" asked Rastun.

The skin around Pistaka's nose crinkled, like someone held a cup full of cat piss to his face. "The men are afraid to go out with all these Ropen attacks. I thought you killing that monster yesterday would calm them, but it just made them more afraid, to the point they refused to fish."

"Understandable," said Petal.

Pistaka scowled at her. "I had to arrange for more men from Zaina's company to come here and accompany the crews. Ropen or not, we cannot afford to have our entire fleet sitting at the dock. The amount of fish we catch has been affected by the recent oil spill."

"And your boats overfishing before then has not helped matters." Mohede aimed an unsmiling gaze at Pistaka.

The executive glowered at him. "We . . . have more effective methods of fishing than others on this island."

"Yes, so effective they put some villagers out of work."

Pistaka's face twisted in anger. Mohede gazed at him, unsmiling.

Rastun's eyes flickered between the two, then settled on Pistaka. "I don't think I've heard of a fishing company having to hire a private security firm."

"We have had . . . issues with the local population. They have damaged our property, including some of our boats, and the police do nothing to stop it." His eyes narrowed at Mohede.

The cop frowned, looking bored. "The National Police has investigated these incidents, but we do not have enough evidence to make any arrests."

Pistaka snorted, then looked at Rastun. "And now you see why we must hire our own security."

Rastun glanced over at Zaina. "I hope you're getting your money's worth."

Zaina fixed him with a hard stare. "Tiger Force is the best private security firm in the country. Everyone we hire has to have five years minimum in the armed forces or the police."

"Which one were you?"

"Air Force, fourteen years. Ten with Paskhas."

"Paskhas, huh?" Rastun nodded. That was Indonesian Air Force special operations, specializing in airfield defense, forward air control, and search and rescue. "Not bad."

Zaina grunted out a laugh and gave him a derisive grin. "Better than your Army Rangers."

"Rangers lead the way, my friend."

Karen rolled her eyes. Rastun pretty much guessed her thoughts. *Knock it off with the sausage fest.*

"So, Mister Pistaka," said Petal. "What would you like to know about our expedition?"

"When you will kill the Ropen."

She frowned. "The only Ropen we will have to kill are the ones that have attacked people. The others will be preserved."

"Preserved so they can attack more of our boats?"

"I understand your concern. I'm sure we can find a solution where the Ropen can be protected and your fishermen can do their jobs safely."

Pistaka held Petal in his hard gaze. "Where are they coming from?"

"We're not sure." Karen got out her iPad. "But Pulau Kangean and the sea to the west have had a large number of sightings, mainly Ropen lights. The attack on Captain Adsit's boat, and the last known positions of the missing boats, have all occurred to the west of the island."

She pushed the iPad to Pistaka. He looked it over and let out a long sigh. "This is in the middle of our prime fishing area."

"It might be time to fish somewhere else," said Geek.

Pistaka shook his head. "Some of our biggest hauls have come from this area."

Rastun caught Mohede muttering something under his breath, probably another disparaging remark about Mainaky.

"The new guards from Tiger Force won't be here until tomorrow evening," Pistaka continued. "And the men will not go out to sea until they arrive. That's two days without any catches. Two days of losing money. We have to make up for it by going to the most productive areas of the Java Sea."

"That could be dangerous," said Petal.

"That is why I have more men from Tiger Force coming here. But that will cost a lot of money for every day they are on our boats. How long will it take to find these monsters?"

Petal shook her head. "I'm sorry, but there is no way I can give you a definite answer. Our best bet is tranquilizing one of these animals and attaching a GPS tracker on it. Hopefully it will lead us back to the other Ropen."

"And when will that happen?"

"It'll happen when it happens," Rastun replied in a sharp tone. He'd had enough of Pistaka's attitude.

Pistaka glowered at him. "It better happen soon. And I want regular updates on your progress."

Rastun ground his teeth. *And I want to slap you upside the head for being an insufferable ass.*

***

Frustration boiled over in Pistaka even as he shook the hands of the American monster hunters. The FUBI was supposedly the best at what they do, yet they could not give him any firm answers on when they would find the Ropen. Even worse, they wanted to protect these damn things. His facility had already lost two boats. What if he lost more? What if fishermen started to quit over fear of the Ropen? How long before corporate headquarters in Jakarta decided he had to go?

Pistaka collapsed in his chair after the FUBI left. His stomach clenched. He hated being on this backwards island, but running Mainaky's newest facility was a big step in his career. A couple of years here and he could move on to a bigger facility in a place like Bali or Surabaya. A place with some fucking civilization.

He turned to Zaina. "What about your company? Can you find these Ropen?"

"We can try. But searching all the jungles and caves around here will take a lot more men and a lot of time."

"Which will cost this company even more money. That will not make my bosses in Jakarta happy." Pistaka slouched. "We need to get rid of these monsters."

"I do have an idea," said Zaina.

"What is it?"

"The FUBI said if they find the Ropen, they will let us know. When that happens, I can assemble a team to go to the site and eliminate them."

Pistaka swung his chair around to face Zaina. "That sounds good. But what if the FUBI is there protecting the monsters?"

Zaina flashed a grin. "That will not be a problem."

SIXTEEN

It took nearly two-and-a-half hours to make the trip from the Mainaky facility to the graveyard at Torjek. Rastun saw no sign of a caretaker on duty like a cemetery would have back in the States. He also saw no evidence that any of the graves had been recently disturbed.

"Well, can't say I'm surprised this turned out to be a bust."

"Maybe we'll have better luck talking to the villagers," said Karen. "They might have some stories about Ropen digging up graves in the past."

"There are a couple of caves nearby." Petal looked at her tablet. "Let's check them out before we interview the villagers."

Rastun glanced at his watch. It was after 2:30. They should have plenty of daylight to reach at least one of the caves, scope it out, and head to Torjek before nightfall.

They trekked into the jungle, Herrera and one MSA sailor on point, and Norgay and Seaman Tama bringing up the rear. After their encounter with the angry Indonesian back in Kalisangka, Rastun had everyone maintain a five-yard interval just in case trouble popped up. He also checked leaves and branches for any sign of disturbance. No bends or breaks were evident. He also saw no footprints.

The group had gone about a mile when Norgay radioed, "Captain. There is movement behind us."

Rastun halted, squeezing the grip of his rifle. "Monster-sized or human-sized?"

"Human. More than one."

"Copy. I'm on my way."

He turned to Geek. "Norgay's reporting movement to the rear. Human, at least two. Keep everyone moving and keep sharp."

"Yes, sir."

"Be careful," Karen said.

He nodded to her and detoured into the jungle. The last thing he wanted to do was stay on a path with unknown, maybe hostile people shadowing them. That would just make him a juicy target.

Rastun slipped through the foliage, then crawled the last twenty yards to Norgay, who lay behind a bush. He held his breath, listening.

He could have been blasting Skillet on his MP3 and still heard them. Branches thrashed and cracked. Whoever was following them made no attempt at stealth.

Some of the thrashing overlapped. He looked to Norgay and held up three, then four fingers. The Nepalese nodded.

Rastun glanced over him. On the other side of the path, Tama crouched behind a tree, AK-47 rifle ready.

"Ow!" someone yelped, a male voice.

"Shut the fuck up, asshole," snapped a second voice. Female. Both sounded American with non-descript accents.

"Ssh!" A third voice, likely male.

Three confirmed, but Rastun felt one more could be with them.

The branches ten yards away swept down. A man appeared, lean, tan-skinned. Spanish? Central or South American?

Two more people followed, a scruffy man and an overweight woman with short blue hair.

As he suspected, the group had a fourth member. A young Asian woman who held her phone in front of her, probably recording.

One other thing he noticed. None of them carried any weapons he could see, not even a utility knife.

Just who the hell were these assclowns?

He gave Norgay a series of hand signals. After he nodded, Rastun took a quick breath, then shouted, "Hands up! Don't move!"

SEVENTEEN

The little group froze. The Asian woman gasped. The scruffy guy whipped his head left to right, eyes wide with confusion and fear.

Rastun popped up from behind the bush. He kept the barrel of his rifle pointed halfway between the ground and the four people, his index finger hovering beside the trigger guard. If any of them made a suspicious move, he could drop them in a split-second.

"He's got a gun!" screamed the blue-haired woman.

"Don't shoot." The tan-skinned man held his palms up in front of him. "Don't shoot. We're unarmed."

"Hands up." Tama came out of his hiding place. The four complied.

"You can't do this, you fascists," snapped Blue Hair. "We have every right to be here."

"Quiet," ordered Tama. He pulled out his radio and spoke in Indonesian, probably to the rest of his squad.

Rastun stepped toward the group, Norgay behind and to his right. "Who are you? Why are you following us?"

"I'm Cesar Marques," said the tan-skinned man. "United Nations Cryptozoological Investigation Division."

"The what?" Rastun's face scrunched.

"I have ID. Let me show you." He put down his hands and went for his pants pocket.

"Whoa." Rastun brought up his rifle. So did Norgay and Tama.

"Don't you shoot him, you Nazi fuckers!" hollered Blue Hair.

"Calm down." Again, Marques held out his palms. "I'm just going to show you my ID."

"Two fingers," Rastun told him.

With his thumb and index finger, Marques pulled out his wallet and tossed it over to Rastun. He flipped it open and saw a laminated card with Marques' photo. To the side it read, "United Nations Cryptozoological Investigation Division: Cesar Marques," in English, Spanish, and French. He showed it to Norgay, then threw it over to Tama.

"Didn't Professor Ehrenberg mention the United Nations is putting together its own cryptid hunting group?" asked Norgay.

"Yeah." Rastun nodded. "He did say that a couple weeks back. I didn't think they'd be ready for an actual expedition for at least a few months, maybe a year."

"What can I say?" Marques grinned. "We move fast . . . Jack."

Rastun let out a short breath. Okay, so the jackass recognized him. "And you just happened to come to Indonesia when we're here looking for the Ropen. I doubt that's a coincidence."

"Talk to the Indonesian government. They invited us here."

"To find the Ropen?"

Marques nodded.

"Bullshit. The government came to us to find it."

"Maybe they wanted two groups looking for it just in case you failed." Marques grinned again, a smug grin that made Rastun want to punch him in his damn face.

Vegetation thrashed behind him. Two of Tama's MSA comrades joined him.

"Backpacks off," ordered Tama. "Must be searched."

"Fuck you," Blue Hair sneered at him. "You have no right to do this, you jackboots."

"Yeah," the scruffy guy added. "This is a violation of our civil rights." He looked to Rastun. "Tell 'em."

With a grunt, he called to Tama. "You guys have the authority to detain them?"

"They suspicious. Maybe threat."

Rastun turned back to the scruffy guy and shrugged. "Well, it's their country, so I'll defer to them."

Blue Hair snorted. "Typical. The American war machine supporting human rights abuses, and against its own citizens."

Rastun rolled his eyes. "Seriously? This is a human rights abuse?"

"You're holding us against our will when we've committed no crime. You've threatened us with your guns. You --"

"Shut up," ordered Tama. "Must be searched."

Blue Hair's mouth hung open as she stared at the MSA sailor. "Don't you dare tell me to shut up. And don't you dare put your filthy pervert hands on me."

"Lenna." Marques looked over his shoulder at her. "Calm down and comply with their orders."

Lenna's face blazed red. She drew a couple of deep breaths and nodded, angry eyes locked on Marques.

The four removed their backpacks. Tama and the other MSA sailors patted them down, then went through their packs.

"No guns, Mister Rastun." Tama stood after searching the last backpack, a couple of items in his hands. "These only weapons find. Not real weapons."

The Indonesian held out a Swiss Army knife that belonged to Marques and three strands of firecrackers. No way would anyone carry out an ambush with stuff like this unless their target was a group of senior citizens from a local garden club out for a Sunday stroll in the park.

So if Marques' bunch didn't intend to attack them, just what the hell were they up to?

Tama showed Rastun their IDs and passports. Marques hailed from Brazil. The other three were American, the scruffy guy named Thomas Griffin, and the Asian woman named Kory Hyo. None of them had the same UN identification as Marques. So what was their story? Freelancers? Interns?

"Phone please, Mister Rastun." Tama pointed. "Must call *Grantin.*"

Rastun gave him the sat phone.

"Ask for Minister Irama from the Ministry of Environment and Forestry," said Marques. "He will vouch for us."

Tama regarded him with a stern expression before dialing. His two buddies kept an eye on the alleged UN team.

So did Rastun and Norgay. Rastun's eyes shifted from one person to another. Marques appeared relaxed, the hint of a damn grin on his lips, like he thought this was some sort of joke. Kory wore a stiff expression. Not angry, more calm, cool, and collected.

Lenna still looked pissed off. Then again, she had the aura of someone who went through life raging pissed off at everything. Griffin kept shifting his attention between Rastun, the Indonesians, the ground, and the trees. Nervous? Impatient?

Rastun glanced at Tama, who was still on the phone with the *Grantin.*

Might as well do something productive. "You guys come here on that yacht?"

"Yeah, we d--"

Lenna hollered over Griffin's response. "We're not guys, you Cis asshole."

Rastun glared at Lenna, and she returned the hard expression. He then focused on Marques. "Pretty fancy boat the UN gave you. I don't think Jacques Cousteau's boat was that nice."

"It actually belongs to a friend of mine, but she is committed to the UNCID's mission."

"Which is?"

"Protecting cryptids, instead of killing them." Marques' grin faded.

"We only kill them when human life is threatened," Rastun countered.

"Last time I looked, human beings weren't an endangered species," Kory spoke with a slight edge to her voice. "I think we can afford to lose a few if it means protecting the most unique animals in the world."

Rastun fixed her with a hard stare. "You might think differently if you've ever seen people eaten or mauled to death."

Kory snorted and looked away.

Tama came over to Rastun, holding out the sat phone. "Lieutenant Bahar for you."

He took the phone. "Rastun here."

"We just checked with the Ministry of Environment and Forestry," said the *Grantin's* XO. "They vouched for Marques and his friends. They are contracted by the ministry to search for the Ropen."

"What?" Rastun's face scrunched in puzzlement. "I don't get it. Your government gave the FUBI the contract to find the Ropen."

"I do not understand, either. But Marques' group has permission to be in Indonesia and look for the Ropen. They are free to go."

A frustrated breath hissed between Rastun's teeth. "Got it." He let the phone drop to his side. Why the hell would the government go behind the FUBI's back and hire another agency to find the Ropen? Especially an agency that had only been in existence for a few weeks?

"All right." Rastun took a step toward the UNCID team. "You're free to go."

"Thank you." Marques smirked.

They collected their gear, while Lenna spoke into her phone. "We're finally being let go by the Indonesian Army and the FUBI. During our captivity, we were subjected to threats and intimidation. We were the victims of illegal search and seizure . . . and psychological abuse."

"That woman is being very dramatic," Norgay said under his breath to Rastun.

"More like melodramatic." He looked over at the MSA sailors. "Come on, let's get back to the others."

They walked a few yards down the jungle path when Rastun checked over his shoulder.

Marques and his friends tailed them.

Rastun raised an eyebrow. "You are free to go now. So go."

He started forward again, still glancing over his shoulder.

The UNCID crew remained on his six.

"What? You a bunch of stray puppies or something?"

"As you said, we are free to go," Marques replied. "So we can go anywhere we want. That includes following you."

Rastun grunted. "Let me guess. You're gonna hang around while we do all the hard work, then take all the credit when we find the Ropen. Right?"

"No. We are going to make sure you do not kill another Ropen."

EIGHTEEN

The team made it to the cave, with Geek and Alana deploying their Alley Cat drone. It sent back images of bat guano caked on the rock walls and several of the flying rodents roosting above the little four-wheeled RC vehicle. Probably fruit bats, Rastun guessed. But they found no evidence the Ropen had used this cave.

The whole time, Marques and his half-assed gang of cryptid hunters dogged them, watching their every move. Even as they sat near the cave eating MREs.

"Okay, those guys are seriously starting to creep me out." Karen grimaced at the UNCID group.

Rastun followed her gaze. Marques perched himself on a fallen tree trunk, arms resting on his legs, focused on the FUBI team. Or was his stare aimed at Karen in particular?

Anger bubbled in the pit of Rastun's stomach, especially with that little smirk on Marques' lips, an expression that straddled the line between mischievous and creepy. Lenna recorded them on her camera phone while Kory leaned against a tree, arms folded and looking bored. Griffin sat on the ground, hugging his knees, eyeing the group. Like with Marques, most of his attention seemed to be on Karen.

Rastun snorted. "To hell with them. They're just trying to play head games with us. Let 'em stare at us if that's what gets their rocks off."

"Well, if they try something else besides staring, they're gonna regret it." Karen patted the pepper spray hanging from her belt.

Rastun eyed the canister. He'd been wondering what they would do if Marques and his group decided to do something more direct than following and staring. They sure as hell couldn't shoot a bunch of unarmed civilians. Rifle butts were an option, though with Lenna constantly recording them, that would cause a Category Five shitstorm in the media. They did have their Aster 7s, but the tranquilizer darts had dosages for Ropen. That amount of the drug might make a person go to sleep forever.

Note to self. Make sure field security specialists carry less-lethals on future expeditions.

They finished eating and trekked further into the jungle. Marques and his friends continued to shadow them.

"Shit." Geek looked over his shoulder. "This is like having your little sister tag along everywhere you go."

"I wouldn't know. I'm an only child," said Rastun. "Although there was this goat that used to follow me around whenever I cleaned the barnyard exhibit when I worked at the Philadelphia Zoo."

"Well, I was the one who tagged along with my sister when I was a kid." Karen glared back at Marques' bunch. "Although I doubt I was as creepy as these jerkoffs."

Rastun looked over his shoulder again. Had these jackasses been following them since they left Kalisangka? The thought aggravated him. He should have noticed them long before they reached Torjek. It wasn't like there was much traffic on these jungle roads.

He slowed his pace, the realization setting in.

"Hey." Karen tapped his arm. "What's wrong?"

"Huh?"

"You have that look on your face, like you're in deep thought and pissed off at the same time."

"Just thinking about those dipshits." He jerked his head toward the UNCID team. "How they got to Torjek."

"I'm assuming they followed us from Kalisangka."

"No." Rastun shook his head. "They'd need a vehicle for that. We would have heard their engine the times we stopped. Hell, they may have decided to just ride our bumper all the way to Torjek. Marques doesn't seem interested in keeping a low profile."

"Okay, so they didn't follow us across the island. So the only thing I can think of . . ." Karen halted and grabbed his arm, mouth agape.

"Looks like you just read my mind," said Rastun.

Karen nodded. "They made it to Torjek before we did. They knew we'd be there."

"Yup."

"How?"

Rastun's eyes narrowed. "Marques must have someone on the inside selling us out."

***

They made it to Torjek before the sun began to set and interviewed around thirty villagers. Only two ever heard of any stories involving the Ropen eating corpses at the graveyard, and those were based on second or third-hand information. After the interviews, they rented spare rooms at cafes and markets to spend the night. Rastun also ordered Norgay to find out where Marques' group was staying.

"Don't bother staying out of sight," he told the Nepalese. "They want to watch us, let them know we're watching them."

The room Rastun and Karen got in the back of a coffee house consisted of two well-worn cots and a rickety stool with a candle.

"Pretty bare bones," Karen noted.

"We'd have to upgrade to get to bare bones," Rastun replied.

After changing out of their sweaty clothes, Rastun wrote his daily report for Colonel Lipeli while Karen uploaded photos from the day's outing onto the FUBI's website and social media pages. He included his suspicions about a mole feeding Marques information on their expedition. They'd just completed their tasks when the sat phone rang.

Rastun checked the ID on the screen and nodded. "What'd ya know," he said to Karen. "It's our favorite deputy marshal."

He hit the speaker button. "Sherlock. Got your homework assignment done?"

"Actually, Captain, I'm just getting started," replied Arthur Sherlock Dunmore. A former Ranger like Rastun, his help had been invaluable to the FUBI during the sea raptor and lizard men expeditions. "But I can give you what I've got so far."

"Shoot. Let's start with that Marques asshole."

"He was hired by the UN less than a month ago. Before then, he split his time as an environmental activist and cryptozoologist. He has his own YouTube channel. Some of the videos are of him helping natives in the Amazon protest logging, ranching, and oil exploration. Others are his expeditions to find cryptids like giant spiders, the Titanoboa, and some lake monster in Argentina called Nahuelito."

Rastun nodded. "So what about the yacht he's on? He said it belonged to a friend, and Karen said it's registered out of California."

"Correct. Her name's Paulette Thompson. She went to UCLA for two years, switched majors twice, then dropped out."

"How does a college drop-out afford a yacht?" asked Karen.

"You can thank her mother and step-father for that. Donna Thompson and Brian Bates."

Rastun turned to Karen, who shrugged and shook her head. He looked back at the phone. "Never heard of them."

"Bates is a Hollywood agent," Sherlock told them. "He specializes in representing reality TV stars. The mother is a chef and nutritionist for several big-name actors and actresses. She also has her own show on the Food Network."

"Sounds like between the two of them, they have more than enough money to buy a huge yacht and let their daughter sail it all over the world," said Karen.

Rastun snorted. "Can you say spoiled?"

"Actually, it doesn't look like Paulette's partying from one ocean to another. She turned her yacht into a protest vessel, similar to Greenpeace's *Rainbow Warrior.*"

"I seriously doubt *Rainbow Warrior* is anywhere near as nice as that yacht," Karen commented.

"I guess she wants to be comfortable while saving the world," said Sherlock. "Looking at her social media history, she's protested ocean dumping in The Philippines, whaling in Iceland, tuna overfishing in Japan, offshore drilling in the Gulf of Mexico. That last one she was taken into custody for almost colliding with a Coast Guard cutter."

"Any jail time?" asked Rastun.

"Not a single day. Her lawyer convinced the jury the Coast Guard was at fault. Paulette got off scot-free. If her folks can afford a seventy-foot yacht, they sure as hell can afford a good lawyer."

"I guess so," Rastun muttered. "What about her crew? By the way, I used air quotes when I said, 'crew'." Sherlock chuckled softly. "Thomas Griffin is a former child star. He was on a show called *Lunar High.*"

"I thought that name sounded familiar," said Karen. "Emily used to watch that show when she was little. He played the snarky kid, Cameron." She cocked her head. "Didn't he lose all his money?"

"More like his mother blew through it all by the time the show ended."

"I'm guessing his acting career ended, too."

"Like a lot of child stars, work dried up when he got older. He's also been busted for DUI and disorderly conduct. His social media is filled with posts on just about every social cause you can imagine."

"It makes me wonder if he's a believer or he's doing it to stay relevant," said Rastun. "Maybe that's why he hooked up with Marques and Thompson. The Ropen's big news."

"So was the oil spill in the Java Sea. The *Earth Warrior's* been there for the past two months harassing oil tankers."

"And now they've decided to switch gears and save the Ropen," said Karen.

"Griffin has at least eighty posts about protecting the Ropen." Sherlock paused. "By the way, some of his posts call for boycotting the Philadelphia Zoo."

Rastun clenched a fist, glaring at the phone. Where did that little shit get off dragging his parents into this? His dad was the zoo director and his mom the head veterinarian. They had nothing to do with what was going on here. Yet Griffin wanted to threaten their livelihood, the livelihood of everyone who worked at the zoo.

An image formed in his mind of his fist smashing into the former child star's face . . . over and over again.

Karen clutched his arm. He took a deep breath before speaking. "Thanks, Sherlock. I'll check in with my parents, see if everything's okay."

Rastun paused, refocusing. "What about the two women?"

"Lenna Sodowsky's an assistant manager at a Starbucks in Mission Viejo. Graduated from Pasadena City College with an Associate's Degree in Humanities. She's a member of half-a-dozen activist groups. Kory Hyo has an Earth Science degree from Cal State Northridge and teaches at Mount San Antonio College. She's also the founder of a local animal rights group in Walnut, California."

"Any run-ins with the law?" asked Rastun.

"I haven't found out yet. Most of what I've learned about them has been online. I sent a request to the Brazilian Federal Police for any information they have on Cesar Marques. I also did the same with the Indonesian National Police for the man who harassed you two at the dock."

"All right." Rastun nodded. "Keep us posted, and as always, thanks for your help."

"You're welcome, Captain. One more thing before I let you go. It's purely circumstantial, but I figured you ought to know."

"What is it?"

"About three months ago," Sherlock began, "there was an eco-terrorist attack at a logging camp in Jewell, Oregon. Someone planted a device on the fuel tank of a truck. Six people were injured in the explosion, two of them critically."

"I assume this is relevant to us somehow," said Karen.

"I checked Paulette Thompson's posts from that time. *Earth Warrior* docked in Astoria, thirty miles north of Jewell, three days before the bombing, and it left a few hours after it happened."

NINETEEN

"Yes, Jack. I've seen the tweets. But we've had a steady stream of people come through yesterday and no one has harassed me or your father, or anyone else at the zoo."

Upon hearing that from his mother, Rastun's shoulders loosened and he let out a relieved breath.

But not too relieved.

"That's good to hear. Still, you guys keep an eye out for anything suspicious."

"Our security staff's been alerted," Joyce Rastun said over the sat phone's speaker. "I think this is just a bunch of idiots who spout off online, but are too afraid to actually do anything."

"Maybe. Still, all it takes is one whackjob to read one post and decide now's the time to cleanse the world of 'evil.' So just be careful."

"We will. You and Karen be careful, too. I think you're in more danger over there than we are here."

They bid each other goodbye. Rastun stared at the phone, hoping what Mom said was right. That the posts to boycott the Philadelphia Zoo, the posts that called his parents horrible people because their son had dared protect himself and others from that Ropen, were just typical keyboard warrior bullshit. Type a couple of rage-filled sentences, feel like you've changed the world, then gulp down some capo-frappo-latte and forget about it.

Karen wrapped an arm around his shoulder and leaned against him on the cot. "I'm sure they'll be okay. Your parents sound like they're taking this seriously."

"Yeah." He kissed Karen on the head. "Speaking of taking things seriously, we might have a group of eco-terrorists down the road from us."

"You really think they had something to do with that bombing in Jewell?"

"Who knows, but that is one big coincidence that Paulette Thompson's boat was in Oregon the same time that truck blew up."

"True," said Karen. "But the Maritime Security people didn't find any bombs when they searched them. Well, they did find those firecrackers, but what can they do with those?"

"Not much. Still, after what Sherlock said, I'm not taking any chances with these dickheads."

Rastun texted Geek, Alana, Norgay, and Herrera to meet him at the café where he and Karen stayed.

And bring along Tama and the other MSA guys, he added.

When everyone had gathered, they came up with a sentry rotation to watch the market where Marques and his dumbass friends stayed. Rastun agreed to take the midnight to one watch.

"Any of them decide to go out for a midnight stroll, let everyone know," he told the group.

He waited until the MSA sailors headed off before waving the FUBI members over to him.

"I wanted to wait until Tama's squad wasn't around before I told you." He laid out his suspicions about a mole helping Marques.

"Do you think it's one of the Maritime Security people?" asked Petal.

"I don't know who it could be. Until we do, watch what you say and who you say it to."

Rastun went back to his room, teeth clenched. Dammit, he was supposed to be working with the *Grantin's* crew. Now he had no idea if he could trust anyone on the boat.

Despite his worry, he managed to fall asleep shortly after he lay down on his cot. His cell phone stayed silent until the alarm went off around 11:45. He relieved Alana and leaned against a tree across from the market. The building was dark, and stayed dark during his entire hour-long watch. No one exited the market before Tama relieved him. Rastun headed back to the café and climbed onto the cot next to Karen. It took just a few minutes for him to fall asleep.

His alarm went off again at 5:30. No emergency calls during the night. The UNCID had done nothing to screw with them. He wondered if that would change today.

Everyone met at the café an hour later. They'd just ordered their food when Rastun's sat phone rang. A check of the screen showed it was Colonel Lipeli.

"Jack, I'm with Ed Lynch and Roland Parker. We need you to get everyone on your team together. We've got some important stuff to talk about."

A twinge of concern shot through him. Lipeli, Lynch, and Parker wanting to talk about something important at 6:30 in the morning local time. *This can't be good.*

"Actually, everyone's already together. We just sat down to have breakfast."

"Sorry, but breakfast will have to wait," Lipeli told him.

Rastun frowned and put the phone on speaker.

"I hate to tell you all this," Director Lynch began, "but we are facing a storm of negative press."

"So what else is new?" Rastun leaned back in his chair.

"For one," said Lipeli, "Cesar Marques posted the video of your team detaining his group. It's gone viral. News agencies all over the world are spinning it every which way. Some are calling it illegal detainment, a few claim you were about to shoot them in cold blood."

"That's bullshit." Rastun sprang forward in his chair. "We had an unknown group following us, acting suspiciously. We detained them, found out they were legit, and let them go."

"Settle down, Jack," Lipeli told him. "We know what they're saying is BS."

Karen tapped on her tablet as Lipeli continued. "The problem is, Marques and his bunch have a lot of sympathetic allies in the media and several well-known activist groups. We're still taking flak for apparently wiping out all the lizard men in South Carolina. An incident like this also gives the people in Congress who think we're some paramilitary group more fodder. Especially after the press conference by Paulo Folgosi."

"Who the hell's that?" Geek's face scrunched in puzzlement.

"The Executive Director of the UN Environment Programme. He's Marques' boss. He criticized us for detaining Marques and his team. 'Unacceptable' and 'barbaric' were a couple of the choice words he threw out. He also said he feared we might kill his people and bury them in the jungle because we're afraid of competition from another group of cryptid hunters."

Rastun slapped a palm against his forehead. "And people actually believe this horseshit?"

"Jack," said Lipeli. "Last year you dealt with a guy who thought the lizard men were part of an alien race that secretly rule Earth. Some people will believe anything."

"What are they even doing here in the first place?" asked Petal. "Why would the Indonesian government hire two different groups of cryptid hunters to find the Ropen?"

"I put that same question to the Foreign Affairs Minister," replied Parker. "It appears the Ministry of Environment and Forestry did an end-run around the rest of the government to bring in the UNCID. From what I gather, Minister Irama is a big-time conservationist. He's done commendable work to enhance the protection of several endangered species throughout Indonesia, including tigers, rhinos, and Komodo Dragons."

"And he sees the Ropen as another species to save," said Rastun.

"Correct."

"Why can't the president here send Marques and those assclowns packing?" Herrera wondered aloud. "After all, we were the ones hired first for this mission."

"The Foreign Affairs Minister wouldn't say," Parker told them. "But from reading between the lines, it seems like there might be some political intrigue going on behind the scenes that makes it hard for their president to do that."

The corner of Rastun's mouth twitched. Who the hell knew what exactly this intrigue could be? A favor owed? Blackmail? Bribery? Indonesia had made a successful transition from authoritarian government to full-fledged democracy over the past twenty years, but corruption remained a major problem.

"Shit." Rastun slammed a hand down on the table, the realization hitting him. "That's it."

"What?" asked Parker.

"Marques and his pals knew in advance we were going to Torjek. I thought he had someone on the inside giving him intel. Well, in a way, he does. It's Captain Teguh."

"The captain?" Tama sat up straight, eyes bulging in shock. "How can you say that?"

"I don't mean he's doing it intentionally." Rastun held up a hand. "The captain files regular reports on our expedition with not just the MSA, but all the ministries interested in the Ropen, including Environment and Forestry."

"And then someone there turns around and gives it to Marques." Geek shook his head. "Now it's making sense."

"What?" asked Rastun.

"Marques' yacht was shadowing us nearly all day. Then right before we flew here, it stopped tailing us and headed for Pulau Kangean. Captain Teguh probably reported what we were going to do, then Marques' minister friend shared it with him."

"We may need to tell the captain to leave out some details in future reports."

"Do not think he will do that," said Tama. "Captain Teguh very . . . strict. Always follow rules."

"In other words, by the book," added Rastun.

Karen nudged him with an elbow and showed him her tablet. It was open to Twitter, showing posts with #FUBI.

"Karen's showing me some of the posts you were talking about." Rastun lay the tablet on the table so everyone could see. He scrolled through it, catching a number of headlines and comments.

"Militarized FUBI Operatives Draw Guns on Unarmed Activists."

"UN workers 'Feared For Their Lives' in FUBI Assault."

"FUBI Nazi thugs kill rar animuls now want kill people to."

"Shut down FUBI now! Just a breeding ground for Nazis."

Rastun rolled his eyes. *Holy shit, everyone's a Nazi these days.*

He then played the video from Lenna's phone. It showed only the first thirty seconds, when Rastun and Tama emerged from the vegetation and ordered them on their knees. Nice editing to make him and the MSA sailor look oh-so intimidating. Another video showed Thomas Griffin taking a couple of deep, anxious breaths, mouth agape, eyes wide.

"I don't think . . . I don't think I've ever been so scared. I mean, I just went numb. I saw those guys coming at us with those machine guns. I thought . . . I thought I wouldn't get out of that jungle alive."

"Oh please," Rastun scoffed. "No wonder this guy has a tough time getting acting gigs. I did a better job as Geppetto when my fourth grade class did *Pinocchio.*"

"Thomas Griffin may be on the melodramatic side," said Lynch, "but it's helping garner support for the UNCID. The number of protestors outside our headquarters has doubled since yesterday. Somewhere between four and five hundred. There are some members of Congress demanding hearings to pull our federal funding. With Marques watching our every move, we are under a microscope. Anything you do from here on out, you need to do with the utmost caution. Don't do anything that could paint the FUBI in a negative light."

"What if Marques and his assholes get in our way if we have to take down another Ropen?" Rastun's voice rose with each word. "What if they put our lives in danger, or civilian lives? What am I supposed to do? Tell them to stop, pretty please with sugar on top?"

"We're not telling you to not protect yourselves and others." Lynch's tone was sharp. "But you have to weigh your options when dealing with the UNCID. After what happened yesterday, I have no doubt they'll be looking for any opportunity to discredit the FUBI. That means being mindful of what you do and what you say when you're around them."

"Like we don't have enough on our plate with man-eating flying reptiles around," said Rastun. "Now we have to worry about every word that comes out of our mouths?"

"Yes, you do," Lipeli emphasized each word. "The last thing we need is for them to take something any of you say out of context to turn more of the public against us."

When the conference call ended, Rastun pressed his back hard into the chair, his eyes narrowed. Karen rubbed his shoulder, though he barely acknowledged it, still glaring at the sat phone.

When their food came, he ate quietly, still steaming over the call. Even as they set out into the jungle for another day of Ropen hunting, he couldn't shake off his aggravation. Especially with Marques and his assclowns shadowing them.

Rastun glared at them, replaying the conversation with Lipeli and the others in his mind. In his nearly two years with the FUBI, he'd always felt the higher-ups had his back and limited their interference in field operations.

He thought back to some of the phrases they'd used. "Utmost caution." "Weigh your options." What the hell did that mean? How much force could he use on Marques' group if their actions threatened the expedition? What if he felt he used reasonable force, but the online outrage mob lost their shit and compared him to Jack Bauer? Would Lynch and Colonel Lipeli still support him? They always had in the past, but if the public outcry got too hysterical . . .

Dammit. Rastun let out a harsh breath. He hated having this kind of doubt in his superiors. Lynch had been a pretty good boss, and Lipeli had always stood by the men and women under him since their time together in the Rangers.

But how many times had he seen it in the news? Someone makes an off-color comment or has some accusation of wrong-doing – proven or otherwise – made against them and are quickly booted out on their asses. No chance to make things right. Loyalty, past accomplishments, none of it mattered. All that mattered was placating the angry mob.

Would that be his fate, the fate of everyone on his team, if Marques stepped up his social media attacks?

TWENTY

Sherlock walked into his apartment, shoulders squared, head held high. He set down his bag of Chinese takeout on the kitchen counter, taking a satisfied breath. For a year he'd been trying to locate one Taylor Clendenon, a former college professor from Albany, New York, who'd been on the run after being busted for running a drug ring with several of his students.

He smiled, thinking of the man's reaction when he and his partner found him at a coffee shop this morning in nearby Strasburg, Virginia. When they identified themselves as U.S. Marshals, Clendenon's jaw dropped, sputtering, "No. No. I was careful. You couldn't have found me."

But they had, and it led to Sherlock's favorite kind of arrest. The one where the suspect offered no resistance.

With his official work done, he could tackle his side project. Sherlock got his laptop and set it on the counter as he started eating. He was still waiting on the authorities in Brazil and Indonesia to send him any information on Cesar Marques and the angry man who confronted Captain Rastun and Karen. Lenna Sodowsky and Kory Hyo's criminal histories had been much easier to obtain, not that there was much to them. A couple of disorderly conducts during protests for the former, and some traffic violations for the latter. He'd also sent photos and info on Marques and his friends to law enforcement agencies throughout Oregon. Maybe someone there knew something about their brief stay in the Pacific Northwest.

The next step was to delve deeper into their social media pages, check on friends, family, and followers, determine which ones would be good to contact to try and develop a profile on them. He also wanted to see if they knew anyone that might be prone to violence, and who might have the knowledge to construct a bomb.

First, he checked Twitter, typing FUBI and Ropen. Both words yielded plenty of results. A number of posts contained the favorite insult of the social media outrage mob, "Nazi." One even showed a black and white photo of three SS soldiers, their real faces replaced by those of Jack Rastun, Karen Thatcher, and Dr. Ehrenberg.

"Idiots." Had these people ever seen a single documentary on World War II? Sherlock doubted it. Otherwise, they would know what actual Nazis had done.

Other posts showed protesters outside FUBI headquarters in Alexandria, one with a short video of people yelling and giving the middle finger to a car turning into the parking lot.

"I hope a Ropen eats you and your kids," someone shouted at the person in the vehicle.

Sherlock let out a slow breath, the muscles in his face tensing. He didn't have a problem with people protesting, whether he agreed with their cause or not. He'd fought for their right to do that. But the constant drumbeat of calling his friends Nazis and wishing death on innocent people worried him. With that sort of hate, how long before someone crossed the line between words and action?

As he scooped out a forkful of chow mein, his cell phone rang. He checked the screen and straightened with anticipation. The caller ID read OR STATE POLICE.

"Hello?"

"Deputy Marshal Dunmore?" The voice was female, young, energetic, likely Caucasian.

"Speaking."

"Hi. This is Detective Maddie Keough with the Oregon State Police. You recently sent out pictures of some possible suspects in the bombing of the logging camp in Jewell."

"Yes, I did." Sherlock got to his feet. "I assume you found something?"

"Maybe. I was assigned to the bombing investigation, and those photos jogged my memory. I went through my notes and it's possible two of your suspects, Lenna Sodowsky and Kory Hyo, were in the area the day of the bombing."

"What were they doing?"

"Well, no one saw them near the logging camp," Keough answered. "But they were with a group of around twenty protestors outside a diner where some of the loggers go for breakfast. They were yelling at them as they were leaving for work. A few of the loggers we interviewed said they remembered an overweight woman with blue hair. There were also three Asians in the group, one man and two women. One of them could have been Kory Hyo."

"Did they just yell or did they get physical with the loggers?"

"Nope. No one got violent."

"Did the protestors do anything else that day?" Sherlock leaned against the wall.

"About seventy of them gathered at the entrance to the camp. They were there for a few hours, blocked a couple of trucks trying to drive out. The police had to move in and arrested about twenty of them."

"I didn't see anything in Lenna Sodowsky or Kory Hyo's records that show they were arrested in Jewell."

"I went through bodycam footage from the protest and couldn't find anyone matching Sodowsky or Hyo's descriptions," Keough told him.

"And I couldn't find any posts from them or anyone else from *Earth Warrior* from Jewell, and they post constantly on social media."

"I checked their social media pages, too," said Keough. "These folks love to protest. It doesn't make sense they'd miss out on the big show at the logging camp."

"Mm." Sherlock stared at the carpet, thinking. "The oil spill in the Java Sea happened the day before. They might have decided to pull out and head to Indonesia. The spill was big news for weeks. Paulette Thompson and her friends probably thought they'd get more attention there than at a logging camp in the middle of nowhere."

"Sounds plausible. Well, I plan on heading to Jewell tomorrow to re-interview the witnesses and show them pictures of *Earth Warrior's* crew. I'll let you know if I come up with anything."

"Thank you, Detective. I appreciate it. Good luck."

The call ended, and Sherlock continued to lean against the wall. A hum of energy grew throughout his body. They were onto something with Marques' crew, something that could prove to the world they were not the saviors of cryptids they made themselves out to be.

He went to the contacts list on his phone and selected Colonel Lipeli. When his former CO picked up, Sherlock said, "I thought I'd let you know, I just got off the phone with a detective from the Oregon State Police. We might have a connection between the *Earth Warrior* crew and the Jewell bombing."

"That's great."

"It is," replied Sherlock. "But there's a lot of work that needs to be done before we can determine whether or not they were directly involved. Which brings me to asking for a big favor."

"What is it?"

"Do you think Mister Parker would let me borrow one of his planes?"

TWENTY-ONE

Ismed shivered and looked up at the darkened sky, half-expecting to see the glow of a Ropen light. He let out a shaky breath when he didn't.

I can't believe we're out here at night. What is Captain Chudori thinking?

He gripped the railing, staring at the water around him, thinking back to this morning before they left Kalisangka. Chudori told him and Omar that they would not start back home before nightfall like they had the past week.

"The Mainaky crews will be out at night now, stealing our fish. Taking money and food from us. I'll be damned if we will sleep while they take what's ours."

Ismed had hoped the captain would change his mind once the sun went down. How could he not after what happened to those foreign tourists and poor Mister Pinurbo a few days ago?

But he didn't. A shiver went up his spine as he gazed around the Java Sea.

"Ismed!"

Chudori's shout snapped him out of his thoughts. He spun around and saw *Asrul's* captain standing next to the pilothouse, face scrunched in anger.

"Stop daydreaming and check the rigging."

"Yes, sir." Ismed hung his head and went off to carry out Chudori's order. Even as he made sure the rigging was secure, he checked the night sky. No Ropen lights. He thanked Allah for that.

Job complete, he stared past the stern, praying there would be a tug on the net, that they would get a big haul. Then maybe Chudori would head back to Kalisangka. Hopefully that would happen soon.

Time dragged on. The net remained slack. Ismed tapped his fingers on his leg. He thought about the American women he met a few days ago, Karen and Petal, imagining a three-way with them, trying to forget about demon flyers. But every minute or so he'd glance at the sky, expecting to see a glowing green light. He swallowed, imagining one of those monsters eating him like they had Mister Adsit.

Come on. Let's catch something already. How much longer would they be out here? Would Captain Chudori just give up soon? Ismed doubted it. Their only catch today was a small batch of cardinalfish. They wouldn't get many rupiah for that.

I wonder if Mainaky's boats are doing better. Probably. He heard they had the best fish-finding sonar available, along with bigger and better storage areas. The crews probably got paid better than he did. Ismed often thought about going to work for them. But he'd seen what happened to those from the village who got hired by Mainaky. People spoke their names like a curse. Some were shunned by not only friends, but family. Even Mister Adsit had said some harsh things about his two sons who worked for the company.

The money might be better with Mainaky, but Ismed had no desire to be hated by everyone in the village.

"There's another boat off the port side," Omar called out.

Ismed swung around. He saw the lights from the other boat in the distance. It had to be a few kilometers away.

Chudori stuck his head out the pilothouse, scowling. "It better not be them."

Ismed walked over to Omar as their boat swung toward the other vessel. Omar peered through his binoculars, then lowered them.

"Who is it?" asked Ismed.

"I don't know for sure." Omar shook his head. "But I have a good idea."

It took a few minutes to close the gap between the two vessels. Omar let him use the binoculars. Ismed could now make out details. The boat was longer and sleeker than theirs, with a much bigger crane. Antennae grew from the top of the pilothouse.

It was definitely a Mainaky boat.

"Hey." Ismed leaned forward. "They're hauling up the net."

"What did they catch?" asked Omar.

"It looks like a big haul. Maybe tuna. Wait! There's a shark in there. Two of them."

"Bastards!" Omar spat.

Ismed couldn't blame the mate for being angry. Shark meat fetched a very good price. The fin alone was worth many times more than the shark's entire body. Several countries throughout Asia and the Pacific, including Indonesia, considered shark fin soup a delicacy.

Omar alerted Captain Chudori about Mainaky's catch.

"Those sons of whores!" He stomped out of the pilothouse. "That should be our catch! These are our waters. We've fished here longer than they have."

Chudori raised a fist. "Mother fuckers!" he shouted at the Mainaky boat.

"What do we do now?" asked Ismed.

Chudori's shoulders rose and fell with slow, furious breaths. He glared at Ismed. "Get the chum, boy."

Ismed nodded and hurried off. He returned with the wretched smelling bucket, scoop in hand. "Where should I throw it?"

"At them!" Chudori jabbed a palm at the Mainaky boat. "We're going to show them we've had enough of them stealing our fish."

Omar let out a big belly laugh. "I love it, Captain."

Ismed winced. "W-Won't we get in trouble?"

Chudori's face twisted in rage, to the point Ismed took a step back.

"Those fuckers are stealing our food and our money! Do you want to see your family and friends starve? Do you want to have money for that stupid cell phone of yours? Do you want Mainaky to empty the seas of our fish?"

"N-No, sir." Ismed looked down at his boots.

"Then it's time we let those assholes know we won't let them get away with this anymore. Now get ready to throw that chum at them. Hell, throw whatever you have at them."

"Gladly, Captain." Omar grinned.

Ismed just nodded. What if they contacted the police? Forget the police, Mainaky had armed security people on their boats. What if they shot at them?

The engine growled. The *Asrul* drew closer to the Mainaky boat. Ismed looked down at the scoop, his stomach knotting. Would he go to jail for this?

Three men appeared at the gunwales of the Mainaky boat, waving and shouting. Ismed held his breath when a fourth man appeared. Definitely not a fisherman. He wore a gray uniform and ballcap and clutched a rifle.

Ismed swayed as the *Asrul* heaved to starboard and pulled alongside the Mainaky vessel.

Chudori stormed out of the pilothouse. "That's it! We've had it with you greedy bastards! Those are our fish. Get the hell out of here."

"This sea does not belong to you," one of the Mainaky men hollered back. "We have every right to fish here, too. Now fuck off."

The men on the other boat laughed. Except the security guard. He watched their boat with a stony expression.

"You fuck off!" Chudori yelled. "Ismed. Omar. Throw the chum."

Omar howled with laughter. He grabbed a scoop and flung the rancid, bloody meat chunks across the gap between the boats. The chum splattered against the side. Some of it landed on the deck. The fishermen jumped back.

The security guard did not.

Omar laughed and threw another scoopful of chum at the Mainaky boat.

"What the hell are you waiting for?" Omar threw out his arms as he stared at Ismed. "Do you like these greedy shits? Hoping to get a job with them?"

The words jerked him out of his stupor. He could not afford to let Omar and the captain think he liked Mainaky.

Ismed scooped out some chum and threw it at the other boat. He heaved a second mass of meat chunks. A third. The other crew cursed and yelled at them. By the time he scooped out another batch of chum, Ismed was smiling.

Until the security guard fired his rifle.

Ismed yelped and threw himself to the deck, trembling.

More sharp cracks echoed in the night. None hit him. Ismed didn't even feel any thuds against the hull of his boat. His shivering subsided. Had the security guard just fired into the air?

"Are you fucking crazy?" screamed Chudori.

Ismed pushed himself to his knees and peered over the gunwales as the security guard spoke, "You are assaulting Mainaky Fisheries employees and damaging company property. Stop now or I will take more forceful action."

"Suck a goat's dick," Chudori yelled.

Omar laughed again and scooped out more chum.

"Keep your hands down," demanded the security guard.

"Come over here and make me." Omar thumped his chest with a fist.

The guard aimed his rifle at *Asrul's* waterline. "If you throw any more chum, I will ventilate that shitty boat of yours."

"You shoot my boat and I'll ram yours."

Ismed's head snapped toward Chudori. He looked at the captain with wide eyes. He couldn't be serious. This boat was the captain's livelihood. Hell, it was *his* livelihood.

Ismed took a shaky breath. He knew it. He knew they'd get in trouble for fucking with Mainaky.

Someone shouted from the other boat. Not a shout of anger, but of fright. Ismed turned. He gasped and stumbled backward.

A Ropen dropped down on the Mainaky boat. The security guard barely turned around when the monster chomped down on his shoulder. The rifle fell from his grasp. The Ropen shook the man and tossed him across the deck.

Another Ropen appeared, knocking over one of the fishermen. The monster's snout descended, and came back up with dripping chunks of flesh dangling from its mouth.

Chudori jumped back into the pilothouse, swinging the boat away from the Mainaky vessel. Ismed sat on the deck, palms pressing against the damp wood, shaking with every breath.

Anguished screams went up from the Mainaky vessel. Fear consumed Ismed. He didn't want to be ripped apart and eaten.

He pushed himself to his feet, eyes locked on a nearby hatch.

Something let out a croak from behind. A flapping noise followed.

"No!" Ismed started running.

Pain exploded across his back, so intense he couldn't scream as he fell on his face. Invisible hammers pounded his skull. He rolled over.

Ismed opened his mouth. Talons tore through his chest and gut before he could scream. Fountains of blood poured out his shredded body. A black curtain fell over his eyes.

TWENTY-TWO

Another day, another bust. Rastun grunted as he took the stairs to the second floor of the café. His team had checked half-a-dozen caves around the village of Pandeman in Pulau Kangean's interior. They found lots of bats, along with lots of guano, but no sign of any Ropen. And they had Marques and his jagoffs on their heels the whole time, phones out, probably hoping he or someone else in the expedition would do something they could use to paint the FUBI in a bad light.

No such incidents happened. Rastun's group pretty much ignored Marques' bunch . . . to an extent. Rastun couldn't afford to let his guard down around them, given the connection between the *Earth Warrior* and the bombing in Oregon Sherlock told him about.

He opened the door to his and Karen's room. Light from the narrow hallway revealed a long white string hanging from the ceiling, connected to a light bulb. Rastun pulled it.

"Looks like we got stuck in a storage closet." Karen scrunched her face.

Crates of tea and coffee lined the far wall. A cot sat next to it. That was it.

"I'll definitely be dreaming about our own bed back home tonight." Karen slipped off her camera bag as she entered the small room.

"You act like this is the first time you've had to rough it," Rastun said to her.

Karen looked at him, head tilted. "There's a big difference between having to sleep in a place like this and enjoying it."

Rastun chuckled, then took off his pack and placed it on the floor.

Once settled, they sat on a crate and got out their tablets, Rastun writing his daily report, Karen uploading photos to the FUBI's social media pages, at least when she could connect to the internet.

It was during one of those periods that Karen said, "Jack. There's an email from Randy. It looks like they finished the autopsy on the Ropen we killed."

She slid her crate closer to him so he could read it. Human remains had been found in the creature, including fingernails and pieces of bone. Whether they came from Adsit and his crew or the Dutch students had yet to be determined. Either way, it had been a maneater.

After finishing his report, Rastun lay down on the cot, falling asleep shortly after closing his eyes. The alarm on his phone woke him up less than an hour later. He groaned, rubbed his eyes, and swung his legs off the cot, leaving Karen to shift and moan. Her eyes opened halfway.

"Sorry. It's almost time for my watch." He got his Steyr AUG and slung it over his shoulder. "I'll try not to wake you when I get back." He kissed the side of her head.

Karen pushed herself up on an elbow, strands of her brown hair falling over her left eye and cheek. "I may not mind if you wake me up." She gave him a wry smile.

Rastun kept his gaze on his fiancée, straightening as he sucked down an exuberant breath. "I already can't wait for my watch to be over."

Karen softly giggled and lowered her head back on the cot.

Rastun went downstairs. At almost ten o'clock, the café was empty and the lights off. He opened the front door to find Tama standing on the wooden porch. Rastun brought up his hand to give the MSA seaman a friendly slap, then caught himself. Indonesians considered a backslap disrespectful.

Tama turned just as Rastun spoke. "Okay, my turn."

"Yes, sir."

"Any problems?"

"No, sir. All quiet."

"Good." Rastun nodded. Just the way he liked it. Hopefully, it would stay that way for the rest of the night.

He bid Tama a good night before the seaman went inside. Rastun stepped to the edge of the porch, scanning the darkened homes and businesses around the café. Not a soul stirred. The only sounds came from the chirps and screeches of the jungle wildlife.

Rastun then glanced up at the night sky. He saw a few stars, but no Ropen lights.

Letting out a breath, he settled in for what he hoped would be an uneventful two-hour watch.

Something moved in the darkness.

Rastun's head whipped to the left, his hand clenched the strap of his rifle. A lean, human shape ambled along the rutted road.

Tensing, Rastun locked his eyes on the figure. It was roughly thirty feet away, walking casually, not looking the least bit threatening.

Or is that what he wants me to think?

The figure was now twenty feet away. Fifteen. At ten feet, Rastun could make out the person's face in spite of the shadows.

"Hello, Mister Rastun." Cesar Marques gave him a short wave.

"What the hell are you doing here?"

Marques responded with an innocent shrug. "I'm just out for a late night stroll."

"Then keep strolling." Rastun glared at him.

Grinning, Marques walked by the café. Rastun never took his eyes off him.

Marques stopped. Rastun removed his hand from the rifle strap, ready to go hand-to-hand in case this fucktard wanted to try something.

Arms folded, Marques rocked back on his heels. "On second thought, I think I'll stay right here for a while."

He locked gazes with Rastun, a prominent smirk on his face.

"You know what I think?" Rastun's eyes narrowed. "I think you should get out of my sight."

Marques chuckled. "What if I don't?"

Rastun clenched his teeth, fury burning within him as the son-of-a-bitch continued. "Are you going to beat me up?" He held up his cell phone. "I can get that on video. I think it will go more viral than when you terrorized us in the jungle."

A harsh breath shot out Rastun's nose. He wanted to say, "Go fuck yourself," and follow it up with a fist to the prick's grinning face. But he kept silent, stewing, remembering his orders from his superiors about taking care when dealing with the UNCID.

They just stared at one another, Rastun's face stiff, Marques still wearing that damn grin. A minute of silence passed, then two.

"Your life must be pretty pathetic if you have nothing better to do than stare at me all night long." Rastun finally spoke.

"I am simply doing my job, keeping an eye on you and making sure you do not hurt any Ropen."

"And is part of your job threatening my parents' livelihood, and the livelihoods of everyone who works at the Philadelphia Zoo?" Rastun's brows scrunched together.

"Ah, the boycott." Marques shrugged. "We have to do everything we can to preserve a species as rare as the Ropen. It's nothing personal."

"Well it's personal to me," Rastun said in almost a growl. He then aimed a finger at Marques. "Leave my parents out of this."

Marques smirked again. Rastun took a deliberate breath. Damn, he just wanted to hit this fuckstick in the mouth so hard he would taste his rectum.

"You know," Marques relaxed his stance, "when I was fifteen . . ."

"Yeah, I don't give a shit about your life's story," Rastun interrupted him.

Marques let out a brief chuckle. "As I was saying, when I was fifteen . . ."

Fuck me. Rastun rolled his eyes. The SOB was going to continue anyway, and being on watch, Rastun was a captive audience.

"My school was visited by a member of Chamber of Deputies," Marques continued. "That's similar to your Congress. Anyway, he talked about how he was committed to stop the cutting and burning of the Amazon Rainforest. He talked to my class about how the forest had to be preserved, how species and tribes unique to it could be lost forever, how its loss could affect the entire planet. He told us to do our part to help, which included contacting the Chamber of Deputies to urge them to support his legislation to protect the rainforest."

Marques looked away for a moment before continuing. "He wanted us to get our friends, our parents, and other relatives involved. So that's what I did. I emailed the Chamber, I got my family and some of my friends to do the same. I read articles and watched interviews with this deputy. He always seemed so passionate, so committed to this cause. And in the end, his legislation passed."

His ever-present grin faded. "But every time I looked at stories and figures about Amazon deforestation, it did not stop. It kept getting worse. His legislation didn't do a damn thing."

"Wow. A politician lied," Rastun said in a deadpan tone. "That's never happened before."

Marques scowled for a moment. "Two years later, this same deputy came back to my school. He said the same things as before, how he was committed to saving the rainforest. So I challenged him. I told him the legislation that was supposed to protect the forest did no such thing. Trees kept being cut down, animals were being killed, and people were being forced to leave their villages. Do you know what my reward was for calling him a liar?"

"What?" Rastun's tone held little interest.

"I was suspended from school for two days. That's when I realized there were two kinds of people in the world. Those who talk about solving problems and those who actually do it. I chose to be one of the doers."

Marques took a step closer to Rastun. "Thanks to my direct efforts, I've saved endangered species, kept villagers in their homes, and prevented trees from being cut down. Some of my actions have landed me in jail. So believe me when I say that I will do whatever is necessary to protect the Ropen."

He punctuated his promise with a smirk.

Rastun stepped up to him, his face inches from Marques'. He glared right into the other man's eyes. The smirk vanished.

"Well believe me when I say that I'll do whatever's necessary to protect my --"

The ringing of his satellite phone interrupted Rastun. He stepped back from Marques and checked the screen. Ehrenberg was calling.

"Yeah, Doc?"

"I want you, Karen, and Geek back on the *Grantin*. It looks like Ropen activity is picking up in the Java Sea. We just got distress calls from not one, but two fishing boats."

TWENTY-THREE

The beeping of Sherlock's cell phone woke him from his nap. He blinked and rubbed his eyes, stretching out in the plush seat of Roland Parker's Gulfstream. He took out his phone, glancing at the time in the corner of the screen. It read 10:45 a.m. Pacific Time. About a half-an-hour before he landed at Warrenton-Astoria Regional Airport.

"About time," he muttered when he checked the email alert. The Indonesian National Police had finally gotten back to him.

Two photos were attached to the message; the picture Karen had taken of the angry Indonesian man and a head shot of the same man, this one showing him clean shaven and wearing navy dress whites.

The police identified him as Kiswanto Herfanda. He'd spent six years in the Indonesian Navy, four with the Kopaska, an elite unit of combat divers. Honorably discharged, he now worked as a tour guide and diving instructor, and also founded an environmentalist group in Jakarta. He'd been arrested once for blocking traffic during a protest, and prior to joining Paulette Thompson's crew had reportedly taken part in protests over the Java Sea oil spill.

He forwarded the information to Rastun, adding, "Watch out for this one."

The Gulfstream started its descent as Sherlock went on Twitter. Photos and videos showed hundreds protesting outside FUBI headquarters. Calls for boycotts of Roland Parker-owned companies continued. One university in California caved to social media pressure and announced it would end its partnership with the FUBI in a Sasquatch monitoring project. Federal agents were investigating death threats made to the Secretary of Agriculture, with most of them demanding she cut off the department's funding of the Foundation, or else.

For all its critics, the FUBI also had a number of supporters. Most, however, did not seek to change the minds of their opponents. Exchanges usually consisted of one side saying something along the lines of, "Militaristic Nazi murderers," and the other responding with, "Libtard pussy assholes."

The Gulfstream touched down on a rain-soaked runway. Sherlock stepped out the side door and looked up into gray skies and a drizzle. Not worth opening his umbrella.

He walked across the tarmac and into the wood-sided terminal building. A trim woman in her late twenties or early thirties with short blond hair and a round face stood beside a bench in the waiting area, a Starbucks cup in her hand and a badge clipped to her belt.

"You must be Marshal Dunmore." The woman's face brightened as she strode up to him, or more like power-walked. Sherlock sensed an aura of endless energy radiating from her. Hard to tell if it was natural or from the caffeine. Perhaps a combination of the two.

"And you must be Detective Keough." He extended his hand. "A pleasure to meet you."

"Same here." She gave him an energetic handshake. "How was your flight?"

"Not bad."

"So, ready to go?"

"Lead the way."

Keough gulped her coffee and almost raced across the terminal toward the parking lot.

The woman does not like to waste time. Sherlock grinned and followed her.

He put his bag in the trunk of Keough's standard issue police sedan and got into the passenger seat. The rain picked up as they pulled onto the Warrenton-Astoria Highway.

"So you help the FUBI hunt monsters, too?" asked Keough.

"A couple of times. Mostly I act as a liaison between them and local law enforcement. And they prefer the term cryptids, not monsters."

"Cryptids. Right. Gotcha. Still, gotta be pretty cool. A few months ago, me and my boyfriend went hiking around Eagle Creek. It's supposed to be a Sasquatch hot spot. Didn't run into any."

"That could be a good thing," said Sherlock. "Encounters with cryptids aren't always fascinating."

Keough glanced at him as she drove over the Lewis and Clark River Bridge. "Spoken from experience?"

"I got knocked across a room by a lizard man last year. Bruised two of my ribs."

"Ouch. Well that sucks."

Sherlock gave a low grunt. "It could have been worse. That thing could have ripped out my throat."

When they hit a red light, Sherlock pulled out his phone and showed Keough the picture of Kiswanto, telling her the man's background.

"Sounds like he could be big trouble," said Keough. "Was he with Paulette Thompson's crew when they were here?"

"I doubt it. They probably met up when her yacht got to Indonesia."

Keough bobbed her head from side-to-side. "Still, can't hurt to show his picture around. You never know."

Sherlock nodded. *Leave no stone unturned, no matter how unlikely.* The trait of any good investigator. He had a feeling he and Keough would work well together.

They arrived in Jewell forty minutes later, the rain never letting up. Keough decided to start with the six logging company employees injured in the explosion.

The first one they visited was the worst of the lot. Clay Sweeney, thirty-six, camp foreman. Sherlock and Keough were met at the door by his wife, Wendy.

"You finally arrest the fuckers who hurt my husband?" the portly brunette asked, her eyes narrowed.

"No, but we do have some possible suspects," replied Keough. "We'd like to ask your husband if he may have seen any of them."

Wendy let out a long, frustrated breath. "Sure. C'mon."

She stepped aside and let Sherlock and Keough enter. Wendy led them through the small one-story house to a back bedroom. Sherlock heard a TV playing from it.

Clay Sweeney lay on the bed, half his face and neck disfigured by burn scars. A patch covered his right eye, or rather, where the eye had been. Keough had emailed Sherlock about the injuries suffered by the six victims in the bombing. Sweeney suffered second and third degree burns over half his body. He also took shrapnel in the knee, stomach, and shoulder, limiting his mobility.

Sherlock had seen injuries just as bad during his time in Iraq and Afghanistan. It still did not make the sight any easier to stomach.

"Clay, it's the detective you talked to after the explosion," Wendy told him. "She also brought along a U.S. Marshal. They wanna talk to you about it again. You up to it?"

"Yeah, sure." Sweeney's voice sounded rough and distorted, as the right side of his lips had been burned away.

Keough walked over to his bedside. "We have some new suspects in the bombing. I want to see if you remember seeing any of them before the incident."

She held out her phone and scrolled through the photos of the *Earth Warrior* crew. Wendy, meanwhile, stood against the doorframe, arms folded, watching. Sweeney recognized Lenna from the protest at the diner. That short blue hair definitely made her stand out. He thought Griffin looked familiar, but couldn't remember seeing any of the others.

"Did you see any of them around the logging camp?" asked Keough.

"No." Sweeney gave a slight shake of the head. "Like I told you before, I was working. Didn't pay a lot of attention to those nutcases." He turned away from Keough, as though ashamed he could not give the answers she wanted.

Keough managed a sympathetic smile. "It's okay, Mister Sweeney. We appreciate your time."

He grunted an acknowledgment, still not looking at her.

They left the bedroom, Wendy shutting the door. "So who the hell are those people? Did they set off that bomb?"

"They're environmental activists," Sherlock answered. "They've been harassing the FUBI expedition in Indonesia looking for the Ropen. We placed their yacht in Astoria a few days before the bombing, and it left a few hours afterwards."

"Yacht?" Wendy's eyes widened. "Does that mean they're rich assholes?"

"The yacht's owner comes from a wealthy family," said Sherlock.

"Then we're gonna sue their asses," Wendy spoke in a sharp tone. "Clay may never be able to work again. He doesn't even want to leave the house the way he . . ."

Her lip trembled. She took a shaky breath and continued. "We've got medical bills, rent, groceries, electric bills. How the hell can we pay all that if he can't work? Those rich shits ruined my husband's life, but they get to sail all over the world on their damn yacht? Fuck them."

Keough held up her hand. "Mrs. Sweeney, we still have a lot of ground to cover to determine who planted that bomb."

"Then you find out, and you tell me when you do, and they're gonna pay for what they did to Clay."

"We will."

Wendy did not show them out. She stood in the middle of the living room, wiping her eyes.

Sherlock took a final look back at the house. He could sympathize with the Sweeneys. Their lives had been altered forever by someone who hated the idea of chopping down trees so much they felt it gave them the right to hurt innocent people.

He knitted his eyebrows together, thinking of the enraged posts directed at the FUBI. Sherlock hoped the same fate didn't happen to any of his friends and colleagues or their families.

Keough took him to the other men injured in the blast. Three of them recognized Lenna from the diner protest, and one of them thought he saw Griffin around town.

The rain finally stopped by the time they reached the camp itself. None of the employees there remembered seeing any of the *Earth Warrior* crew at the camp. Keough and Sherlock then went to the diner.

"I remember this guy," said one waitress when they showed her Griffin's picture. "Came in to get some takeout coffee when those crazies were here yelling at the guys. My granddaughters used to watch his show. I had him autograph a couple pieces of paper for them. I remember him going on about this big movie he was going to be in."

"Did you see him in Jewell after that?" asked Keough. "Maybe during the night?"

The waitress shook her head. "Nope. Just when he came in for the coffee."

After showing the *Earth Warrior* photos to the rest of the diner staff and customers, Sherlock and Keough headed back to her sedan.

"Well that was a bust." The detective sagged into the driver's seat.

"That was just the start," said Sherlock. "I suggest we try the port in Astoria next."

Fifty minutes later, they arrived at the administrative offices of Port of Astoria, after a quick coffee stop for Keough. They met with the Director of Operations, a chubby, bald Asian man named Vinh.

"I definitely remember that yacht." He pointed at the photo of *Earth Warrior,* one which Karen took on Pulau Kangean. "Big sucker. Definitely some well-to-do types. Caught the attention of a lot of the guys at the port, especially the blond woman on board. Really good looking."

"Did you notice them doing anything suspicious?" asked Sherlock. "Maybe leaving late at night?"

Vinh shook his head. "No, can't think of anything. But I can't give all my attention to one boat. And I'm not here at night. You'd have to talk with the people on our night shift."

Keough asked for and got their home addresses and phone numbers.

"Let's try the security guards first," suggested Sherlock. He looked at his watch. Just a little after six. They should all be awake by now, eating or relaxing before heading to work.

The first guard they visited said he saw little of the *Earth Warrior* crew while docked in Astoria. Same with the second guard.

The third guard lived on the Washington side of the Columbia River. Night had fully taken hold by the time they knocked on the door of the apartment house where Fred Ellison lived. A fit young black man of medium height greeted them.

Sherlock did a quick survey of the small living room. Very tidy. His gaze stopped on a photo on the wall of four men in desert pattern camouflage uniforms standing beside an elongated, wheeled armored vehicle.

"You served?" Sherlock nodded to the photo.

"Yes, sir. Four years." Ellison turned to the photo. "Stryker gunner. Were you in, too?"

Sherlock nodded. "Fourteen years. Airborne MP, then Army Rangers."

"Damn." Ellison's eyes bulged, impressed.

Sherlock noticed the younger man relax his posture. He'd seen this happen before when interviewing other vets. That common ground of military service often helped break the ice.

"So what do you need to see me for?" asked Ellison.

"It's about a yacht that docked at your port a couple of months ago. The *Earth Warrior.* " Sherlock showed him the picture on his phone.

"Yeah, I remember that one. All of us were talking about it. Really nice yacht, and a hell of a nice-looking captain." He looked to Keough, grimacing. "Um, sorry, ma'am. I hope I didn't offend."

"Oh please. I grew up with two older brothers. It takes a hell of a lot more than typical male hormones to offend me."

Ellison smiled.

"You talk to the captain?" asked Sherlock.

"Never got the chance. I waved to her once when I was making my rounds and she was on deck. That's about it."

"What about these other people?" Keough scrolled through the photos of the yacht's crew.

"Yeah, him I talked to." He pointed at Griffin's picture. "The actor."

"Was it a lengthy conversation?" Keough put her phone down.

"Yeah, it went on for a bit."

"When was that?"

Ellison cocked his head to the side, thinking. "Had to be after midnight. I was walking by when he pulled into the parking lot. Had some plastic crates packed to the gills. The yacht left later that morning, so I guess he was making a supply run."

"How did Griffin seem to you?" asked Sherlock.

Ellison scrunched his face. "Kinda nervous, actually. I offered to help, but he told me no. Kinda sounded rushed. But when he took that first crate on board and came back for the second one, he was pretty talkative. Telling me about all these big stars he met, how he finished shooting this movie that was gonna put him back on the map."

They finished interviewing Ellison five minutes later. As they walked to the car, Keough turned to Sherlock. "I wonder what got Griffin so jumpy about that crate?"

"Maybe he had some incriminating evidence in there. Muddy clothing, flashlights or other tools. Maybe some explosives he didn't use." Sherlock slowed his pace. "What kind of device did they use?"

"After our bomb techs and ATF sorted through the debris, they determined it was a limpet mine. The suspect attached it to the tractor trailer's fuel tank."

Sherlock nodded. "I've heard of those. Allied naval commandos used them during the Second World War. They were magnetized so they could attach them to the side of warships, set a time delay fuse, then swim away. That's not the sort of explosive your average eco-terrorist uses."

"Yeah, one of the ATF guys gave me the low down on those things. It sounds like something that Kiswanto guy would use."

"Except all indications are he was in Indonesia when the Jewell bombing took place." Sherlock crossed his arms. "What time did the bomb go off?"

"Eight in the morning," answered Keough.

"And when did *Earth Warrior* leave Astoria?"

"Ninety minutes later."

Sherlock tilted his head, thinking. "Ellison said he ran into Griffin after midnight. Let's say anywhere between twelve and one. It's about forty minutes from Astoria to Jewell, say between a half-hour to an hour to sneak into the camp, plant the mine and leave, forty minutes back to Astoria, another half-hour to shop for supplies."

Keough stared up at the night sky. "So Griffin could have left the port any time between nine and ten at night, right when the shifts were changing, and be back within that midnight to one time frame. Now here's my next question. How does a down on his luck former child actor know how to make something like a limpet mine?"

Sherlock opened the passenger door of the sedan. "Let's find out."

TWENTY-FOUR

Rastun zoomed in with his binoculars, scanning the fishing boat. It bobbed in the ocean, at the mercy of the waves. He saw no one in the pilothouse or on deck. A survivor could be hiding below, terrified that the Ropen could return. He dismissed that as very wishful thinking.

He turned to Karen, then Ehrenberg, who flanked him near the *Grantin's* bow. His fiancée took pictures of the deserted fishing boat while Ehrenberg checked it over with his binoculars. The vessel had been spotted by a navy patrol plane an hour ago and vectored *Grantin* to its position.

"Oh no." Karen gaped at the boat.

"What is it?" asked Rastun.

Karen lowered her camera. "I just saw the name on the side. It's the *Asrul.*"

Rastun gritted his teeth. That was Chudori's boat. Letting out a slow breath, he looked back at the vessel, thinking of the interview they had done with the captain and young Ismed, who couldn't stop gawking at Karen and Petal. He closed his eyes, imagining their horrific fates.

Footsteps sounded behind them. Lieutenant Bahar approached.

"We're ready," he told them.

Rastun, Karen, and Ehrenberg followed him to the boat ladder at *Grantin's* stern, where Geek and McClure met them. They climbed down into a waiting Zodiac, Bahar handing Rastun a Glock 17 from the boat's armory to replace the one he'd lost back on Pulau Kangean. Bahar maneuvered them up to *Asrul's* platform, securing the inflatable to the side. Jaw set, Rastun stepped onto the fishing boat.

A mass of dried blood stained the rear deck near a hatch. A bucket rolled about, bits of chum lying nearby.

Rastun stepped around the blood, the stain broken up by oblong patterns. Talon marks from the Ropen.

He lifted his head as he neared the pilothouse, then halted.

"I've got a body."

Rastun made his way over to the corpse, grimacing. He thought it was the other crewman, Omar, going by the build. There wasn't much else to identify him. Much of the flesh had been torn from his face. His head rolled from side-to-side with the motion of the boat, connected to his body by dark red strands of sinew. The torso had been ripped wide open, most of the internal organs gone or in bloody pieces.

"Oh my God." Karen put a hand to her mouth and turned away.

Ehrenberg closed his eyes, while Geek shook his head. It wasn't the first time any of them had seen such a grisly sight. Still, Rastun was hard-pressed to recall any worse than this.

"I will check below," said Bahar. "Mister McClure, will you accompany me?"

"You got it." The former paratrooper followed the lieutenant to the hatch leading below deck.

Karen regained her composure and took pictures of what remained of Omar. Rastun stepped toward the pilothouse, finding more blood around it, along with a knife, probably one used to skin fish. Chudori's, maybe? One last desperate fight before being carried off by the Ropen?

The sat phone rang. It was Norgay.

"Cesar Marques and Lenna Sodowsky are gone."

"Where did they go?" asked Rastun.

"I do not know. They must have slipped away during the night. Thomas Griffin and Kory Hyo are still with us."

Rastun's jaw stiffened. Much as he hated the UNCID dipshits following them, at least he knew where they were. He didn't like the idea of the two of them, especially Marques, out of sight.

"Have Mohede call his people in Kalisangka, see if the yacht's still docked there. And stay sharp. Who knows what these ass-hats could be up to."

"Yes sir."

Rastun told the others about Marques and Lenna vanishing. A few minutes later, Bahar and McClure returned topside.

"Not that it should come as a surprise," said McClure, "but no one's down below."

Ehrenberg gazed around the deck. "Maybe there were just two Ropen. One took Chudori, the other Ismed. They couldn't carry Omar, so they ate him here."

"And what? Stashed the others away to eat later?" asked Geek.

"Crocodiles are known to do that," Ehrenberg answered. "It could be the same for Ropen."

The team continued to gather evidence while a group of MSA sailors came over in another Zodiac to retrieve Omar's remains. Two of the men were assigned to stay on the *Asrul* to refill the fuel tank and sail it back to Kalisangka. The group was about to head back to *Grantin* when Rastun's sat phone rang. Norgay again.

"One of Mohede's officers called back. The *Earth Warrior* is gone."

Rastun groaned. He looked out at the Java Sea, wondering when he'd see that damned yacht.

***

The navy patrol plane found the second missing fishing boat roughly fifty miles north of *Asrul's* position. It, too, was adrift and devoid of life.

The name on the side read *Mainaky 07.*

"So much for the added security," Rastun commented before they took a Zodiac over to the boat.

The scene on the Mainaky vessel was even worse than on the *Asrul.* They discovered five bodies, all shredded and partially eaten.

"Mainaky boats have a crew of six." Bahar stared at the body of a man with gray fatigues, shredded and covered with blood. "Seven including the guard from Tiger Force."

"So we can assume the other two were taken away," said Ehrenberg. "Meaning we have at least four Ropen in this area."

Rastun picked up the compact rifle lying near the dead guard. A Heckler & Koch MR556. He checked the 30-round magazine.

"Looks like he got off five rounds before the Ropen got him."

"Doesn't look like it did him much good," added Geek. "Damn things musta came down on 'em fast."

Ehrenberg sighed and reached for his sat phone. "I better give Mister Pistaka a call. He wanted us to keep him in the loop."

"I don't think he's gonna like this news very much," Geek said.

After getting through to Pistaka, Ehrenberg put him on speaker and told him about the attack on *Mainaky 07.*

"How could this have happened? We had a guard on the boat. Why did he not kill the monsters?"

"We believe the attack happened quickly," Ehrenberg told him. "There were at least two Ropen involved. He could have been overwhelmed."

"Did he put up any kind of fight?" A new voice came over the speaker. Rastun recognized it as the Tiger Force leader, Zaina.

"I checked his magazine. He got off five rounds. He might have been the first one the Ropen got."

A pause. "Kho had a wife and two children."

"I'm sorry." Rastun didn't care much for Zaina, but he sure as hell didn't envy the man having to break this news to Kho's family.

"Our fishermen only went back to sea because we put armed guards on their boats," said Pistaka. "What will they do when they hear this?" A moment of silence passed. "We must put more guards on our boats."

"Tiger Force does not have an unlimited pool of men," replied Zaina. "We also have other clients who need our services."

"But we . . . I . . ." Pistaka grunted. "We shall talk about this later. Doctor Ehrenberg?"

"Yes?"

"Can you return the boat to our facility?"

Lieutenant Bahar leaned forward. "I will assign two of my crew to pilot it back to Pulau Kangean."

"Good."

"Though I am afraid the bodies of your crew must remain with us for further examination."

"Very well. Get the boat back to me as soon as possible, and do something to stop these Ropen attacks!" Pistaka's voice shot up with his final words.

The call ended, with Karen scowling and shaking her head. "What an ass. He didn't even say one word about his crew."

Rastun felt his own face contort, probably mirroring Karen's. Pistaka looked to be in his early thirties and given his high-strung personality, someone looking for a fast climb up the corporate ladder. The Kangean facility might be his first true leadership position, and it was starting to go to shit with the recent Ropen attacks. Now he panicked, showing more concern over his career than his employees. Definitely not someone Rastun would want to serve under.

The team collected evidence, while MSA sailors removed the bodies. They had almost finished when Geek pointed to the horizon. "Looks like we've got company, Cap'n."

Rastun saw a white shape in the distance. He raised his binoculars and zoomed in on a triple-decker yacht.

"Fuckin' wonderful," he grumbled as *Earth Warrior* sailed toward them.

***

Rastun took one last look at Marques' yacht a mile away before heading below deck on the *Grantin*. He knew it would be a matter of time before the UNCID dipshits showed up. The ever-efficient Captain Teguh would have radioed their positions to his superiors, who then relayed it to all the various ministries in Jakarta, with Environment and Forestry passing it on to Marques.

With the UN cryptid hunters working for the Indonesian government too, there wasn't a damn thing the FUBI could do to keep them in the dark.

Rastun headed to his berth. Ehrenberg ordered the team to get some sleep during the last few hours of daylight. With the Ropen apparently more active in the area, everyone would be in for a long night.

He checked his email. Nothing new from Sherlock. He and a detective from the Oregon State Police were following up a lead in California, hopefully one that would prove *Earth Warrior's* involvement in the Jewell bombing. That would remove one problem from his plate.

Next, Rastun went to Twitter, finding some photos of protesters outside FUBI headquarters. Some posts estimated their size at a hundred, others at around three hundred. Many signs had the usual ridiculous insults of "Nazi" and "Murderer." One did read, "Stop Cryptozoological Genocide." Also ridiculous, but somewhat original. Another picture, held by a dark-haired woman in her late teens, had a decent drawing of a Ropen chomping down on a man – Rastun assumed it was him – with blood pouring from his waist.

His teeth clenched when he saw a photo of another group of protesters across the street from the Philadelphia Zoo. Not a very big group. Maybe twenty or so. Still, he didn't like enraged wackos so close to where his mom and dad worked, especially when they carried signs like, "Mr. & Mrs. Rastun . . . Worst Parents Ever!" and "You Should Have Aborted Your Son!" He prayed those protesters didn't do anything beyond hold up stupid signs.

Rastun climbed into his bunk. Sleep did not come as quickly as usual, concerns over his parents gripping his thoughts. And concerns about Emily. No incidents had happened at her school, but would that last with so many people whipped up by this online hatred toward the FUBI?

He finally managed to fall asleep, waking up when his phone blared out Epica's "Beyond the Matrix" at 1830 hours. After stopping at the crew mess for a quick dinner with the rest of his team, they headed topside. Several MSA sailors were on deck, wearing helmets and armed with AK-47s. Two others manned the boat's MINIMI machine guns mounted fore and aft. The crew was well prepared for any prehistoric threat.

They scanned the night sky. Rastun saw plenty of stars, but no glow of Ropen lights. He looked to the south, to the white running lights on the surface. *Earth Warrior*, still a mile away. He returned his attention to the sky.

An hour passed with no sign of Ropen, then two hours. Karen sidled up next to him, yawning.

"Didn't get much sleep?" He grinned at her.

"Like we ever get much sleep on these expeditions."

"Just gotta suck it up, hon."

She cocked an eyebrow at him. "Don't I always?"

Rastun chuckled and snaked an arm around her. She pressed against him. He breathed deep, relishing the feel of Karen's body against his. He shook his head in amazement. Here he was, in the middle of the Java Sea, looking for a creature from the dawn of history with the woman he loved. A woman he'd be married to five months from now.

Married. The thought made him excited and nervous at the same time. Not only would he gain a wife, but a step-daughter in Emily, who was just a couple of years away from becoming a teenager. Talk about a scary thought. He prayed he could do a good enough job to –

"Jack." Karen slipped out of his grasp, looking to the sky.

Rastun raised his head. He tensed when he spotted a green light wink in the distance.

Then two lights . . . three.

TWENTY-FIVE

Urgent shouts echoed up and down the *Grantin*. A klaxon blared. Rastun had his Steyr AUG in his hands as footfalls pounded toward him. Ehrenberg, Geek, and McClure, the cryptozoologist holding an Aster 7 dart gun.

The lights glowed for a few seconds, then faded. The next time they appeared they were closer to the water, and closer to the *Grantin*.

Something crackled near the bow. One of the boat's machine guns. A yellow line of tracers zipped across the darkened sea. All fell short of the Ropen.

A searchlight snapped on, its white beam sweeping through the night sky until it fell on the Ropen. They had to be a thousand yards out. Karen snapped pictures while Rastun clenched the grips on his rifle.

"Damn, those are some big SOBs," said Geek.

Rastun grunted. "Wait till they're right on top of you. Then you'll see how big they really are."

"I say we drop the ugly bastards before that happens." McClure stepped to the railing as another string of tracers flew at the Ropen, again missing.

Ehrenberg put a hand on his shoulder. "Remember. We need at least one alive to fit it with a GPS collar. It could be the only way to find the rest of them."

McClure grimaced. "If you say so, Doc, but it's not my favorite idea."

"Not mine, either," added Rastun. "But like he said, it's probably our only option."

The machine gun fired again. So did rifles from some of the MSA sailors. One of the Ropen twitched, definitely hit. Its beak opened wide, probably crying out, Rastun guessed. Distance and the din of gunfire prevented him from hearing it.

The wounded Ropen banked right.

"It's going for the yacht." Karen pointed at the *Earth Warrior*.

Rastun looked to the sleek vessel, concern sweeping over him. He may not like Marques and his jagoff friends, but he didn't want them to die. They had to help.

But they couldn't do it until they dealt with these two Ropen.

The machine gun chattered. More rifles banged away. The Ropen on the left jerked, but kept flying. Tracers from the MG connected with the one on the right. It twisted in the sky, head thrashing, maw wide open.

"It's going down!" someone shouted.

Rastun snapped his head to the right. Lieutenant Bahar stood a few feet away, decked out in a helmet and holding an AK-47 rifle. Three other MSA sailors stood around him.

"Concentrate fire on the remaining Ropen," he ordered.

"No!" Ehrenberg sliced an arm through the air. "Let it land."

Bahar's eyes bulged. "What are you saying? You know how dangerous those things are."

Ehrenberg jumped in front of the *Grantin's* XO. "I need to put a collar on it to track it. The only way to do that is to tranquilize it. We do it over the water, it might drown before we get it aboard."

"I am not letting that thing set foot on this ship," Bahar countered, his tone sharp.

"The Ropen hunt in groups. They might live in a colony. We need one of them alive to lead us back to it. It could be the only way to prevent more attacks."

Bahar's harsh gaze held Ehrenberg, then shifted out to sea. One Ropen tumbled across the waves. The other continued flying, closing in on the *Grantin*. Rifles from other crew members cracked. The machine gun opened up again, but its tracers missed.

"Someone make a decision." Rastun held his fire. "This thing's gonna be on top of us soon."

Bahar stared at Ehrenberg, then the Ropen, then back to Ehrenberg.

"Cease fire!" Bahar rushed by, waving his arms and hollering. "Cease fire!"

The machine gun fell silent and the rifle fire tapered off.

The Ropen glided toward them, now fifty yards out.

"Back up, back up, back up," ordered Rastun.

They retreated past the tied down helicopter and toward the stern. He, Geek, and McClure tracked the Ropen with their rifles. If the tranq dart didn't work fast enough, they had to be ready to take it down permanently.

The Ropen straightened, flapping its wings, and set down on the deck. Rastun's heart hammered as he stared down the sights of his rifle. This creature seemed smaller than the one they'd fought on Pulau Kangean, but not by much.

It let out a croaking sound and took a short hop toward them. One of the MSA sailors gasped and fired. Three bullets punched through the Ropen's wing.

"No!" Ehrenberg shouted.

Bahar shoved down the sailor's rifle, shouting something in Indonesian.

Ehrenberg turned back to the Ropen as it set down on all fours. A dull thump of air spat from the Aster 7. Rastun spotted the blue-tailed dart embedded in the creature's neck.

"Get behind the chopper," Rastun ordered.

They hurried to the other side of the AS565 Panther. Rastun hoped to keep it between him and the Ropen until the tranquilizer took effect. Maybe another minute or so.

He stared at it from beneath the helicopter's tail boom. The Ropen grunted, its head hung low. It leaped toward the end of the stern, wobbling as it came down.

"Looks like it's almost out." Karen held up her camera and took another picture.

"Congrats, Doc." Geek slapped him on the shoulder. "Looks like your crazy-ass plan worked."

"Thanks." Ehrenberg took off his pack and reached inside for a GPS collar.

The Ropen flapped its wings, lifting off the deck a few feet, then coming back down. It tried to rise a second time, failing again. Rastun took steady breaths. Any second now.

The creature tried to take off, but swayed, landed on shaky legs . . .

And tumbled over the side.

"Shit." Rastun dashed for the stern.

"No, no, no." Ehrenberg followed, along with the others.

Rastun saw the unconscious Ropen bobbing in the water, getting further away as the *Grantin* plowed through the waves. He looked to Bahar. "We need to turn this boat around, and get some ropes."

The XO nodded and brought up his walkie-talkie.

One of the lookouts shouted. Then another. Rastun caught sight of the sailor atop the ship's island pointing to the northeast. He raised his binoculars.

Four more Ropen dove at the *Grantin*.

TWENTY-SIX

Marques flung open the door to the deck and almost went outside, but stopped at the last second. He had no idea if the Ropen was still attacking the bridge or if it had moved on to another part of the yacht. The animal could be perched right above him for all he knew, ready to tear his head off.

He waved for Kiswanto and Lenna to hold up, then peeked outside. Left, right, up. All clear.

Screeches echoed from the front of the *Earth Warrior*. Marques leaned outside and caught sight of the Ropen's wing near the bridge. A slight tremor rippled through the yacht as the giant reptile struck the island. A stab of worry went through him. He hoped Paulette was all right.

"Let's go." Marques hurried across the deck, carrying the crate with one hand. Kiswanto clutched the other end of it. Lenna followed, her eyes wide.

He set the crate down near the bridge. The Ropen shoved its head through the shattered front windows, squawking and wailing, trying to get at Paulette. He doubted she was anywhere close to the creature.

Marques and Kiswanto opened the crate, each one pulling out a tubular fireworks mine. They lit the devices and flung them at the Ropen. The creature ignored them, its head still shoved inside the bridge.

The mines hissed, then cracked. Orange and white sparks spat from the tubes.

The Ropen pulled its head out of the broken windows and shrieked.

Lenna touched her lighter to a row of bottle rockets. They snapped toward the Ropen, riding colorful, sparkling trails. Bright bursts surrounded the creature.

Marques lobbed another mine at the Ropen. Kiswanto did the same a couple of seconds later. More brilliantly colored sparks and flames erupted around the creature. It cried out, flapping its wings.

Lenna set off more bottle rockets. Marques grabbed another mine from the crate when the Ropen jumped away from the bridge. It spread its wings, flapped a couple of times, and lifted off.

Marques exhaled loudly in relief, staring back at the crate. He had hoped this plan would work when he got the fireworks in Jakarta. The loud and bright explosions could send any animal into a panic. He didn't think the Ropen would be different.

Plus, it would still be alive, unlike if it ran into the FUBI.

Speaking of which . . .

He hurried to the bridge, the others following. Paulette stood near the console, strands of her hair fluttering from the breeze flowing through the shattered bridge windows.

"Are you all right?" Marques put an arm around her waist and drew her into him.

"I'm fine," said Paulette. "We're gonna need a new window, but our controls are all fine."

"Good. Let's head for the *Grantin.*"

"We're not going to help them," Lenna spoke in a sharp tone. "Let those Nazi assholes get eaten."

"We are going to help them." Marques gazed at everyone on the bridge. "And in turn, it's going to help our cause."

***

The MSA lookout atop the bridge just brought up his AK-47 when a Ropen swooped down on him. The man screamed as sharp talons sank into his shoulder and chest.

Rastun raised his rifle, aiming for the monster's head, trying to compensate for the boat's rocking. He fired four times. None of the rounds appeared to have connected.

The Ropen lifted the sailor from the superstructure and flung him through the air. His body slammed against the helicopter's windshield. Spiderweb cracks spread out along the glass. The sailor tumbled to the deck, blood pouring from his wounds.

Rastun and Bahar ran toward the fallen man. Rastun trained his rifle on the Ropen and fired. It twitched and croaked. He glimpsed Bahar turning over the sailor. Blood soaked his torso. He did not move.

The Ropen cried out and jumped from the island.

"Get back!" He pulled Bahar away from the dead sailor and fired. Bloody holes appeared in the Ropen's body. McClure, Geek, and a few MSA sailors opened up. The Ropen screeched and jerked as it landed near the chopper's nose. It lunged forward, snapping its jaws. Rastun heard the dull puff of Ehrenberg's Aster 7. He did not see the tell-tale blue tail embedded in the creature.

The group fell back to the tail boom. Rastun leaned around the helicopter's fuselage and fired, hitting the monster's left wing. How many damn rounds had they put in this thing, and it didn't look close to going down. Of course, he'd heard war stories of soldiers who got shot multiple times and continued fighting.

And Ropen were much bigger than the average soldier.

The beast croaked and jumped atop the helicopter, shaking it. It peered down at the group.

Rastun aimed for the head and fired. Geek and McClure did the same, as did Bahar and his men. The Ropen's head jerked back, blood flying in all directions. It raised its beak and squealed. Rastun put his last two rounds into its throat and reached into his tactical vest for another 30-round clip. He'd just shoved it into his rifle when the Ropen toppled off the helicopter and crashed to the deck. Blood spread out from its head, ripped apart by multiple bullet wounds.

"There are two more Ropen attacking the foredeck," said Bahar, a walkie-talkie in his hand. "Everyone on me." He repeated his order in Indonesian, then turned to the sailor who had manned the aft machine gun. Again, he spoke in his native tongue. The sailor nodded and dashed back to the MG.

The group started toward the foredeck when Rastun caught movement in his peripheral vision. Something big.

He turned and saw the machine gunner's mouth open wide.

"Look out!" Rastun shouted.

Bahar also yelled.

A Ropen soared over the stern and pulled up. Its feet smashed into the machine gun, knocking it off its mount. The gunner fell on his back as the weapon spiraled through the air and into the water.

Rastun opened fire as the Ropen landed on the sailor. More rifles cracked and banged around him. The Ropen let out a pained and angry screech, its talons ripping down the length of the sailor's torso. The reptile flapped its wings and flew over the stern railing and into the darkness.

They hurried over to the sailor, but Rastun knew they were far too late. Blood streamed from the poor man's chest and gut. Pieces of intestine hung out his shredded stomach.

With Bahar on point, the group raced past the helicopter and along the island. A trio of sailors stood ahead of them, firing their rifles at the two Ropen attacking the island.

One of the monsters jumped down on them. A sailor screamed and dove away. The other two kept firing. The Ropen screeched as it crashed down on the pair. It sank its talons into the torso of one man, while its jaws clamped down on the head of the other.

Rastun's team fired. The Ropen jerked, cried, and leaped over the side, gliding away.

Ehrenberg and Bahar checked the two MSA sailors. One was clearly dead, head mangled and throat cut wide open, blood pouring from it. The other sailor was alive, barely. Blood covered his chest and stomach, while his right arm and right leg lay at unnatural angles. Ehrenberg and Karen tended to him while Rastun looked down the deck. The forward MINIMI machine gun was unmanned. He had a bad feeling about the fate of the gunner.

"I'm going for the MG." Rastun ran past Bahar.

The XO shouted something short and urgent. One of the MSA sailors gave a quick response and dashed after Rastun, probably to act as back-up.

The pair made it to the foredeck. A Ropen perched on the bridge, its beak buried in something fleshy and red. It lifted its head, stringy pieces of flesh hanging from its mouth.

It spotted Rastun and the sailor and let out a piercing cry.

Rastun fired until his rifle emptied. The MSA man's AK-47 chattered. Rastun slung his rifle over his shoulder and pounded toward the machine gun. Several feet away lay a sailor in a pool of blood. The gunner.

He reached the MINIMI just as something slammed onto the deck. Rastun spun around. The Ropen had the MSA man in its jaws, swinging him around, then tossing him aside. The bloodied body struck the island with a dull, fleshy thud.

"Dammit," he cursed. He grabbed the machine gun and started to bring it around.

"Jack!" Karen yelled.

The Ropen sprang toward him.

Rastun jumped to the left and rolled along the deck. The Ropen's jaws clamped down on the machine gun. It reared back its head, tearing the weapon from its mount and hurling it away.

Gunfire roared. Rastun glanced past the Ropen. Another of the pterosaurs landed on the port side, cutting off Geek and McClure from helping him.

The Ropen near Rastun wailed and got on all fours. He pulled out his Glock, for what good the little pistol would do against this monster. But he sure as hell wouldn't go down without a fight.

The Ropen's jaws opened, revealing sharp, blood-stained teeth, pieces of flesh stuck between some of them. It advanced on him.

Something snapped overhead. Bright orange light illuminated the *Grantin.*

Rastun looked up. Orange sparks fell from the air. Another explosion lit up the night, throwing out a shower of white sparks. Bright, colorful dots swirled before his eyes.

Fireworks?

More sparkling streaks flew across the water. Fireworks burst across the foredeck. Rastun rolled away so as not to get burned. He peered past the *Grantin's* bow.

Earth Warrior charged toward them, more fireworks flying from its deck. White, red, orange, and green sparks erupted around the *Grantin.* The Ropen shrieked and leaped off the foredeck, flying high into the night sky.

Rastun got to his feet and looked around, blinking away the colorful dots dancing before his eyes. The Ropen on the port side also flew off, joining the last one as more fireworks went off.

The display went on for another minute or so, then ended. Karen and the others rounded the island. She rushed to Rastun, throwing her arms around him.

"You okay?" She squeezed him hard.

"Still breathing." He kissed her forehead.

"I don't believe it." Karen let him go and turned toward the *Earth Warrior,* less than a hundred yards off their port bow. "Fireworks?"

Rastun walked over to the railing, watching as the yacht neared them.

"Ahoy, *Grantin!*" a megaphone-enhanced voice blared across the water. It was Marques. "Are you in need of assistance?"

Lieutenant Bahar shook his head and waved off the yacht.

"All right. We will be nearby, just in case."

Rastun clutched the railing, eyeing the figures standing by the *Earth Warrior's* bow. Marques, Kiswanto, and Lenna. He snorted as Karen stood beside him.

"Well isn't this a kick in the nuts," he grumbled.

"What?" asked Karen.

"We actually owe our lives to those dickheads."

TWENTY-SEVEN

Sherlock stepped out of the Gulfstream and stared at the terminal of Long Beach Airport. A few other corporate jets were parked in front of the white rectangular building. He gave a slight nod. One of the benefits of traveling in a smaller jet. They could land at a municipal airport like this instead of putting up with the insanity of LAX, one of the five busiest airports in the world, just fifteen miles away.

He walked down the steps and onto the tarmac, Keough behind him. She glanced over her shoulder at the Gulfstream. "Damn, I wish my agency had a billionaire philanthropist to loan us his private plane."

"Yeah. Helping out the FUBI does have some nice perks."

"How did Roland Parker make all his money?" Keough asked as they went through the glass doors of the terminal.

"He runs an investment firm," answered Sherlock.

Keough looked back at the Gulfstream. "Must be one hell of an investment firm if he can buy a plane like that."

"It's among the top ten in the world."

They checked in with the rental car station, got the keys, and headed for their vehicle.

"Now the fun begins." Keough opened the passenger door. "LA traffic."

"Are you speaking from experience?" asked Sherlock.

"My friends and I came down here a couple of times for spring break when we were in college. It amazes me half the population here hasn't been killed in car wrecks. What about you?"

"Once, back when I was married." Sherlock slid behind the wheel. "We did a family trip to Disneyland. The drive was a bit hairy."

Keough guffawed. "Understatement of the century there."

Sherlock got on the 405 at the tail end of rush hour. Still, the freeway was packed, many of the drivers acting like they were in time trials for the Indy 500. More than once he had to hit the brakes or swerve when some daredevil raced across two or three lanes to make their exit. At least Keough wasn't screaming every ten seconds like his ex-wife had done. Though she did clutch the door grip and stare ahead with a stiff expression.

They survived their drive on the 405 and reached their destination, a six-story exclusive apartment complex along the water of Lower Newport Bay. They showed their badges to the security guard at the front gate.

"We're here to see Matt Allen," Sherlock told him.

The guard's brow furrowed. "Can I ask what this is about?"

"We're investigating a case and think he might know someone involved. We just want to ask him some questions."

The guard nodded, then got on the phone in his booth. Less than a minute later, he opened the gate and directed them to a parking spot.

Keough let out a loud breath, staring at the beige brick building in front of them. "You know, part of me hopes he isn't involved in all this."

Sherlock turned to her. "I know what you mean." Matt Allen had spent twenty years with LAPD before retiring. To Sherlock, any cop involved in criminal activity was one of the lowest forms of life on the planet.

They walked up to the apartment building and through the glass doors. A squat man in a dark blazer with thinning gray hair and a paunch stood up at the polished wooden desk. Matt Allen. Keough had learned about him on IMDB while checking on Thomas Griffin. The two had worked together on an upcoming movie titled *Cutting the Wire*. Sherlock guessed it was the film Griffin had bragged about to the folks in Oregon, the one that would revive his career.

Looking at the cast listing, his was the sixth name from the top. Most likely a supporting character. Sherlock doubted it would put the former child star back on the map. But if certain pieces fell into place, it might put him in jail.

The plot of *Cutting the Wire* dealt with a woman trying to make it onto the Los Angeles Police Department Bomb Squad. Griffin played a bomb tech, and Allen had been a consultant on the movie. Six years in the Army as an MOS 89D – explosive ordinance disposal specialist – and twenty years in the LAPD, fifteen with the bomb squad, Allen knew his explosives.

Sherlock and Keough introduced themselves and shook Allen's hand. The ex-cop tilted his head. "A U.S. Marshal and an Oregon State Police detective? Kind of an unusual pairing, especially in LA."

"Our cases happened to cross paths," said Keough. "We wanted to talk to you about Thomas Griffin. You worked with him on a movie called *Cutting the Wire.*"

"Yeah. He in trouble?"

"We're still trying to determine that," said Sherlock. "Is there someplace we can talk?"

"There's a conference room down the hall. Let me just get someone to cover the desk."

He pulled out a walkie-talkie and called for another security guard.

Keough looked around the spacious tiled lobby with its large windows and decorative potted plants. "Nice place. Has to be a lot less stressful than your former job."

"Damn right it is." Allen put his hands on his hips. "Sit on my ass, do background checks on prospective tenants. Occasionally I check out a noise complaint. May sound boring, but it gives me something to do between consulting gigs."

Sherlock glanced at Keough. Good job on her, trying to put Allen at ease. Then again, the man had been a cop for twenty years. He probably knew what she was doing.

Another, younger guard took over the front desk. Allen led them to the conference room. All three sat in plush leather swivel chairs.

"Okay." Allen leaned back. "Sorry for being so forward, but let's shoot straight. You two wouldn't be talking to me unless Griffin fucked up big time."

"You say that like you expect him to get in trouble." Keough rested her elbows on the table.

Allen snorted. "Twenty years in the LAPD, I've heard plenty of stories about former child stars busted for everything from drug possession to beating the shit out of their girlfriends. Thomas Griffin was by no means the worst of the bunch, at least when I worked with him. But nothing surprises me with people like that."

"How well did you get along with him?" asked Sherlock.

"He was okay. Full of himself, sometimes tried too hard to get people to like him, but not a total prick. And believe me, I've been around actors who are raging mega-assholes."

Sherlock nodded. "So what did you do on *Cutting the Wire?*"

"I helped the actors get the terminology correct, worked with the props and special effects people to make sure bombs and explosions were as authentic as possible. Also showed them how we actually dispose of bombs. That whole cut the red wire thing is so much Hollywood bullshit."

"Did Griffin pick up on everything you said?" asked Sherlock.

Allen glanced up at the ceiling, as though trying to recall. "Pretty much. The kid seemed eager to learn."

Sherlock and Keough glanced at one another. Rolling his chair closer to the table, Sherlock asked, "Did Griffin ever ask you any detailed questions about bombs?"

"Not that I can . . ." Allen's voice trailed off. His gaze flickered between Sherlock and Keough. "Oh, don't tell me the dumbass got involved in some kind of domestic terrorism shit. And I guess that would make me a person of interest at the least, and a suspect at the worst."

Sherlock studied the other man's face. He didn't detect any outrage. Also, no nervousness. No facial ticks or sudden scratching or shifting in his chair. Nothing to indicate he was trying to hide something. Just a veteran cop who knew how the investigative process went.

"Thomas Griffin has been working with a group of environmental activists who may be connected to the bombing of a logging camp in Jewell, Oregon," said Keough. "This group is also operating in Indonesia, following the FUBI expedition looking for the Ropen, which is why Marshal Dunmore is involved. He's the law enforcement liaison for them."

"Aw jeez." Allen leaned back and shook his head. "Well, I can tell you this. I never told the kid how to make bombs and he didn't ask me for instructions."

"Did you ever see Thomas Griffin with any of these people?" Keough held out her phone, showing him photos of the *Earth Warrior* crew.

"Nope." Allen shook his head. "Never seen any of 'em."

Nothing in the ex-cop's body language indicated to Sherlock he was lying. While disappointed they seemed to be back at square one, he was glad that a brother law enforcement officer had not actively helped a possible eco-terrorist.

They thanked Allen for his time and headed back to their car.

"Well, at least the three women on *Earth Warrior* live in the LA area," Keough pointed out. "We might have better luck digging into their backgrounds. Why don't we start with Paulette Thompson's parents? Hell, she did try to ram a coast guard cutter and got off scot-free."

"Forget them." Sherlock pulled out the keys to the rental car. "They're rich Hollywood folks. As soon as we identify ourselves, they'll be on the phone to their lawyers, who'll tell them to keep their mouths shut."

Keough sighed. "Yeah, I guess you're right."

Sherlock looked over the roof of the car at the detective. "Our best bet is to check out their friends and followers on social media. See which ones are in the Los Angeles area, which ones they might be closest to, and which ones might support violence to further an agenda."

"That's gonna be a lot of people to sort through."

"I know," said Sherlock. "So I guess we better get to work."

TWENTY-EIGHT

The rows of sharp teeth descending toward Rastun vanished when he opened his eyes. He lay in the bunk paralyzed, body damp with sweat. He forced himself to draw a breath, then another.

Fucking nightmares. Not the first time he'd had such dreams. It certainly wouldn't be his last, especially if he kept adding to his list of near-death experiences.

His body relaxed; the dream-induced paralysis gone. Rastun slid out of the bunk and went through his morning routine of push-ups and sit-ups. All the while, he replayed last night's Ropen attack. They had hoped to recover the one creature that had been tranqed and fallen overboard, but a search afterward turned up nothing. It had likely drowned and become a feast for any sharks in the area.

All his exercising did nothing to rid his frustration and sense of failure. Both clung to him as he went to the head, changed into fresh clothes, and walked to the crew mess. Lunch service had already begun and Rastun counted a dozen MSA members sitting at the rectangular tables. None of them talked. All wore sullen expressions. A few stared at their food for several seconds before taking a bite. The very air of the mess felt heavy.

Rastun lowered his eyes. He'd been in similar atmospheres in Iraq and Afghanistan. Six crew members had died in last night's attack. The *Grantin* had a complement of between 80 or 90. Everybody knew everybody. The entire crew had to be feeling the loss.

He made his way to the serving line, still eyeing the quiet Indonesians. Could he have done anything different to save even one of their fallen comrades? He replayed the attack in his head as a food service specialist heaped chicken noodles on his plate. He then grabbed a packet of *krupuk* crackers, nearly crushing them when he couldn't come up with any actions that would have prevented a single death.

Rastun picked up a plastic mug, pausing at the coffee dispenser. His mind took him back to Iraq nearly a decade ago. He was just a few months removed from his commission as a second lieutenant and leading a platoon of 82nd Airborne soldiers. On his second patrol, the unit had been attacked by insurgents. They'd beaten back the enemy, but at the cost of two of his men.

Later, he'd asked his platoon sergeant what he could have done differently to have kept those men alive.

"Probably nothing," he had told Rastun. "That's war, L-T. Even if you make the right decision every time, you're still gonna lose people."

His sergeant had been right. Not that it kept him from feeling guilty, then or now.

When he was done eating, Rastun headed topside. The blood from last night's battle had been mopped up. New windows from the ship's stores had been installed on the bridge to replace the shattered ones. Other MSA personnel made repairs to the machine gun mounts and replaced the windshield on the helicopter.

He stared past the stern. *Earth Warrior* continued to tail them. Irritation, even embarrassment, flooded through him. It would have been one thing if Geek, Karen, or Lieutenant Bahar had saved his ass, but now he owed his life to a dickhead like Marques. Someone who was trying to undermine their expedition.

Would you rather be dead, dumbass?

Rastun always believed in giving credit where credit was due, but he wondered if he could actually thank Marques if they met face-to-face again.

He went back to his berth to write up his after-action report for Colonel Lipeli. He was two pages into it when Bahar stopped by his quarters.

"How's the crew holding up?" asked Rastun.

"As well as can be expected." Bahar's lips pressed together. His shoulders sagged.

"You ever lose anyone before?"

"No." Bahar shook his head. "This is the first time men under me have died. Six." He let out a heavy breath. "Six. Yet somehow we have to go on and do our duty."

"I know. I've been in your shoes more times than I care to count." Rastun's tone was flat.

"It sounds like it does not get easier."

"No it does not, and if it does, there's something seriously wrong with you."

Bahar nodded, stepping inside. "Perhaps we can stop the Ropen before any more of our people, or anyone else, is killed by them. The captain informed me we're getting reinforcements."

"More patrol boats?"

"Yes. Two, along with four others from the Sea and Coast Guard. The Navy is also sending two corvettes."

"Pretty decent-sized fleet," said Rastun. "When should they get here?"

"In two or three days."

Rastun nodded. It did appear this part of the Java Sea was the Ropen's prime hunting territory. The extra ships should make it easier to find the creatures.

Except . . .

"We better get together with Captain Teguh and the Doc." Rastun stood. "We need to coordinate with the other boats, and make sure their crews have tranquilizer darts and GPS collars."

"A good point. I will speak with the captain and arrange it."

Rastun was about to thank the MSA officer when the man's walkie-talkie crackled. The person on the other end said something in Indonesian and Bahar replied in his native tongue.

"It appears we have a situation. Come." He waved Rastun to follow.

The two hurried through the passageways and up to the deck. They strode toward the aft, where an MSA member and McClure stared through binoculars.

"What do we got?" Rastun halted next to the ex-paratrooper.

"Look off *Earth Warrior's* starboard side."

Rastun brought up his binoculars. Two cabin cruisers approached Marques' yacht. When they got within a hundred yards, the people on the two vessels waved to *Earth Warrior.* Marques, Paulette, and Lenna came out on the yacht's bridge wing and waved back.

"There is another boat approaching," said Bahar.

Through his binoculars, Rastun saw a white sail in the distance. It, too, was headed for the *Earth Warrior.*

He turned back to Bahar. "It looks like Marques just got reinforcements, too."

TWENTY-NINE

Maybe I shouldn't watch the news anymore.

Joyce Rastun held her coffee mug halfway to her mouth, watching TV from a sofa in her living room. After the local news finished with the rundown of overnight murders and fires in the Philadelphia area, they turned their attention to the Ropen hunt in Indonesia.

The coffee churned in her stomach as she thought about the attack on the patrol boat. The news reported the FUBI members were all right – including Jack and Karen. She wished her son would have called to tell her himself. Sure, he must be busy, but my God, he'd almost been killed by a cryptid. Again!

Joyce put her mug on the side table and leaned forward, staring intently at the TV. A video played from the UN cryptid hunter that had been giving Jack's group so much trouble.

"What we showed is that it is possible to save *both* people and cryptids in these situations," Marques said from the deck of a boat. "Using non-lethal methods, we were able to save the lives of everyone onboard the Indonesian patrol boat, while at the same time preserving one of the rarest animals in the world. Now, will the FUBI follow our lead, or will they continue to let their soldiers-for-hire slaughter these remarkable creatures?"

The screen cut to the studio anchors, one male, one female, with a shot of the Philadelphia skyline behind them.

"The video from Cesar Marques inspired other boats that had been demonstrating against oil companies following the Java Sea spill to join his cause," said the female anchor. "It has also resulted in more anti-FUBI tweets, including these, 'Hashtag, Save the Ropen. Shut down the FUBI,' and, 'Best Wishes Cesar Marques. End the FUBI's monster genocide.' Other tweets also call for the continued boycott of the Philadelphia Zoo, where the parents of famed FUBI security specialist Jack Rastun work."

Joyce huffed. This was getting ridiculous, and worrisome. Posts making Jack, Karen and their co-workers look like psychopaths would only stir up the crazies. Like some of the zoo protesters a couple of days ago who accosted a group of children on a field trip. They told the kids going to the zoo meant they wanted the Ropen to die. None of those children had been older than eight. What the hell was wrong with people these days?

She didn't bother finishing the rest of her coffee, just poured the remnants into the kitchen sink. After brushing her teeth, she and her husband got in their car and headed to work. About thirty or forty protesters stood across the street from the zoo.

"I'm actually starting to recognize some of them." Robert Rastun nodded to the group as he flicked the turn signal. "They've been here since day one. Jeez, don't they have a job to go to? Or classes?"

Joyce let out a slow breath. "I wonder how many guests we've lost because of those jerks."

"I have noticed a dip in attendance over the past few days. There have been two or three groups that canceled their outings. One woman even said they have to stand in solidarity with the Ropen." Robert rolled his eyes as he drove through the parking lot. "Like a prehistoric animal ten thousand miles away can actually appreciate her concern."

He turned to Joyce and patted her shoulder. "Don't worry. We can ride this out."

"But can Jack? Or Karen?" She bit down on her lip.

"I'm sure they'll be okay. They've been in tough spots before." Robert looked straight ahead, hands squeezing the steering wheel.

Joyce stared at her husband. Brave face aside, she knew he was just as worried about Jack and their future daughter-in-law as she was.

After parking, they headed toward the zoo entrance. Ten minutes till opening, and already a dozen or so people stood in line, many of them senior citizens. Retirees, likely. Joyce caught sight of a chubby woman in her early twenties with short half-blond, half-pink hair. The younger woman's eyes locked on her. Joyce's forehead crinkled. Had she glared at her?

She put it out of her mind by the time she reached her office. Joyce switched on her computer, bringing up order forms for medicine and other essentials, and checking to see which animals needed teeth cleanings and check-ups. Robert had told her they were expecting delivery of an Australian brown falcon from a small zoo in Idaho that would close soon. She emailed them a request for the bird's medical history and dietary needs. After that, she put together next week's schedule for her staff.

Joyce leaned back in her seat, her gaze shifting to the framed photos on her desk. One showed Jack decked out in his Army uniform, receiving his commission upon graduating from Marshall University. The other was of him, Karen, and Emily from their trip last year to Sedona, where Jack had popped the question. She smiled, happy for her son. Worry quickly replaced her joy, thinking about the creatures he and Karen were searching for in Indonesia.

Please be careful.

Joyce left the office to start her rounds. Her first stop would be the maned wolf exhibit. One of the animals, Charro, had not been eating much the past couple of days and appeared lethargic. She clenched her jaw, concern building within her. She had performed successful surgery on him for gastric dilatation volvulus a couple of years ago and removed a cyst near his spinal cord last year. Still, Charro was 13 years old, right around the maximum life expectancy of a maned wolf in captivity. Would she be forced to perform her most unpleasant duty on the poor animal?

She slowed as she looked across the walkway from her office. The blond/pink-haired woman she'd seen earlier sat on a bench near the barnyard exhibit, staring at her phone, a soda cup next to her. The woman glanced up, again unsmiling, stared at her for a second or two, then looked back at her phone.

Joyce kept walking, glancing over her shoulder, holding her breath, suspicious. The woman remained on the bench, staring at her phone.

Great. I'm turning into Jack. One of his favorite sayings was, "A little paranoia can keep you alive." A shame he had to go through life like that. Besides, dozens upon dozens of zoo guests meandered around her. Like anyone would try something with so many people here.

Joyce wandered past the big cat exhibit, the carousel, and the horse ride pen. She greeted a zookeeper delivering food to the bald eagle habitat, then chatted with another keeper returning from Monkey Junction. She imagined Jack doing these jobs, a habit she'd gotten into when he'd been deployed to Iraq or Afghanistan, or lately when he searched for dangerous cryptids. Lord knew she and Robert had encouraged him to get into zoology. But after the passing of his Uncle Roger, who fought with the Army Rangers in World War II, Jack had been determined to follow in his footsteps.

Sometimes she wondered if they should have steered him away from the Army more forcefully. She had not wanted them to become overbearing parents, to control Jack's life. But maybe if they had done it, she wouldn't have to worry about him being shot, stabbed, beaten up, or eaten.

Of course, there's no guarantee he would have listened to us. She sure as hell had not listened to her father, a successful surgeon, when he told her to go into nursing. Telling her that veterinarians were not "real doctors" and calling it "a waste of a career" just made her more determined to get into the field and prove him wrong.

Joyce passed a small group of people chatting underneath a shade tree, including a trim black woman with coiffed hair. She wore a gray hoodie with ARMY emblazoned across the chest and a prosthetic leg. The others around her also had artificial arms or legs. Probably veterans. It made her think of Jack again.

Joyce greeted them, "I hope you're having a good time today."

"We are, ma'am," replied the female vet. "Thank you."

Joyce continued to the maned wolf enclosure. She sighed when she spotted Charro lying on his belly beside a bush. Just by looking into those sad, dark eyes she knew something was wrong. She needed to schedule an exam, the sooner the better. Could she help him, or was there nothing

—

"Hey you."

Joyce swung around, and held her breath. The blond/pink-haired woman approached, holding her cup.

"Yes?"

"Your son's that cryptid-killing motherfucker Jack Rastun, right?"

Straightening, Joyce held up a hand and replied, "Yes, he is my son, and there is no need for language like that here. Now we have nothing to do with the FUBI, so I'd apprec--"

"Fuck you, lady! You imprison innocent animals and your Nazi son kills them. You're all pieces of shit. You should all die!"

The woman's arm shot out. Joyce gasped and jumped back. Yellow liquid splashed all over her. She yelped, recognizing the stale stench immediately.

Urine.

The woman cried out and grabbed the collar of Joyce's jacket. She stumbled forward.

"Let go of me!" Joyce clawed the crazy woman's wrist.

"Fucking bitch! You're gonna pay for --"

An arm snaked under the blond/pink-haired woman's armpit and across her chest. She cried out as she lost her grip on Joyce's jacket. The woman whirled away from her and crashed onto the walkway, the female vet with the prosthetic leg on top of her. Two of her friends helped subdue the woman.

"Get the fuck off me!" she yelled. "Nazi fuckers!"

Joyce leaned against the railing running along the enclosure, taking shaky breaths, a hand over her chest. My God, that lunatic was going to beat her up. Or would she have . . .

She swallowed, her legs quaking.

"You okay, ma'am?" The female vet put a hand on her shoulder.

"Um . . . yes. Yes, thank you. Thank you so much."

The vet nodded and looked back at the other woman, kept on the ground by the other two amputees. "What the hell's her problem?"

"My son. He works for the FUBI."

Joyce took a few deep breaths, gagging on the stink of urine that soaked her, then pulled out her walkie-talkie. She contacted the head of zoo security and told him of the situation. Her husband also heard it.

"Are you okay?" The words shot out of Robert's mouth.

"Yeah. I'm-I'm fine."

"I'm on my way there now."

Two security guards arrived a couple of minutes later, followed by a very concerned-looking Robert, who wrapped her up in a hug. A little bit later, two Philadelphia Police officers showed up to arrest the lunatic woman.

"And we are pressing charges against her." Robert stabbed a finger at the now-handcuffed woman. "And I want her barred from this zoo . . . forever."

Joyce watched the officers haul off the woman, who continued her insane screaming. Her fear spiked, not for her, but for Jack and Karen. If some random woman felt justified throwing a cup of urine in her face, what might the crazy protesters in Indonesia do to her son and his fiancée?

THIRTY

Agung Adsit tried to maneuver his scooter best he could around the ruts in the dirt road. He failed more often than he succeeded. Every jolt made him grit his teeth. It would ensure him a sore ass by the time he reached Kalisangka. A small price to pay to see his mother and make sure she was doing well.

His jaw stiffened as he swung around a deep hole in the road. Did his mother still cry as she had during his last visit? Was she coming to grips with this loss?

Am I? Agung could not count the number of times he wanted to cry. But he was a man, the oldest son. With his father gone, he needed to be strong for his family. That meant keeping his grief private.

He glanced down at the basket attached to the front of his scooter. It contained a water jug for him, and bread, rice, tea leaves, and some rupiahs for his mother. Not as much as he wanted for the woman who birthed him, but whatever he could do to help her during this terrible time, he would.

It would be nice if I could stay a little longer. Yes, his mother had Aunt Soehaemi around, along with his grandfather and his brother, Hamdan. But he was lucky Mainaky gave him this one day off to see his family. Agung did not think he would have additional time off for a while. Besides, he and Sitor would have to put in more hours to make extra money to help their mother. And Hamdan needed to get his ass out on a boat to earn a living. His youngest brother did not want to fish, but too damn bad. You did what you had to for your family, especially during a time like this.

Sweat drenched Agung's face and his throat was dry. He stopped near the edge of the road and picked up his water jug. Removing the cap, he tipped his head back and downed one gulp, two gulps.

A large dark form soared above him.

"Shit!" Agung tried to jump off his scooter. He pitched over and fell face first on the ground. The jug tumbled with him.

"Allah help me," he sputtered, scrambling to his feet. He shivered, imagining the beast ripping him apart, like what happened to his . . .

No, no, no! He whipped his head about. Where was it?

There! The large, winged monster glided through the jungle. Agung drew quick, deep breaths. Allah be praised, the demon flyer ignored him. He was still alive.

And what if it comes back?

He jumped on his scooter and rode off, leaving behind his water jug. He glanced behind him, still breathing hard, making sure the monster did not follow him.

Then he remembered. There was a cave nearby. Many believed the demon flyers lived in them. How many more could be around?

Agung rode faster, not caring about the ruts that shook his scooter. He did not stop until he reached Kalisangka. Instead of his mother's home, he stopped first at the National Police station. Mohede was not around, but he told his story to one of the Chief Brigadier's men.

"You are lucky you got out of there alive," said the cop, who then reached for his phone. "Chief Brigadier Mohede left instructions to call the FUBI if anyone sees the demon flyer. Hopefully, they can kill them all."

Agung nodded. He wanted that as well.

***

"You sure you're all right?" It had to be the fifth time Rastun had asked the question since his mother called him about the assault at the zoo. Usually, it was her asking him that over and over again. He might have laughed had his rage not reached Krakatoa level proportions.

"Yes, I'm fine. I'm still a little shook up. I mean . . . I know people are angry over what you're doing and it's spilled over to us, but . . . I don't know, Jack. People are going insane over this."

Rastun clenched the sat phone. He stalked back and forth, as much as possible in his confined quarters on the *Grantin*. Karen leaned against the bunks, watching him, her face stiff with a mixture of anger and worry.

"Your father told security to conduct more thorough searches of zoo guests for the time being." Mom's voice came through the phone's speaker. "He's also thinking of bringing on a few more part-time guards."

"I want cops there," Rastun said firmly. "Dad knows people in Philly PD. Have him get a few uniforms to sit on the zoo. I want people there who are armed in case something more serious happens."

"He is going to talk with them about that."

"It needs to be more than talk. He needs to make it happen." Actually, what Rastun wanted to happen was for him to be at the Philadelphia Zoo, with Geek, Herrera, McClure, and Norgay. Fully armed and standing at the front entrance, eyeballing every person that went in with a look that said, "Don't even think of fucking with my family."

"Jack, we are taking precautions, and I am fine. You and Karen are probably in more danger over there than we are here."

"Mm-hmm." After what happened with Mom and that psycho woman, he wasn't so sure about that.

"You guys keep me posted on security there, got it?"

"Jack, you have enough on your plate with --"

"I said keep me posted. Maybe I can give you some advice to improve security." *That way I can do something useful from ten thousand fucking miles away.*

"All right. We will."

After he finished the call with his mother, Rastun phoned Colonel Lipeli and ran down the situation for him.

"I was afraid something like this was going to happen," said Lipeli. "We had three of our employees doxed, and someone put a photo of the school where Ed Lynch's kid goes, saying, 'None of you are safe.'"

Karen hugged herself, wincing. "Has anyone done anything like that with Emily's school?"

"Not that I've seen. I'll double-check, but so far the field security specialists I've sent by there report all's quiet."

Let's hope it stays that way, Rastun thought before his boss continued. "I'm sorry your mother got dragged into this."

"Thanks, but we need to stop this shit. Next time it may not be a cup of piss. It might be a knife or a gun."

"I know. Director Lynch and Mister Parker and I are trying to come up with ways to counter this social media barrage."

"Yeah, well I have a few ways how to counter it."

Lipeli let out a breath. "Jack, I know you're pissed off and concerned about what happened with your mother, but getting confrontational with Marques and his group is the absolute last thing I need you doing."

Rastun's facial muscles tightened as his fury peaked. "You want me to do nothing?"

"Yes."

"You gotta be kidding me. Those shit-sucking maggots can threaten us, threaten my family, and you don't want me to do a damn thing about it?"

"That is exactly what I'm saying," Lipeli repeated in a firm tone.

"Well that's going to be hard since those pukes are constantly on our ass."

"Then get McClure or Geek or someone else to deal with them. I *do not* want you having direct contact with the UNCID from this point on."

"Well if they pull any shit, I'm not gonna --"

"Dammit, Jack," snapped Lipeli. "That's exactly what they want. For you to lose your head and say or do something stupid that they'll blast all over social media. Our reputation is already hanging by a thread, and something like that will put it right in the toilet, maybe even jeopardize the FUBI's future. I know you're worried about your family and you want to kick Marques' ass, but you need to keep it together."

"Easy for you to say. It wasn't your mother that got attacked!" Rastun crushed the sat phone.

Karen moved her hands up and down, mouthing, "Calm down." A mix of surprise and worry flared in her eyes.

Rastun looked back at the phone. Nothing came from the speaker. Just a heavy silence. He gritted his teeth, knowing he had just crossed the line with Lipeli.

"You listen to me, *Captain.*" Lipeli didn't yell, just spoke in a low, deliberate tone. Sometimes that could be worse than getting yelled at.

"This outburst is *exactly* the reason why I do not want you engaging with the UNCID in any manner. I *will not* allow you to let your emotions jeopardize this organization. So, you have two choices. Pull your shit together or come home with an official reprimand in your file. Do I make myself clear?"

"Yes, sir." Rastun's reply slipped through his clenched teeth.

"Then you focus on the Ropen and we'll focus on the UNCID. Understood?"

"Yes, sir." Again, his teeth clamped together as he spoke.

After Lipeli hung up, Rastun glared at the wall, shoulders rising with slow breaths. Do nothing? People he cared about were threatened, and the Colonel, who himself had been handcuffed by idiotic rules of engagement by pussy politicians and generals during his time in the Army, now handcuffed him?

"Fuck!" He swung around and slammed his hand against the closet door.

"Jack." Karen took a step toward him. "You have to calm down."

"Calm down? Are you kidding me?"

"No, I'm not." Her voice rose with each word. "You probably don't want to hear this, but Colonel Lipeli has a point."

"Are you serious? You're taking his side?"

"It's not about taking sides."

"Those fuckers are the ones stirring up all this shit." Rastun stabbed a hand at the wall. "They're the ones who pushed that lunatic over the edge to attack my mom."

"You're not the only one pissed off at them," Karen fired back. "You don't think I want to slap the hell out of Cesar Marques or any of his friends? And what's that going to accomplish? It'll just give them another excuse to make you and the entire FUBI look bad."

"So we just let them keep whipping everyone into a frenzy until maybe someone winds up in the hospital, or worse. Maybe someone like Emily --"

"Don't you dare use her to try and make me agree with you!" Karen shoved a finger inches from his face. "This whole thing is hard on both of us, not just you!"

Karen stormed past him and out of the room.

Rastun's face tightened. Tremors of rage shot up and down his body.

"Fuck!" He pounded the closet door with his fist again. Then he just stood in place, silently seething.

"Jack?"

"What?" His head snapped around to find Ehrenberg standing in the doorway. The cryptozoologist swallowed, his head drawing back.

"Sorry," Rastun muttered. "What?"

"Um, we just got a call from the police in Kalisangka. Captain Adsit's son, Agung, was riding home when he spotted a Ropen. He says it might have gone into a cave near where he saw it. We're going to meet Petal and the others there."

"Okay, I'll get ready."

Ehrenberg tilted his head. "Everything okay, Jack?"

Rastun let out a long, frustrated breath. "No. Everything is not okay."

***

Pistaka sat at his desk, frowning at the report concerning a faulty engine on *Mainaky 11* when his assistant informed him over the intercom a policeman in Kalisangka was on hold.

"Is it something important?" he asked in a curt tone.

"I believe so. He said it is regarding the demon flyer."

Eyes widening, Pistaka said, "Put him through."

A few seconds passed before a voice said, "Is this Mister Pistaka?"

"Yes. Who is this?"

"This is Adjutant Brigadier Vikri of the National Police. We had a report of a Ropen sighting from one of your employees, Agung Adsit."

"Oh yes?" Pistaka straightened in his seat. "Where and when did this happen?"

"This morning. Agung was riding home when the monster flew over him. I'd say he is lucky to be alive."

"Uh-huh. Where did this happen?"

"On the main road between your facility and Kalisangka. Agung figures perhaps five or six kilometers from your plant. I thought I should call since it is very close to you."

"Yes. Good. Did Agung say where the demon flyer went?"

"He said there is a cave near the road," replied Vikri. "It might have gone in there. The American monster hunters seem convinced the demon flyers live in caves. Who knows? Again, I wanted to give you a warning."

"Good. Thank you. I will warn everyone here."

Pistaka hung up without saying goodbye, then told his assistant to send for Zaina. About five minutes later, the security force leader arrived at his office.

"The police just called. One of our fishermen saw the demon flyer near here."

"Where exactly?" asked Zaina.

"About five or six kilometers down the main road. The monster may have gone into a nearby cave. I'm sure the FUBI has already been informed, but if you and your men hurry, you can get there before them and kill those damn monsters."

THIRTY-ONE

The helicopter ride to Pulau Kangean gave Rastun the chance to tamp down on his emotions. Definitely not easy with everything that had just happened, but what choice did he have? They could encounter a deadly animal. He needed to be focused, to put to the side the assault on his mother, going off on Colonel Lipeli, then going off on Karen.

He glanced across the Panther's hold where Karen sat, deliberately not looking at him. Shit, he had messed up, let his temper get the better of him. He needed to apologize, and soon. Something Geek told him shortly after he proposed to Karen popped into his head.

"The biggest piece of advice I can give you, Cap'n, is be prepared to say 'I'm sorry,' a lot."

His former sergeant knew what he spoke of.

The chopper landed in a clearing near the coast. The group hopped out and hiked about a mile to the road, where Mohede and his pickup waited for them. They would rendezvous with Petal and her team where Agung's sighting occurred and head to the cave together. He wanted to go in full force to deal with this Ropen, or multiple Ropen.

Five minutes into the trip, Rastun's sat phone rang. It was Norgay.

"We just arrived at the sighting location," the ex-Gurkha's voice came through the speaker. "There is another truck here with a Mainaky logo."

Brow furrowed, Rastun looked to Geek, who sat next to him in the pickup's bed. "What the hell are they doing there?"

"I don't know," replied Norgay. "No one from the company is with the truck. I checked the ground and vegetation and found footprints and disturbed branches. Someone went into the jungle."

"No way is it any of the fishermen," said Geek. "They wouldn't want to be within fifty miles of a Ropen."

Rastun nodded. "And I doubt it's Pistaka. The guy's an office puke. No way would he roam around the jungle."

The pair stared at each other, jerking back and forth when the pickup hit a rut. Geek then straightened. "I bet it's those private security clowns."

Jaw tightening, Rastun glanced at the sat phone in his hand. What the hell were Zaina's guys doing there? Hunting the Ropen themselves? How did they learn its location so fast?

It's not like any information on this expedition has been compartmentalized. Again, the difference between dealing with a civilian organization compared to a military one. Of course, it wasn't like no one had ever coughed up military secrets.

"Stay out of sight and observe until we get there," Rastun told Norgay.

"Copy."

They made it to the rendezvous point twenty minutes later, where Norgay, Petal, and the others emerged from the jungle to meet them. Rastun leaped out of the bed, his gaze settling on the two people who had not concealed themselves among the trees. Kory Hyo and Thomas Griffin. His eyes narrowed at the former child actor, rage building by the second. He was the one who started the damn boycott of the Philadelphia Zoo on social media. Then he and his fuckhead friends kept stoking the fire, the absolute hatred, until the inevitable happened. Some nutjob acted on it and made his mother the target.

And there he stood, maybe thirty feet away. Rastun's brain screamed at him to run down the little shitstain, slam him against a tree, and punch him over and over.

He gritted his teeth, taking deep breaths, trying to control himself. Wondering how he could just stand there after what Griffin had done.

"Sir."

Norgay's voice pulled him back to reality. "Yeah?"

"No one has returned to the truck." Norgay nodded to the Mainaky pickup, parked on the side of the dirt road.

"I'm just worried they'll kill any Ropen they come across." Petal grimaced as she looked toward the trees.

"We haven't heard any gunfire," Herrera chimed in. "So I guess that's a good sign."

"Or it could mean the Ropen attacked them before they could shoot," said Petal.

Rastun looked toward the trees. "Whatever the case, we're at full strength, so let's get in there and check it out."

They proceeded into the jungle, Herrera and one of the MSA sailors on point, and Norgay and another *Grantin* crewman named Kabo bringing up the rear. Rastun stayed in the center of the group, far away from Kory and Griffin, who tailed them.

He drew in more deep breaths, scanning around him, coming up with contingencies on what they would do if they ran into any Ropen, if they got into a confrontation with Tiger Force, if Kory or Griffin tried anything. Especially Griffin.

Please try something. Please give me justification to beat the living shit out of you.

Herrera's left fist shot up. Everyone stopped. "I hear movement ahead," he radioed.

"Take cover," ordered Rastun.

Everyone slipped behind trees and bushes. Except Kory and Griffin. They just stopped and looked around, their expressions a mix of curiosity and confusion.

Vegetation ahead of them thrashed. Four men came into view, all wearing the slate gray fatigues of Tiger Force Security. At the head of the squad was Zaina.

"Nice day for a stroll in the jungle," Rastun called out from behind a tree.

The four men tensed, their hands gripping the straps of their rifles, which they had slung over their shoulders.

Rastun stepped halfway out from the tree. Zaina and his men relaxed, somewhat.

"Mister Rastun," said Zaina. "I thought you would show up eventually."

"Yeah, well, looking for Ropen is what we do, and we heard there was one here."

"There was. We found it in the cave. It will not bother anyone again."

"You killed it?" gasped Kory. "You sick bastards."

"Yeah." Griffin jabbed a finger at them. "You . . . You're genociding Nazi fuckers."

Zaina raised an eyebrow, then gave a slight shake of the head. "The monster was dead long before we arrived. We did find a lot of bats. That's probably what that fool fisherman saw."

The four guards made their way past the FUBI team. "You're welcome to see it for yourself, what's left of it."

With that, Zaina and his men headed back toward the road.

"Norgay, you and Kabo follow Zaina and his guys. Make sure they don't pull any shit."

"Yes, sir."

The pair slipped through the trees, while the rest of the group headed for the cave. Unfortunately, Kory and Griffin followed.

When they reached the mouth, Ehrenberg gazed at it for a few seconds before turning to Rastun. "You think Zaina was telling the truth?"

"Maybe, but I trust that guy about as much as I trust the average politician." He looked back at Geek and Alana. "I think it's time to break out your toy again."

Alana removed the Alley Cat drone from her pack, then took out her iPad. After checking the camera mounted on top of the little four-wheeled vehicle, she sent it into the cave. Rastun, Karen, Ehrenberg, Geek, and

Petal all gathered around Alana, staring at the screen as she flicked on the drone's night vision lens, turning the interior green. She swung the camera a full 360. Nothing but rocks.

Rastun glanced at Karen, flashing her a quick, hopefully apologetic grin. She did not acknowledge it.

Yeah, I'm really going to have to apologize.

The Alley Cat kept going, bouncing over uneven terrain. Alana stopped it twice for a 360 scan. The camera found nothing.

Rastun caught Ehrenberg chewing the bottom of his lip. Petal's gaze never shifted from the screen. Would they finally come across a Ropen nest or would it be another bust?

"Looks like we got a little dip here." Alana slowed the Alley Cat, stopping it at the edge. She panned the camera down.

"Holy shit." She drew her head back.

The snout of a Ropen appeared in front of the camera.

"Take it in closer," said Ehrenberg.

"Roger." Alana thumbed the controls on the touch screen, slowly rolling the Alley Cat down the incline.

The Ropen didn't move. Rastun knew it would never move again. The skin was pressed tight against the head. A dark hole took the place of where the creature's left eye should be.

"Looks like it's been dead a while," Karen noted.

"Mm." Petal nodded. "Hard to tell how long, or how it might have died until we see it up close."

"I don't think that's such a good idea," said McClure. "There could be a lot more Ropen in there, ones that aren't dead."

Ehrenberg looked to the ex-paratrooper. "Well, let's find out. Alana, take us deeper."

"You got it, Doc."

The Alley Cat motored past the dead Ropen. It went on for roughly another mile before the cave started to narrow. After another half-mile, Alana did a 360 scan. Rastun tilted his head as he examined the image.

"That looks like it'd be a pretty tight fit for any Ropen."

"I doubt there are any others deeper in this cave." Ehrenberg leaned closer, brow furrowed. "Alana, pan up. I thought I caught some movement."

Alana did as instructed. Rastun spotted elongated shapes hanging from the ceiling. Big ones. Not Ropen big. Not even close. But . . .

"Those look like some damn big bats," said Geek.

"Probably flying foxes," Ehrenberg explained. "A species of megabat. Some people think that Ropen sightings – well, before now – were people who misidentified bats like these."

Herrera drew his head back, puzzled. "How the hell do you confuse a bat for a prehistoric monster?"

Ehrenberg answered, "If you've grown up with stories about creatures like the Ropen and you're out and about and suddenly see something large fly overhead, especially at night, it startles or scares you. Your mind might jump to a monster instead of a more logical explanation. Never underestimate how fear can cloud someone's judgment."

Norgay reported back that Zaina and his men had driven off. *Thank God for that,* Rastun thought. One less thing he had to worry about.

They proceeded into the cave, leaving behind two MSA sailors to guard the entrance. Thankfully, Kory and Griffin stayed outside. Maybe going into a cave was too much of an effort for their activism.

"Don't we already have one dead Ropen to study?" said McClure. "Do we really need another one?"

Petal spun around to face him. "A species like this, you can never have enough specimens to examine. If it died of natural causes, we can get an idea of the Ropen's lifespan. Maybe it got into a fight with another of its kind. That could give us some insight into their social interactions."

McClure held up his hands. "Okay, I'm convinced."

In a few minutes, they came upon the dead Ropen and shined flashlights on it. Rastun gazed over it from tip to tail, or rather, what was left of the tail. The creature appeared in an advanced state of decomposition. Large chunks of skin were gone, the work of maggots. Clumps of white grew around much of the body. Fungi.

"It doesn't smell bad at all." Petal pulled on some Latex gloves, bent down and felt around the Ropen's head and back. "What's left of the skin is completely dried out."

"Look at all the fungus." Ehrenberg crouched beside the torso, then twisted around to the wing. "Some of the bones have also separated. This far into the cave, not exposed to the elements, I'd say it's been here six to eight months."

Karen snapped pictures as Petal continued to examine the body, saying, "Maybe it got hurt or sick and took shelter in here. Maybe it lost a fight in its rookery and got forced out."

"Whatever the case," Ehrenberg chimed in, "this gives a little more credence to the theory that Ropen live in caves."

He put his hands on his hips, staring at the corpse. "I can't see dragging the entire body out of here without causing significant damage. Much as I hate to say it, we may have to take it out in pieces."

Petal's mouth opened, about to argue. She paused, looking down at the Ropen, shoulders sagging. "Yeah, I guess we have no choice. We can definitely take the head, probably parts of the wings and the talons."

They exited the cave, Ehrenberg calling the *Grantin* to tell them about the find.

"We're going to need tarps, cutting tools, crates, and probably more people, too . . . all right, thanks, Lieutenant." He lowered the phone and looked at the others. "Bahar says they should arrive offshore within the hour, then probably another hour for them to reach the cave."

"Sounds like hurry up and wait time," said Geek.

They set up a perimeter around the cave. Mohede and the policeman who'd driven Petal's group here drove to the beach to await Bahar's group. Kory and Griffin kept their distance, talking among themselves. Actually, Griffin did most of the talking. Kory looked bored.

Even his own team can't stand the son-of-a-bitch, thought Rastun.

He spotted Karen sitting under a tree, looking at her camera screen. Steeling his back, he walked over and sat beside her. She glanced at him, then returned her attention to her camera.

"I'm sorry."

Now she looked fully at him.

"I didn't use Emily to try and get you to agree with me. I'm just worried about everyone back home." His face tightened. "There are so many threats out there and I feel like there's not a damn thing I can do about it, and I'm told to leave the people responsible for this shit alone. I'm not wired to sit on the sidelines when people I care about are at risk. I'm sorry I took it out on you."

A smile slowly grew on Karen's face. She rubbed his shoulder. "I know it's hard. I can't tell you how helpless I've felt at times. We just have to get through it . . . together."

Rastun took her hand and kissed it. "I love you."

"I love you, too."

She slid next to him, resting her head on his shoulder. Rastun relished the feel of his fiancée's hair against his cheek.

It was late afternoon when Lieutenant Bahar arrived with half-a-dozen men, all of whom carried tarps or crates. One man also had an ax, while another brought a saw. They sliced off the dead Ropen's head and talons and wrapped them in tarps. Mohede and his officer shuttled the group to the beach in their pickups, with Kory and Griffin following on their scooters.

It was near dark when the pickups returned to take Rastun, Karen, and the rest of the team to the beach. The *Grantin* floated a mile offshore.

So did *Earth Warrior* and its protest fleet. Not all of the crews stayed on their boats. A few dinghies sat in the surf. About a dozen protesters milled about, shouting their usual epitaphs of "murderers" and "Nazis."

Rastun did not spot Kory or Griffin among the crowd. They were probably back aboard *Earth Warrior*.

The protesters did nothing more than shout as Rastun and the others took the Zodiacs back to the *Grantin*. Bahar greeted them when they came aboard.

"Where did you put the Ropen remains?" asked Karen.

"They are in the storeroom. Doctor Ehrenberg and Doctor Garland are down there examining them."

Karen turned to Rastun. "Wanna see if they found out anything?"

"Why not?"

They headed belowdecks, where Ehrenberg and Petal knelt by the decomposed skull of the Ropen.

"So, any scientific breakthroughs yet?" asked Rastun.

Ehrenberg stared up at him. "Not even close. There are a few paleontologists back in the States we might be able to Skype with, including one in Colorado that specializes in pterosaurs. They might be able to give us a few insights."

He stood. "I think we need to put all our focus into searching Pulau Kangean. This Ropen could have been kicked out of its rookery on a different part of the island. Or maybe it was too sick or hurt to return to the rookery and that cave was the closest it could get."

Rastun nodded. "I can check the topographic maps on the eastern side of the island to locate any caves."

"There are also a lot of smaller islands around Kangean." Petal got to her feet. "Even if we use *Grantin's* whole crew in this search, it's still going to --"

A thunderclap tore through the boat, throwing everyone off their feet.

THIRTY-TWO

Rastun's skull rattled. A dull hum clogged his ears. He pressed his hands against the metal floor, groaning. A word burst through the cloudiness in his brain.

Explosion.

He got to all fours and looked around the storeroom. Karen and Ehrenberg pushed themselves onto their sides, grimacing. Neither had any injuries he could see.

Petal lay motionless on her stomach.

"Petal!" Rastun barely heard his own shout, his ears still ringing from the blast. He crawled over to the fallen scientist. His stomach clenched when he saw a line of red extending from her head.

"Petal! Petal!"

She stirred, her hand slowly sliding across the floor to her head.

Rastun gently rolled her over as Ehrenberg and Karen joined him. Petal managed to open her eyes halfway as blood flowed from a gash below her scalp. A lot of blood, but that usually happened with head wounds, even small ones. He prayed it wasn't too serious.

He thought someone called his name, but it sounded muffled. Then Ehrenberg slapped his shoulder and pointed to the door.

Water poured into the storeroom.

"We need to move." Rastun hoisted Petal to her feet. She still only had her eyes half-open. He feared she had a concussion, maybe a bad one.

He clutched Petal to his side with one arm and headed for the door, followed by Karen and Ehrenberg. Water sloshed over their boots. Klaxons wailed.

Rastun stepped into the passageway and tensed at the sight ahead of him. Water gushed through a tear in the hull. A handful of MSA personnel scrambled through the flooded corridor, some in just their underwear, obviously asleep when the explosion occurred. An Indonesian emerged from a room near the hole, carrying a limp man with blood covering his head and shoulder.

Rastun moved forward, Karen and Ehrenberg following. The gusher pushed against his legs. He tightened his grip on Petal and pressed against the opposite wall, sliding along it. The water rose past his ankles.

Ehrenberg slipped and fell.

"Randy!" Karen hollered.

"Doc." Rastun turned.

"I'm okay." Ehrenberg got back on his feet, helped by Karen. "Keep going," he said with an urgent wave.

Rastun did as told, eyeing the ladder ahead. Maybe fifteen feet to go.

Feet pounded on the metal steps. Four crewmen appeared, carrying damage control kits. One snapped his arm toward the top of the ladder and yelled something in Indonesian. Rastun guessed it was, "Get out!"

He lugged Petal up the ladder, Karen and Ehrenberg behind him. The MSA damage control party splashed through the passageway, shouting something over and over. Probably checking to see if anyone else was in the compartment.

The deck tilted. Rastun's jaw stiffened. *That's not good.*

They made it to the *Grantin's* main deck. Several sailors hurried by them, probably making for their damage control stations. Rastun's destination was the upper deck, ready to abandon ship if necessary, and hopefully find one of the boat's medics for Petal.

"Cap'n. Cap'n." The words penetrated the hum in his ears.

Geek and Norgay charged toward them.

"You guys . . ." Geek's eyes widened. "Shit, Petal."

"She hit her head," said Karen. "She's bleeding. Probably has a concussion."

"Here. Give her to me." Geek took Petal and held her against his large frame.

Rastun exhaled. Petal was a lithe woman, probably around 120 pounds. It was still 120 pounds of dead weight he had to drag through water and up a ladder, with one arm. And that arm felt like lead.

But he couldn't think about it. He was on a ship filling up with water. He needed to get his team topside.

The *Grantin* continued to list as they made it outside. Rastun found McClure, Herrera, Alana, and Wikana near the bow, all wearing yellow life jackets. No sign of Lieutenant Bahar or Captain Teguh. Probably overseeing damage control efforts.

"Norgay, tend to Petal," Rastun ordered. "Herrera, track down one of the medics."

Herrera dashed off while Geek laid Petal on the deck. Norgay got out his first aid kit, then cleaned and bandaged the wound.

"What happened?" asked Wikana, his eyes wide with fear.

"Some kind of explosion." Rastun glanced between him and Petal.

"Will . . . Will we sink?" The translator shivered.

"Let's hope not. Even if we do, at least we're a mile from shore. Better than the middle of the ocean."

"Sir."

Rastun turned around to find Alana with life jackets in her arms. He took one, as did Karen and Ehrenberg, who helped Petal into hers.

The list grew more pronounced as Herrera returned with one of the *Grantin's* medics. The man did a quick stitch job on Petal's head wound and diagnosed her with a concussion. He told them to make sure she did not fall asleep.

"Doc, keep her awake." Rastun slapped Ehrenberg on the shoulder, then gazed around the deck. All his people were accounted for and Petal was being tended to. Not much else he could do now. Whether or not the *Grantin* survived or sank was in the hands of her crew.

What the hell caused that explosion? He didn't think it was anything mechanical. The blast hadn't occurred anywhere near the engine room.

That meant it had been deliberate.

"I want everyone sharp," he said. "Someone set off that explosion. Herrera, take up position port side, Norgay starboard. McClure, Alana, you're aft. Geek, with me on the bow. Be ready for another threat."

Everyone acknowledged the order and hurried off. They had to lean from one side to the other to keep their balance against the list.

Rastun made for the bow, rifle in hand. Geek had already taken up position there, staring through his binoculars.

"Got anything?" asked Rastun.

"Just looking at those yahoos on the beach. They're all watching us. Not getting in their dinghies and coming to help, just watching." He leaned forward. "I think some of them are cheering. Little fuckpukes."

"McClure," Rastun radioed. "Any activity from *Earth Warrior* or any of the boats around it?"

"Negative. They're all keeping their distance. Probably hoping we'll sink."

"Yeah, wouldn't surprise me." Rastun felt anger lines creasing his face. This had to be the doing of someone on *Earth Warrior*. They had to be responsible for the bombing at the logging camp in Oregon, and now they planted a bomb on the *Grantin*. How the hell had they gotten the device on the boat? What could he have done differently to prevent this?

Kick your own ass later, Jack. Right now he had to make sure none of those shithead activists got near this boat.

The deck angled a bit more. Rastun gritted his teeth. Dammit, he felt powerless. For obvious reasons, the Army didn't train its people in shipboard damage control. All he could do was pray the *Grantin's* crew knew their shit and could keep this boat afloat.

A wave of dread washed over him. They may only be a mile from shore, but if the boat went down, they would be forced into life rafts. Exposed. Vulnerable. What if that's what these wackos wanted? Wait until they abandoned ship, then try to run them down in their boats. Or God help them if some of these activists brought an arsenal with them.

Rastun's finger hovered closer to the trigger of his Steyr AUG.

"I've got lights in the sky," radioed Alana. "Gotta be fucking Ropen. Four . . . No, wait! Five. Five Ropen lights coming in from the west."

Rastun and Geek looked to the boat's rear. A ball of light flickered in Rastun's night vision goggles, then another.

"Shit, this is all we need." He turned to Wikana. "Get to the bridge and tell them we have Ropen inbound from the west."

"R-Ropen." Mouth agape, the translator slowly lifted his head.

"Move your ass, man!"

Wikana jumped and sprinted away.

Rastun slung the rifle over his shoulder and ran for the fore mounted MINIMI machine gun. "McClure, get on the aft MG."

"On it."

Rastun raised the MINIMI. The *Grantin's* list prevented it from fully covering the Ropen's approach. He disconnected it from its mount and held it Rambo-style.

His eyes swept over the area. Half-a-dozen boats and a dozen activists on the beach. This was a made-to-order buffet for the Ropen.

Yeah, well just try to turn us into dinner. He lifted the machine gun's barrel skyward. Another Ropen light flashed above them. Another. Another. He could make out the creatures' dark silhouettes in his NVGs. Six in all. Any moment they'd dive for their meals.

All the Ropen passed overhead and continued down the coastline.

"Da'hell?" Geek lowered his rifle. "Are we not appetizing anymore?"

"I don't know." Rastun moved to the starboard side, tracking the Ropen as they angled toward the island. Just where in the hell were they going?

THIRTY-THREE

Pistaka sighed as he stared at his desk. All his work was done for the day, now turned to night. Most people would probably look forward to going home to relax or perhaps get together with friends.

Not him. As facility director, he couldn't afford to make friends here, and the ones he did have lived in actual cities, not in the middle of the fucking jungle. There was also not much for a single man to do. Many of the employees that lived in the Mainaky village had families of their own. There were a couple of cafés, but he had no desire to be in there by himself. He also couldn't socialize with his employees.

The only way out of here was to work hard, to make this facility a success, to impress his bosses to the point they transferred him someplace where trees did not outnumber buildings.

And for that, I have to depend on those idiot fishermen. Even with longer stays out at sea, their hauls still fell below the quotas Mainaky headquarters set. Because of those lazy, incompetent bastards, he may never get off this damn island.

Pistaka grunted and left his office. He straddled his scooter, ready for another lonely, boring night at home when he noticed lights in the harbor. Two of his fishing boats had returned. He could use the opportunity to personally check their hauls. If they brought back a lot of fish, good. If not, he would tear into them. These morons sometimes – many times – needed a swift kick in the ass to motivate them.

Pistaka rode his scooter out of the main compound and across the road to the docks. The boats that pulled in belonged to Joko and Habib. One of Habib's crewmen leapt off the vessel and headed toward one of the pickup trucks in the compound. Following him were the Tiger Force guards assigned to the boats. Pistaka shut off his scooter's engine, eyes flickering between the two boats. Which one to inspect first?

Joko. He was the de facto leader of the fishermen. Therefore, the biggest troublemaker. Pistaka would delight in dressing him down over a small haul.

He strode up to the boat, sighting Joko near the bow. The fisherman's shoulders sagged. "Mister Pistaka," he greeted him in an unenthused tone.

"Joko." He went up the gangplank. "Show me your catch."

The other man sighed. "All right."

They headed for the stern as the pickup rolled up to the docks, ready to load whatever fish they'd caught. Joko opened the hatch to the cargo hold. A short grunt reverberated in Pistaka's throat. The hold was maybe a quarter full.

"This is all?"

"It was a bad day," said Joko. "They happen."

"Is that what you want me to tell my bosses back in Jakarta? 'It was a bad day?' You people have had too many bad days."

Joko's face stiffened. "I am not happy about it, either."

"You shouldn't be happy." Pistaka's voice shot up a couple of octaves. "These bad days are costing this facility and this company money. Any more bad days and you and all these other lazy-asses may be out of a job."

"Do not threaten me." Joko raised a finger. "And do not insult my men. We are out there trying to --"

"Demon flyers!" yelled the crewman by the pickup. "Demon flyers!"

Both Pistaka and Joko looked to the night sky. Pistaka shuddered when he saw three . . . no, four Ropen. Then five, then six. All diving toward the boats.

He screamed and pushed past Joko. He ran full-bore down the deck, slipping a couple of times, crying out each time he did. Pistaka righted himself, pounded down the gangplank, and dashed for his scooter. He looked behind him and shivered.

One of the monsters knocked over Joko, biting down on his back. Its head snapped up. Strands of flesh soared through the air. Other pieces of human meat hung from the Ropen's mouth.

Pistaka imagined his body being torn apart like that. He screamed and jumped onto his scooter. His fingers fumbled with the starter.

"C'mon! C'mon!"

The engine buzzed to life. The little bike sped forward.

Something crashed into Pistaka's back. He howled in pain and tumbled off the scooter. Another stab of pain raced through his head and back. He grimaced, his eyes fluttering.

A Ropen crouched over him on all fours. Pistaka opened his mouth to scream.

The monster's jaws ripped into his stomach. Its head lurched back, pulling out a long string of intestines. Pain tore through every part of Pistaka's body. He watched with bulging eyes as the Ropen chewed on his guts, gobs of blood falling on the ground and on him.

Again, Pistaka tried to scream, but his vocal cords were paralyzed. A dark curtain settled over his eyes as the Ropen's snout drove into his torn midsection.

***

"Mister Rastun."

Rastun turned to find Lieutenant Bahar approaching him, managing to keep his balance on the deck despite the *Grantin's* list.

"You guys got that hole plugged?"

"Damage control is working on it, but we have another problem."

Rastun snorted. "Of course. Because God forbid we deal with just one problem at a time."

"We picked up a distress call from a Mainaky boat," said Bahar. "The Ropen are attacking their production facility."

Crap. Rastun gritted his teeth. *Maybe that's why they passed on us.* They had an even bigger buffet there, not just of fish, but people.

"The captain wants you to go there and assist them," Bahar told them.

"How many of your men can you send with us?" asked Rastun.

"None, I'm afraid."

"What, you can't even spare a handful?" Geek chimed in.

"I'm sorry. Captain Teguh needs every man here for damage control and to protect the ship from further sabotage." Bahar glanced at the activist fleet.

Rastun growled in frustration. Boats like the *Grantin* did not carry that big a crew, and this one had lost several sailors in the Ropen attack a few days ago. They also had to have some casualties from the blast.

Rastun looked around at the FUBI team. "All right, if it's up to us, it's up to us. Let's get moving."

"You will have to take the Zodiacs. We cannot launch the helicopter with the boat listing."

They wished Bahar good luck keeping *Grantin* afloat and headed for the stern. Rastun, Geek, Ehrenberg, and Herrera climbed into one Zodiac, with Karen piloting it. The others boarded the second dinghy, Norgay at the controls. They roared over the waves, heading south. Rastun glanced at the *Earth Warrior* and the other boats. None of them made any move to render assistance to the *Grantin.*

Isn't that a violation of maritime law? Of course, if one of them planted the explosive, they certainly didn't give a shit about any laws.

Rastun and Geek took up position at the front of the Zodiac, resting their Steyr AUGs on the prow. Karen steered them closer to the shoreline. It should only take a few more minutes for them to reach Mainaky.

And how many people will die before we get there? He shook off the thought. Much as he wanted to, he couldn't will the Zodiac to go faster.

Lights appeared ahead of him. Bright white, near the surface. They came from a Mainaky fishing boat. Two Ropen snapped and clawed at the deck, trying to tear through it to get at the fish below, and probably any crewmen hiding there.

"Fire at will," hollered Rastun. He glanced at Ehrenberg, who slipped the Aster 7 dart gun off his shoulder. Rastun would have liked to tranq one of these Ropen, but with human life immediately threatened, they had to employ lethal force.

He sighted the Ropen near what remained of the pilothouse, compensating for the bouncing of the Zodiac, and pulled the trigger. Geek joined in with his Steyr AUG. The Ropen jerked as 5.56mm rounds punched into its hide. It flapped its wings and lifted off from the fishing boat.

The second Ropen let out a throaty cry and leapt off the deck. It spread its wings, flying straight at the Zodiac.

"Incoming!" Rastun switched out his spent magazine for a fresh one and opened fire. So did Geek and Herrera. A metallic racket consumed the dinghy as their rifles cracked non-stop.

The Ropen shuddered, but kept coming, its mouth open. Rastun tensed as the monster drew closer.

The beast snapped its head back and let out a strangled gasp. It dropped toward the water.

"Look out!" Ehrenberg shouted.

Rastun and Geek slid to the Zodiac's port side. The Ropen crashed next to them. Huge curtains of water shot up around them. Its head and shoulder came down on the starboard side.

The Zodiac flipped over. Rastun flew through the air and slammed into the water. Shock and disorientation hit him. He was underwater . . . at night. Primal fear clutched his brain. Where was up? Where was down? His lungs tightened. He hadn't had a chance to take a breath before going under.

He forced himself to calm down. Panic would be fatal. He swung his head left, then right. A glimmer of white shone above him. Light from the fishing boat. He kicked once, twice . . .

And broke the surface. He sucked down a big lungful of air, grateful to be close to shore.

The Ropen floated in front of him, unmoving. Rastun swung his head in all directions. Where were . . .?

"Karen! Geek! Do--"

A head bobbed in the water a few feet away. "Yo, Captain." Herrera raised an arm as he tread water.

Another head appeared. Geek. No sign of Karen or Ehrenberg. Rastun took another deep breath, ready to go under to find them.

Karen's head poked above the water. Ehrenberg followed a second later.

Relief washed over Rastun. It vanished a second later. There were still other Ropen around here.

"You guys okay?" McClure asked as the second Zodiac appeared.

"We're fine. Get to the facility." Rastun pointed to the Mainaky plant.

McClure gave him a quick salute and directed Norgay to the shore.

Rastun and the others swam after them. The second team was already racing through the main gate when his group slogged onto dry land. Rastun couldn't find the other Ropen. It had to be around somewhere.

"My camera!" Karen exclaimed. "Shit!"

Her camera, and its bag, had been lost when they capsized. So had her trademark boonie hat.

And so had Rastun's rifle.

He scowled. That was the second damn weapon he'd lost on this expedition. He pulled out his pissant Glock and looked to the others. Ehrenberg had kept hold of his Aster 7 and Herrera still had his rifle. Geek did not.

Shots echoed from the Mainaky facility.

"You three get in there and help," Rastun ordered. "We'll check for survivors on the boat."

Geek, Ehrenberg, and Herrera dashed toward the facility. Rastun hurried for the damaged fishing boat, Karen on his six. He stared at the pistol in his hand, still pissed at losing his Steyr AUG. He glanced out at the dark water. He could probably search the bottom for an hour and not find the rifle.

I may have to start duct taping guns to my hand.

"Oh God." Karen's hands went to her mouth. She closed her eyes and looked away.

Just beyond a pickup parked at the docks was a scooter lying on its side. Someone lay next to it. Pistaka, or what was left of him. The guy had been torn in half, entrails hanging out his torso.

Rastun grimaced. Asshole or not, Pistaka did not deserve that.

"Come on." He touched Karen's shoulder. "Nothing we can do for him."

They took a couple of steps toward the fishing boat when a whooshing noise came from behind them. They turned.

A Ropen stood barely fifteen feet away.

THIRTY-FOUR

"Go! In here!" Rastun pushed Karen toward the pickup.

The Ropen wailed and charged on all fours.

Please be open. He gripped the handle and pulled.

The door flew open. Karen scrambled inside. Rastun jumped in, twisted around and slammed the door shut.

The pickup rocked as the Ropen crashed into it.

Rastun started to bring up his pistol when he noticed something about the window. Whoever used the truck before had rolled it down.

The Ropen stuck its beak through the opening.

"Jack!" Karen shouted.

Rastun leaned back, putting a hand under the Ropen's jaw, trying to push it aside. No use. The thing was too big, too strong. It opened its mouth, raw, stale breath wafting through the cab.

He jammed his Glock under the monster's jaw and fired three times. Blood spattered the seat, the dashboard, and his pants. The Ropen shrieked and yanked its head outside. Rastun fired four more shots at it.

The engine revved. He turned to Karen as she backed up the pickup and swung it to the left. Its hood was aimed directly at the Ropen.

"Better buckle up." She slipped on her seatbelt.

Rastun put on his seatbelt and smiled. "I love you."

Karen flashed him a grin, then stomped on the gas. The pickup roared forward. The Ropen, still on all fours, raised its head, blood pouring from beneath its jaw.

A loud thud shook the pickup. Both Rastun and Karen snapped forward, right into the airbags.

Another thump. The pickup shot into the air. Rastun had no doubt he and Karen would have smashed their heads into the cab's roof had it not been for their seatbelts.

The pickup bounced again as the rear tire rolled over the Ropen. Rastun peered over the deflating airbag. The hood was mangled. He stuck his head out the window, looking to the rear. The Ropen lay in a heap, unmoving, its head bent at an awkward angle.

They got out of the pickup. Someone shouted from the fishing boat. The lights illuminated the man at the bow enough for Rastun to recognize him. Habib, the fisherman Petal had interviewed. He shouted something in Indonesian. Unfortunately, Wikana wasn't here to translate.

"You and your crew okay?" Rastun aimed his left hand at him and made an okay sign with his right hand.

Habib nodded and gave him a thumbs up.

"Stay below." Rastun pointed at the boat, then at the ground three times. Habib nodded and retreated below.

"Jack, I got one." Ehrenberg's voice burst from his earpiece.

"What? Got what?"

"A Ropen. I hit it with a tranquilizer dart. It's taking off to the west."

"Yeah, it looks like the ugly fuckers are pulling out." This from Geek. "Some of those Tiger Force guys were also mixing it up with them. They managed to off another Ropen before we got here."

"Copy. Great job, guys."

Rastun ran for the compound. He saw a Ropen clear the fence, flying sluggishly. That had to be the one Ehrenberg tranqed. The creature dropped closer to the ground. It put out its foreclaws, stumbling when it landed. The Ropen took a few steps, then collapsed.

"All right, it's out cold," Rastun radioed. "Get that GPS collar on it."

"I'm on it." Ehrenberg hurried through the gate, Norgay and McClure following. The two field security specialists covered the cryptozoologist as he put the tracker on the Ropen, just in case it was not completely knocked out.

The beast did not stir. Ehrenberg attached the collar to its leg and backed away. He then took his tablet out of his waterproof pack and checked the screen.

"We've got a good signal. We can track it all the way to its nest."

"Hell yeah!" Geek headed over to Rastun and Karen. "Success."

He and Rastun bumped fists as the rest of the FUBI team joined them.

"So how long before this thing wakes up?" asked Alana.

"I'd give it an hour or so," said Ehrenberg.

"And me without my camera." Karen's face twisted. "Dammit."

"You got your cell phone. You can use that," Rastun offered.

Karen slowly turned to him, eyes blazing in fury. Rastun winced and turned away. Telling a professional photographer to use a cell phone camera was probably an unforgivable insult.

Still, she got her phone out of her pack. "Guess I have to. Though these photos are gonna look like crap."

Rastun said nothing as Karen stood over the Ropen, snapping pictures.

"Looks like you learned another rule of marriage, Cap'n." Geek clamped a meaty paw on his shoulder.

"What?"

"To stay out of your woman's way when you done pissed her off."

"Shut up, Sergeant." Rastun glared at him.

Geek laughed.

An unsmiling Karen took another photo when someone hollered, "Get away from that monster."

Everyone whirled around. Zaina and three of his Tiger Force men approached.

"It's okay." Ehrenberg held up a hand. "This Ropen's been tranquilized. We have a GPS tracker on it that will lead us to its nest."

"That thing killed Mister Pistaka and another one of my men. We must kill it."

"No, wait." The words flew from Ehrenberg's mouth. "I'm sorry for your loss, but we need this Ropen alive. It could lead us back to the others responsible for all these attacks."

"Or it could live alone," Zaina countered. "Which means if you let it go, it could return and kill more people. I will not allow it."

The Tiger Force guards advanced.

Rastun stepped in front of the creature. "Not happening, pal. This thing's our best chance to find the other Ropen."

"Get out of the way." Zaina raised his HK416 rifle. So did his three buddies.

"Don't even think about it, asshole." Rastun brought up his Glock. Geek, Alana, and the other field security specialists also covered the Tiger Force guys with their weapons.

"No, no, no!" Ehrenberg extended his arms. "Everyone calm down. Put your guns down."

Zaina's men didn't lower their weapons. Neither did Rastun's.

"We're all on the same side," Ehrenberg pleaded. "We all want these attacks to end."

"You really want to do this?" Rastun aimed his pistol at Zaina's chest.

"My job is to protect this facility. If that means shooting you, then I will."

"Okay. Go ahead." Rastun lowered his pistol.

Zaina tilted his head, surprised.

"Cap'n, what the hell?" Geek spoke out the side of his mouth.

"Trust me," he whispered back, then faced Zaina. "There are some things you better keep in mind before you pull that trigger."

"What is that?"

"Who you're shooting."

Zaina barked out a laugh. "I can always say I'm shooting trespassers."

Rastun glanced at Karen, who aimed her phone at them, probably recording the situation in case it went south. "Wrong. You'll be shooting a group of people who are working on behalf of the government of Indonesia, and who are partnered with the Maritime Security Agency, a law enforcement organization. You think you're going to get away with that? You think my government won't make a stink about a private security force gunning down American citizens? The guy who funds our organization has lots of connections in Washington, so trust me, they will hammer the shit out of Tiger Force and this government."

Zaina's shoulders rose and fell in a slow breath.

Rastun continued. "The FUBI checked you guys out. Tiger Force has a pretty good reputation. You want to flush it down the crapper by starting a firefight with us?"

Zaina just stared at them. Tense silence surrounded the two groups.

The Tiger Force leader lowered his rifle. His comrades followed suit.

"Put 'em down, everyone." Rastun waved a hand toward the ground. The others lowered their weapons.

Zaina blurted something in Indonesian. The Tiger Force team marched back to the compound.

Rastun let out a long breath. His muscles unwound.

"Damn, Cap'n," said Geek. "You're a born diplomat. Next stop, the State Department."

"It was more luck than diplomacy. And no way in hell would I work for the State Department. I'm not into wearing a suit and tie and kissing the asses of scumbag dictators."

"So what do we do now?" asked Alana.

"I say stay here and make sure Zaina and his asshat pals don't try anything," said McClure.

"That's exactly what we're going to do." Rastun nodded to the former paratrooper. "Hopefully, they got the message and'll just sit and stew in their compound."

About ten minutes later, Zaina appeared with eight other Tiger Force guards.

"What the hell now?" Geek grumbled.

Rastun eyed the group as they approached. His brows knitted together when he noticed something.

None of the Indonesians carried rifles. It also looked like their hip holsters were empty.

"What are you shitheads playing at?" he muttered under his breath.

Zaina halted. "This is your last warning. Leave on your own or we will make you leave."

"Ha!" barked Herrera. "Without any guns, I'd like to see you try."

Arms stretched out to his sides, Zaina said, "Yes, we are unarmed. But I am certain your organization, your government, and our government will not look kindly on you shooting unarmed people. And one of my men is back in the compound recording everything."

Rastun's face stiffened. The little fucker just outmaneuvered him.

Grinning, Zaina and his men strutted forward.

THIRTY-FIVE

Rastun's muscles coiled. Zaina and his guards planned to go hand-to-hand with them, and he'd have to oblige. The little prick had been right about shooting them. Forget about negative press for the FUBI and criminal charges for his team, shooting unarmed people went against Rastun's moral code. Especially since Zaina and his men were not "bad guys." They may be assholes, but assholes just doing their job.

Well, he had a job to do, too.

"Everyone give your weapons to the Doc and Wikana."

The others scowled at the order, but complied. Rastun didn't like the order himself, but didn't want to risk an accidental discharge during the coming brawl.

"Doc, Karen, Wikana. Get back. Karen, pepper spray." Rastun held out his hand.

Karen threw him the cylinder, then backed up, extending her asp.

Rastun looked to Geek, Alana, and his field security specialists. "They do not get to that Ropen."

They all nodded and formed a perimeter around the monster.

Tiger Force didn't break stride.

Rastun inhaled, glancing at his people. Six against nine. But his six were damn good. Three Rangers, a Gurkha, an 82nd Airborne soldier, and a Marine.

Unfortunately, the nine facing them were not simple thugs. They had to be damn good, too. Putting Karen, Ehrenberg, and Wikana into the fight would even the numbers, but only on paper. The doc wasn't a fighter. He could probably say the same for the translator. Karen had taken several self-defense courses, but was not anywhere near the level of hand-to-hand combat as experienced ex-soldiers and cops.

Six against nine. Well, not the first time the odds had been stacked against him.

Rastun's gaze swept over Zaina's men, wondering if they might whip out tasers. They didn't. That surprised him. Maybe they thought electrocuting people – especially ones contracted by the Indonesian government – would be too extreme. Maybe Zaina wanted unarmed to truly mean unarmed and not give any excuse for the FUBI to draw down on them.

He waited until Tiger Force was a few feet away before his right arm snapped up. A stream of foul-smelling liquid shot through the air. It nailed two men in the face. They groaned and stumbled back. Rastun swung the pepper spray toward a third man. He ducked and tackled him. Both fell to the ground, the pepper spray tumbling from Rastun's hand.

The two grabbed arms, shoulders, shirts. Rastun grunted, trying to push the Indonesian off him. Down on the ground was the worst place to be in a melee like this.

Rastun shoved a hand into the Indonesian's face and raked his eyes. No matter how tough or good someone was, everyone's eyes were vulnerable.

The man growled in pain. Rastun rolled him on his back and punched him in the mouth.

Another Indonesian kicked him in the side. Rastun grunted and turned. One of the Tiger Force guards he'd sprayed had recovered quicker than expected. He rammed his boot into Rastun's gut. Air burst out his mouth. He pushed himself away from the man. He needed to get to his feet to have a fighting chance.

Rastun planted one foot. The guard's boot shot toward his face. Rastun knocked it away, putting the man off balance. Sucking down a ragged breath, Rastun got to both feet. The Indonesian threw a punch. Rastun blocked it and moved in. He rammed a knee into the guard's gut once, twice. An elbow strike to the side of the man's head put him on the ground.

Fights raged around him, more chaotic than any line brawl he'd ever seen in hockey. McClure and one guard exchanged furious punches. Alana slugged another guard trying to wrestle her to the ground in the side of the head. Norgay got kicked in the back, then kicked his opponent. Geek scooped up one Tiger Force guy in his massive arms and body-slammed him. Another guard jumped on his back. Herrera came over and landed three kidney punches to the Indonesian, who dropped off Geek's back. One guard snaked his arms around Herrera's chest and pulled him back.

Rastun started over to help when a blow to the back knocked him off balance. He gritted his teeth, pushing down the pain, and swung around.

Zaina faced him.

Rastun launched a sidekick. Zaina blocked it. He also blocked a punch, then threw one of his own. Rastun deflected it. Zaina punched again. Rastun grabbed the other man's wrist and started to twist it. Zaina moved in and kneed him in the thigh. Teeth bared, Rastun fought off the pain and rammed his elbow into Zaina's face. The man stumbled back.

Rastun landed an uppercut to Zaina's chin. Fire exploded across his left hand. He ignored it and pressed the attack.

Zaina's right palm shot out and into Rastun's mouth. He tasted blood. Zaina punched him twice in the gut. Rastun retaliated with a right cross. Both men grabbed each other, swung around, and fell to the ground.

Rastun caught glimpses of the brawl as he wrestled with the Tiger Force leader. McClure was on the ground, wrists secured with zip ties. Geek was on one knee, fending off two attackers. Another Tiger Force guard subdued Alana. Karen went to help, striking the man on the back with her collapsible baton. Another Indonesian hurried over. Karen turned . . . and got a backhand to the face.

Rage erupted in Rastun. He roared and struggled to get out of Zaina's grip. His elbow struck the other man's side twice. Almost . . .

A Tiger Force guard kicked him in the gut twice. Rastun doubled over. His fury spiked when he saw Karen grabbed around the torso and shoved to the ground.

Zaina kicked him in the back. The other man jumped on Rastun. The two Indonesians pushed him to the ground. He felt them grabbing his wrists. Zip ties would be next.

No, no, no! No way were these shitkickers beating him. He pitched and rolled, turning into a pale imitation of a bucking horse, trying to rid himself of his opponents.

He felt plastic slide over his wrists.

Something cracked nearby. An automatic rifle. Rastun recognized the distinctive rattle. An AK-47. Zaina and his partner stopped what they were doing.

Rastun lifted his head. Lieutenant Bahar and five other MSA sailors stood before them in full battle gear. The *Grantin* XO had his rifle pointed to the sky, eyeing the scene.

"All Mainaky security personnel. You will release the Americans . . . now."

For emphasis, the MSA pointed their AKs at the Tiger Force guys. Zaina and the others backed away from the FUBI team.

"Now," Bahar continued. "You will all be placed under arrest for assaulting people in the employ of the government of Indonesia." He repeated it in Indonesian.

Zaina blurted something in his own language. Rastun couldn't understand the words, but definitely picked up the indignation in his tone.

Whatever his argument, Bahar didn't buy it. He directed his people to cuff the Tiger Force team.

Rastun picked himself off the ground and made a beeline for Karen. The welt on her left cheek set his emotions on fire.

"You okay?" He gripped her by the shoulders.

Karen said nothing. Her face twisted in rage. Even in the night he could see red spreading across her cheeks. She broke his grip.

"Karen?"

She stomped over to one of the Tiger Force guards. The man was on his knees, hands behind his back, an MSA sailor watching over him. He shot a confused look at Karen as she approached.

With a primal scream, she kicked the Tiger Force man right in the balls. He gasped and toppled onto his side. Nearly every man in the vicinity cringed, Rastun included.

"Don't ever touch my breasts, you filthy piece of shit!" She stormed away from the guard, whose mouth formed an "O" of intense pain.

The MSA sailor looked to Bahar, who said something in Indonesian. The sailor burst out laughing, along with the rest of his comrades.

Karen walked up to Rastun and exhaled. "Bastard got a little too handsy when he tried to cuff me."

Rastun grinned and kissed her cheek. She glanced down, her eyes going wide. "Jack, oh my God. Your hand."

"What?" He held up his left hand. "Oh."

His pinky was bent at an unnatural angle. Probably dislocated during the brawl.

"We need to get you to a doctor," said Karen.

"Bullshit." He took hold of the injured digit with his right hand. Rastun huffed once, twice.

"Jack, what are you doing?"

He huffed a third time.

Snap!

Flaming bolts of pain swept through his pinky. Rastun clenched his teeth and growled.

"Oh my God, I'm gonna be sick." Karen clamped a hand over her mouth.

Rastun exhaled and cautiously bent his pinky. "See. Good as new."

He patted Karen on the shoulder and headed over to Bahar. "Lieutenant, your timing could not have been more perfect. But I thought Captain Teguh wanted everyone to remain with the *Grantin.*"

"We got the flooding under control and are sealing the hole. I convinced the captain to spare some men to help you."

Rastun gave Bahar's hand a vigorous shake. "You are officially my favorite sailor in the world. Thanks for your help."

"I am just doing my duty."

Rastun grinned. That was the type of answer he would give.

Bahar and the MSA took away Zaina's men while the FUBI hid in the trees, waiting for the Ropen to wake.

It took less than an hour for the tranquilizer to wear off. The Ropen shakily got to its feet, croaked, and looked around the area. Rastun and the others aimed their weapons at it, just in case it decided to attack.

The creature didn't. It flapped its wings and took off to the west.

Ehrenberg held up his tablet. "Well, nothing to do now except wait and see where it lands."

THIRTY-SIX

More often than not for Sherlock and Keough, questioning the friends of the *Earth Warrior* crew proved an exercise in futility. Many flat out disliked the police. In a few cases, "dislike" was an understatement. They accused him and Keough of being fascists and jackboots and oppressors. One person even demanded to know how Sherlock could betray his own race by being a cop. He hadn't answered the question. Why entertain the warped view of someone who only saw him as a skin color instead of a person?

Their next interview took them to the SpaceX facility in Hawthorne, and Don Wilkins. They spoke with him in one of the breakrooms.

"Just so you know, you're not in trouble," said Keough. "We're investigating several people we believe were involved in an eco-terrorist bombing in Oregon. You were a classmate of one of them." She gave Wilkins the name.

"Yeah. Well, more than a classmate. We dated a good part of our freshman year."

Keough scribbled in her notebook. "Did your relationship end amicably or not?"

"Amicably." Wilkins shrugged. "Kind of, I guess."

"Why 'kind of'?" asked Sherlock.

"Well, she was great. We had a good time. But then she got involved in all these causes. Save the environment, stop climate change, that sort of stuff. To the point she started going to meetings and protests more than spending time with me. We split up, but still stayed friendly. We are connected on Facebook and Instagram."

"How often do you stay in touch?" asked Sherlock.

"Not a whole lot. Usually I just see her posts and that's it."

Keough shifted in her seat. "What were some of the more recent posts you saw from her?"

"That she's over in Indonesia, protecting those pterodactyls or whatever they are."

Sherlock nodded. "When she became more active in social causes, did she ever talk about using violence or supporting people who advocated violence?"

Wilkins screwed up his face. "I think maybe once or twice. Said sometimes it was necessary. That's pretty much when I figured we were done."

"How did you two first meet?" asked Keough.

"In our basic thermodynamics class."

Sherlock's brow furrowed. "That doesn't sound like the sort of class someone with her major would have taken."

"Well, she was a mechanical engineering major, like me, before she switched majors."

Sherlock and Keough exchanged knowing looks.

After a few more questions, they thanked Wilkins and headed back to the car.

"If she had a mechanical engineering background, she'd certainly have the skillset to build a limpet mine," said Sherlock.

"You think it's enough to get a search warrant for her place?" Keough opened the passenger door.

"Worth a shot."

Sherlock phoned the U.S. Marshal's office in LA to find out which local judges would be the easiest to get a search warrant from based on the evidence they had. They got three names. He and Keough went with the first name on the list. After a five-minute meeting, the judge signed off on the warrant.

Three hours later, Sherlock and Keough stood outside the apartment with four BATF agents and two local cops. One of the agents knocked on the door. A portly tan-skinned woman answered.

"What the fuck?" She glared at the assembled LEOs.

"Bureau of Alcohol, Tobacco, and Firearms." One agent held up a piece of paper. "We have a warrant to search the premises."

He marched inside, followed by the others.

"Wha . . ." the woman sputtered. "Wait. You can't do this."

"The warrant says we can," Sherlock told her. "Are you a roommate?"

"No. I'm just watching the place while . . . my friend's gone."

Keough tilted her head. "Your friend has a name, and we already know it."

Sherlock headed for the bedroom, Keough in tow. One of the BATF agents asked the woman if she had had any contact with the apartment's owner over the past couple of weeks.

"I don't have to answer that. You're violating my civil rights. I want a lawyer."

Sherlock tuned out the prattling and checked the room, focusing on the desk. It had some knickknacks, a couple of framed photos, and an empty space in the middle.

"Would you say that's where a laptop would go?" He pointed.

Keough nodded. "She probably has it with her."

Sherlock stepped toward the desk while one agent searched the closet and another tossed the bed. He opened the drawer and found pens, a manicure kit, Post-it notes . . .

And thumb drives.

"Agent Greene," he called.

A slender man with blond hair came into the room.

"Check these out." He handed the agent the thumb drives.

Greene inserted one into his tablet. A few seconds later, he smiled wide. "Unbelievable. It's not password protected."

He checked a second thumb drive, then a third. None of them required a password to view them.

"How dumb can you be?" Keough looked to the ceiling. "Especially doing the kind of stuff she's doing."

Sherlock shrugged. "We have officials in the State and Defense Departments who put sensitive information on their computers without proper protection. Why expect a civilian to be different?"

"Hey. I got something here." Greene's voice rose with excitement.

"What?" Keough moved closer to him.

"How about blueprints?" He turned around his tablet so they could see.

Sherlock let out a slow breath. "Yeah. Blueprints for a limpet mine."

***

This should be good. Lipeli tried to keep the smile off his face as he sat at the conference table. Roland Parker took a seat at the head of the table, with FUBI Director Lynch across from Lipeli. A wall monitor showed a split screen of Indonesian Minister of Environment and Forestry Irama and UN Environment Programme Executive Director Paulo Folgosi.

"I want to thank both of you gentlemen for joining us today," said Lynch. "Hopefully we can resolve the issues surrounding the Ropen expedition."

"They will be resolved when the FUBI leaves Indonesia," said Folgosi. "More Ropen died at the hands of your people."

"The Ropen were killed while attacking the Mainaky Fisheries facility on Pulau Kangean," countered Lynch, "which resulted in the deaths of four people."

"That is unfortunate." Irama lowered his head slightly. "But the Ropen could have been driven off without killing them, as Cesar Marques and his UNCID members recently demonstrated."

"Yes, the UNCID." Parker leaned back in his seat. "Interesting that they were brought into this after we were given the contract to find the Ropen."

"That was set up by the Ministry of Foreign Affairs. My ministry is independent of them, meaning we can bring in another agency if we desire."

"And your president is fine with that?"

"Yes, he is."

Lipeli eased forward in his chair. "And that's because the president is committed to protecting the Ropen, right?"

"Yes." Irama smiled briefly. "The president is a true friend of the environment."

"Huh." Lipeli looked down at his notes. "So it has nothing to do with the fact that several environmental groups you're aligned with have funneled money into the president's re-election campaign, and his own personal pockets, in exchange for declaring a whole swath of West Papua a protected area."

Irama's eyes widened. "How . . . No. That is not true."

"My information says otherwise, and it comes from many reliable sources." Lipeli's sources involved people he knew in Joint Special Operations Command, who knew people in the CIA, who got him the report on Indonesia's president, Minister Irama, and the bribes.

"I understand a pretty sizeable resort was to have been built there," Lipeli continued. "Lots of jobs, lots of money pumped into the local economy. All gone now. Well, the developer probably could have bribed the president, but I guess these environmental groups have a lot of donors with deep pockets."

Lipeli's eyes bore in on Irama. "Imagine if all this gets out, especially since your president campaigned on an anti-corruption platform. And I guess your political career won't be so hot afterward."

The minster avoided eye contact with him.

Folgosi cleared his throat. "I for one am shocked by these allegations. My department never would have accepted this assignment had we known of this beforehand."

"Spare me your righteous indignation," said Parker. "You're not innocent in this either."

Folgosi's nostrils flared. "I did not agree to be a part of this conference call just to be insulted by you, Mister Parker."

"Well too bad. Now whether or not you knew about this arrangement between Minister Irama and the President, I really don't care. What I do care about is the social media crusade conducted by the UNCID."

"What of it? Social media helps brings supporters to their cause."

"And whips people into a frenzy, to the point they act in a threatening manner, such as doxing FUBI employees and showing where their children go to school."

At that, Lynch glared at Folgosi.

Parker continued. "And even committing acts of violence, like what happened to Jack Rastun's mother at the Philadelphia Zoo."

"That is hardly my fault. Neither I nor Mister Marques can be held responsible for the actions of people we do not know."

"Maybe, but you do have a responsibility to condemn any threats of violence or acts of violence against FUBI personnel and their families. That could have prevented the assault on Mrs. Rastun. Now thank God she wasn't hurt, but next time, she or someone else won't be as lucky."

Folgosi straightened. "And what do you want me to do? Control the actions of everyone who uses Twitter or Instagram?"

"No," said Lynch. "But we do expect you and Mister Marques to publicly condemn the assault on Mrs. Rastun and order the UNCID to cease its calls to boycott the Philadelphia Zoo and Mister Parker's business interests, as well as the use of any inflammatory language on social media."

"I hired Mister Marques because of his passion. Why would I try to curb that? And again, I have no control over what others do."

"Fine." Lynch stared hard at the screen. "Then in two hours, we will call a press conference at FUBI Headquarters. We will show the cell phone footage of the assault on Mrs. Rastun. Oh yes, someone at the zoo videoed it and put it on YouTube. You can bet it will get a lot more views after our press conference. We will say that you and the UNCID bear culpability in the assault. I can only imagine the kind of backlash you'll receive when millions and millions of people watch a crazed woman attacking another woman in her late fifties. An attack inspired by Mister Marques and his friends."

"I've also been talking to my friends on Capitol Hill," Parker chimed in. "They'll be looking into scaling back their annual contributions to the United Nations, citing this incident as a reason. That won't make you look good to your bosses, will it?"

Folgosi drew a slow breath and forced a smile. "Gentlemen, what can we do to resolve this . . . unfortunate situation?"

"Like I said before," Lynch eyed him. "No more calls for boycotts, no more inflammatory language, public condemnation of all the threats and attacks against FUBI employees and their families, and a public apology to Joyce Rastun and everyone at the Philadelphia Zoo."

Folgosi slowly nodded. "Very well."

"Also," Parker raised a finger, "I saw on the zoo's website they're conducting a fundraising campaign to build a new rhinoceros enclosure. They're about two million dollars away from their goal. I think you should help them reach it."

"You think I can just pluck two million dollars from the United Nations?"

"The UN's annual operating budget is more than five billion dollars," said Parker. "I don't think it's too much to ask to spare two million."

Folgosi exhaled. "Very well. I shall do as you ask."

"Excellent." Parker slapped the table and smiled. "I'm glad we could resolve this . . . 'unfortunate situation.'"

Neither Folgosi nor Minister Irama smiled as the conference call ended.

THIRTY-SEVEN

Thank you, Sherlock. Rastun walked with purpose toward the wardroom on the *Grantin.* His friend had found the connection between *Earth Warrior*, the Jewell bombing, and the blast on the MSA boat. Now he was headed to a briefing to lay out the plan for boarding the activist ship and arresting the person responsible.

Captain Teguh, Lieutenant Bahar, Tama, and six other Maritime Security personnel crowded the small room when Rastun, Geek, and Ehrenberg arrived. Bahar went over the plan. Pretty straight forward. Two Zodiacs with six men each, teams of two sweeping through the boat to secure the crew and any incriminating evidence. Teguh permitted two FUBI members to accompany the boarding party.

"I'll go." Rastun raised a hand. "Me and Norgay."

"Sorry, Jack," said Ehrenberg. "You'll have to sit this one out."

"What?"

Ehrenberg frowned apologetically. "You remember what Colonel Lipeli said. After what happened to your mother, he doesn't want you anywhere near Marques and his team. Last I heard, those orders still stand."

"But we know they're responsible for trying to sink this boat." Rastun stabbed a hand at the floor. "The time for playing nice with these assholes is over."

"Sorry." Ehrenberg shook his head. "But them's the rules."

Rastun snorted. Ehrenberg was in charge of the expedition. If he said he couldn't go . . . *Dammit!*

"I got this one, Cap'n." Geek slapped him on the shoulder.

He nodded at his former sergeant, seething too much to speak. He was still too angry to talk after the briefing ended. He hated being sidelined like this. In the back of his mind, he did realize that he would have a very, *very* hard time not laying out Marques or Griffin, or both.

All Rastun could do was hope the UNCID resisted arrest. Then Geek and the others could take them down hard.

***

Through his night vision goggles, Geek scanned the decks of the *Earth Warrior*. No lookouts. No weapons poking out of portholes. Nothing. The little activist fleet also kept its distance. Maybe they were all asleep. Nothing more to entertain them now that the *Grantin* wouldn't sink.

They reached the dive platform without incident. Bahar jumped out first. Geek grinned. The XO was his kind of officer. Taking the lead, sharing the same danger as the men he commanded. Just like Captain Rastun.

He only wished his friend could be here. What a bullshit rule. Yeah, there was a personal element involved, but he had faith Rastun could still conduct himself in a professional manner.

And if he happened to slug Marques or Griffin . . . *"Gee, I was busy lacing my boots at the time. I didn't see anything. Sorry."*

The rest of the team boarded *Earth Warrior*. Geek got paired with Tama. The two checked compartments on the second deck, finding them empty. Their search done, they proceeded to the bridge. He could hear the blue-haired chick, Lenna, screaming in rage.

"You fucking Nazis! You have no right to do this! This is piracy!"

"Yeah. This is . . . um, a violation of the Fifth Amendment." That sounded like Griffin, getting in his worthless two cents.

The Fourth Amendment is illegal search and seizure, dumbshit. And that was the United States Constitution. Geek had no idea what the Indonesian constitution said on the matter.

He entered the bridge. The MSA had rounded up Marques, Paulette Thompson, Griffin, and Lenna.

"Where's Kory Hyo and Kiswanta?"

"Gone," answered Bahar.

"You're all in big trouble." Paulette glared at them. "My mother and step-father know the best lawyers in Los Angeles. They're gonna sue the shit out of all of you."

"Well you're probably gonna need some good lawyers," said Geek. "Especially since you're facing terrorism charges."

"Bullshit!" Lenna yelled. "You want to throw us in jail and torture us so you can exterminate the Ropen."

"Lenna, please." Marques waved her to be quiet.

"Don't fuckin' tell me to shut up." Lenna's nostrils flared.

Marques ignored her. "What the hell are you talking about? Terrorism? You're lying."

"Oh really?" Geek stepped toward him. "I suppose it was a pissed off tuna fish that rammed the *Grantin* and almost sank her. And I guess a squirrel suicide bomber blew up the truck at the logging camp in Oregon."

Marques' face scrunched in confusion. "We had nothing to do with what happened to your boat, and certainly nothing to do with whatever happened in Oregon."

"Mister Hewitt," Bahar nodded to Geek, "and Mister Rastun have a friend back in America who is a marshal. He investigated the crew of this yacht and found evidence implicating Kory Hyo in the Oregon bombing, which means she is likely responsible for bombing my boat."

"What? Kory?" Paulette shook her head. "No."

"You're a lying sack of shit," spat Lenna.

"Not according to the evidence Marshal Dunmore obtained. Now, where is Miss Hyo and Kiswanto Herfanda?"

"I refuse to cooperate," declared Marques. "I believe these charges against Kory are made up and I will not answer any more questions from you." He tacked on a smirk.

Bahar remained stoic. "Very well. But when we arrest Miss Hyo, you will all be considered accomplices in a terrorist act against the government of Indonesia, and in this country, the death penalty applies to terrorists."

All of their eyes widened. Griffin visibly shook.

"You can't do this." Lenna's voice cracked. "We're American citizens."

"Who have committed a crime on Indonesian soil."

"We are here representing the United Nations," Marques spoke with a firm tone.

"You are an employee of the United Nations, not an ambassador or an ambassadorial staff member," said Bahar. "Therefore, diplomatic immunity does not apply to you."

Paulette turned to Geek with pleading, watery eyes. "P-Please. You have to help us."

"Why?"

"You're an American. You can't let them do this."

Geek glared at her. "Oh, I can't? Let me tell you something. There's a woman lying in the *Grantin's* sick bay by the name of Petal Garland. She's one of the nicest, kindest people I've ever met. And she's in sick bay because you fuckers tried to blow up our boat. So as far as I'm concerned, if the Indonesians are going to be harsher on you than our courts will, they can have your worthless asses."

"But we had nothing to do with what happened to your boat," Paulette hiccupped with a sob.

"Tell it to the judge."

"It's true, man." The words tumbled out of Griffin's mouth. "We didn't know anything about it. It had to be all Kory. She and Kiswanta took one of the cabin cruisers to follow the Ropen with the GPS collar."

"How the hell do they . . .?" Geek groaned and lifted his eyes to the ceiling. "Lemme guess. If the Maritime Security Agency knew the collar's frequency in advance, so did your buddy the Minister of Environment and Forestry, and he passed it on to you fuckknobs."

"Yes, he did," answered Marques.

Geek pulled out his sat phone and called Rastun.

"Cap'n. Afraid I've got some bad news . . ."

**

Rastun stared at the helicopter, wishing they could take off, wait for the Ropen to land, and hopefully get there before Kory Hyo and Kiswanta. But Captain Teguh nixed the idea. No one knew how long it would take the Ropen to reach its nest. It would be a waste of fuel, and they would waste time as well if they returned to the *Grantin* and refueled just as the Ropen got home.

So they would wait.

Rastun stared out at the *Earth Warrior*. Bahar had left four MSA sailors aboard to watch over the crew. They had yet to determine if Marques and the others helped Kory with the bomb or if she had acted alone.

Maybe not all that alone. Kiswanto had been a combat diver. He certainly had the training to swim up to the *Grantin*, attach the limpet mine, and leave without being noticed.

"Bingo!" Ehrenberg blurted, staring at his tablet.

"What?" Rastun hurried over to him.

"The GPS signal's stationary. It's on an island called Pulau Klosot, about fifty-five miles west of here."

"Then let's get rolling."

They hustled to the bridge, where Bahar was on duty.

"Excellent. Lift off as soon as you are ready." With the boat no longer listing, the Panther could safely get airborne.

Bahar looked over at Rastun. "You will need another rifle. I'll requisition you an AK."

"Actually, Lieutenant." Rastun walked over to the bridge window and pointed down at the MINIMI machine gun near the bow. "Do you have an extra one of those?"

THIRTY-EIGHT

Kory grimaced as she glanced down at her flashlight. She wished she didn't need it, wished they could have done this during the daylight. Nocturnal animals like the Ropen were usually attracted to light, believing it a source of food. But they couldn't afford to wait. The damn Maritime Security Agency ship hadn't sunk. With their helicopter, those fucking murderers from the FUBI would probably be here soon.

Her face tightened as her anger boiled. Why the hell hadn't the mine worked? Kiswanto told her he'd been trained to attach explosives to the sides of boats in the Indonesian Navy. Had he fucked up when he planted the mine?

"Shit," Kory muttered under her breath. She thought she'd found a good ally in Kiswanto. None of the others on the yacht seemed prepared to truly do whatever it took to protect these incredible creatures. Even Marques, for all his talk and past deeds, shied away from taking that final, necessary step in the fight for the environment.

Not true for Kiswanto. Maybe it was a combination of his beliefs and his military background, but he had no problem when it came to killing. A few very enjoyable go-rounds between the sheets also helped sway him to her side.

Was it all for nothing? The MSA ship didn't sink. She hadn't killed fucking Jack Rastun and his team of psychopaths. This was why she volunteered to take the cabin cruiser, the fastest boat in their little fleet, to follow the collared Ropen. If it and the rest of these animals were to be saved, she couldn't trust anyone else to do it.

She turned back to the others. The three people from the cruiser, all New Zealanders, wound their way through the jungle. Behind them was Kiswanto. Even if he had screwed up with the *Grantin,* the guy could still be helpful. Besides, she had him by the cock, figuratively and literally. He'd do whatever she wanted, just like any man with the promise of pussy would.

They continued their trek through the jungle, each one carrying a small crate of fireworks. They had scared off the Ropen when they attacked both the *Grantin* and *Earth Warrior.* The same should happen here. Kory hoped it would. They needed to get the Ropen out of here before the FUBI showed up.

The jungle thinned out, leading to a cave where the GPS signal came from. Her nose wrinkled at the stench in the air, like rotting meat. She fought back a wave of nausea. Just one more thing to do before they set off the fireworks.

"Kiswanto." She waved to the former navy diver.

He nodded and sprinted past the trees toward the cave. He switched out his large flashlight for a smaller pen light. Kory didn't know if that would make a difference. Big or small, in the cave, light was light. But Kiswanto couldn't make his way through the dark cave without some kind of illumination.

He slowed as he neared the mouth, then crept inside.

Kory and the others waited. Ten minutes. Fifteen minutes. Was it supposed to take this long? Had a Ropen eaten him? She hadn't heard any screams. Still . . .

Don't fuck this up, too.

A few more minutes passed before Kiswanto emerged from the cave.

"I have it." He held out the band that contained the FUBI's tracker. "Not hard. Demon flyer sleep."

"That's great." Kory beamed at him.

Kiswanto smiled and nodded. She could read the man's thoughts. *I have pleased her, now she will have sex with me.*

"C'mon." She waved the others forward.

They laid out the fireworks around the cave entrance. A few times Kory gazed further down the cave, trying to catch even a shadowy glimpse of the Ropen. But it was too dark for that. She also didn't hear any croaks or squawks. Maybe they were asleep. It was just a couple of hours until dawn.

Fireworks planted, they lit the fuses and hustled back to the jungle. Kory crouched behind a tree, holding her breath. Waiting . . .

Loud snaps and pops echoed from the cave. Multi-colored sparks blazed through the darkness. She thought she heard another sound through the rapid explosions. Screeching.

The fireworks played out when large silhouettes appeared near the mouth of the cave. A horde of Ropen bounded outside, wailing in panic. Several flapped their wings and took to the sky.

"Yes. Yes." Kory stood, smiling. "Go. You're safe now."

"Get down," warned Kiswanto.

She snapped a dismissive hand at him. She turned back to the Ropen, soaring into the night sky. Such amazing creatures. Thought extinct for millions of years. Yet here they were before her, alive. And they would stay alive now that she saved them from the bloodthirsty bastards of the FUBI.

Two Ropen started to jump toward the sky, then looked in her direction. They cried out and charged.

"They're coming this way," hollered one of the New Zealanders.

Kory gasped. "No, no."

The Ropen croaked, closing in on them.

She turned and ran. So did the others.

The creatures burst through the trees. Kiswanto pulled out a knife and swung around.

One of the Ropen clamped its jaws around his mid-section. He let out a gurgling cry before the beast shook him back and forth, then threw him against a tree.

The second Ropen leapt on a fleeing New Zealander. The young man screamed before claws slashed down his back.

Kory heard other screams. The remaining crew from the cabin cruiser. She didn't turn around to see what happened. She had to keep running. Fear and adrenaline set her heart racing. She didn't want to be torn apart, didn't want to be eaten.

Her lungs burned. She gulped air, trying to run as fast as she could, trying to stay alive.

Kory tripped and tumbled down an incline.

THIRTY-NINE

"I see a boat to starboard," the co-pilot's voice came through Rastun's helmet. "No sign of anyone on board."

Rastun grunted. Kory and Kiswanto had beaten them here.

The helicopter set down on a beach on Pulau Klosot's northern tip. The FUBI team scrambled out of the hold. The whirling blades whipped up a storm of sand that pelted Rastun's body. He spat out a few grains.

Ehrenberg took point, tablet in hand. Herrera stayed attached to his hip, just in case. They moved through the jungle, Rastun scanning the area, not just for Ropen, but anything else that could threaten them. Venomous snakes had to be lurking around, and some species hunted at night.

They did not have far to go. The island was small, less than a mile long and less than a mile wide, and uninhabited. By people, anyway. The perfect place for a colony of Ropen to stay hidden from the world.

Herrera's hand shot up. Everyone froze. Rastun clutched the MINIMI tighter. He picked up a sound ahead. Soft. Human. A moan.

He moved up to Herrera and Ehrenberg and signaled them to keep going. They went twenty paces before Herrera moved aside some leafy branches. Rastun took a breath and held it, finger hovering near the machine gun's trigger.

Someone lay against a tree ahead of them. A woman, clutching her ankle, face contorted in pain.

Kory Hyo.

"Do not move," Rastun spoke in a low, threatening tone.

She looked up at him. "My ankle. I think it's broken."

"I don't give a shit." He moved toward her. So did Herrera. Both had their weapons trained on her. Rastun glanced behind him. Norgay covered the left flank, McClure the right, and Geek and Alana the rear.

"Where's Kiswanto?" Rastun demanded. "And the crew of the boat you came on?"

"D-Dead." Kory shivered. "They're all dead. The Ropen got them."

Rastun's eyebrows scrunched together. "Geek. Norgay. With me. We'll scout ahead for her friends, just in case she's lying."

"I'm not."

Rastun snapped his head toward Kory. "You blew up a truck in Oregon and tried to sink our boat."

Her eyes widened in shock.

"Yeah, we know. So excuse me if I don't believe a word that comes out of your damn mouth."

Rastun led Geek and Norgay further into the jungle. It did not take long to discover Kory actually told the truth. They found Kiswanto and the boat crew, their bodies ripped open, the ground around them soaked with blood.

The three headed back to the rest of the group. "Herrera. Cuff her and guard her. We'll take her back to the chopper when we're done."

Kory looked up at him, mouth hanging open in a worried expression. "Wha . . . What are you going to do to me?"

Rastun shrugged. "Probably our government and the Indonesians will go back and forth over who should try you for terrorism. Honestly, I don't care which one gets you, so long as you end up in a jail cell."

"But . . . But . . ." Kory choked off a sob.

Rastun grunted and waved the group forward. They neared the top of the rise when Ehrenberg said, "It's really close."

Rastun, Norgay, and McClure moved ahead, weapons up. Ehrenberg put away his tablet and slid the Aster 7 off his shoulder.

Rastun tensed and peered over the rise.

Nothing.

"It should be right here," said Ehrenberg.

"Well it's not." McClure turned to him. "And I don't think we can miss something that big."

"I see something." Norgay walked a few feet ahead and bent down. He picked up a band and held it up.

"It's the GPS collar," Ehrenberg sighed. "Kory and her friends must have somehow removed it from the Ropen."

"Doesn't matter, Doc." Rastun shook his head. "We know where these things live now."

Ehrenberg nodded and told Geek and Alana to send the Alley Cat into the cave.

"Ugh. Anyone else smell that?" Karen's face contorted.

Rastun took a whiff of the rotten stench hovering in the air and grimaced. He had a bad feeling what caused it.

The Alley Cat rolled toward the cave. Karen, meanwhile, looked over her camera, huffing in disapproval. With her usual camera lying somewhere beneath the water, she got the MSA to loan her one they used for evidence collection on high seas busts. Karen, however, complained about everything from the zoom to the resolution.

"Be happy that at least you have a camera," Rastun had told her.

She had given him a withering glare.

Looking back on it, Rastun figured that had been the wrong thing to say to a professional photographer. To him, a camera was a camera. Of course, if the shoe were on the other foot and he complained about the FUBI replacing their Steyr AUGs with, say, M1903 Springfield rifles, Karen would probably say, "A gun is a gun." Never mind that the Steyr was semi-automatic with a 30-round magazine and the Springfield was a bolt-action relic with a five-round capacity.

"What the hell's all this shit?" Alana's face scrunched as she stared at her tablet.

The others gathered round. The Alley Cat's camera showed several crates near the cave entrance, some with scorch marks. Torn pieces of paper littered the ground.

"Fireworks." The veins in Ehrenberg's neck stuck out. "They may have used them to scare the Ropen out of the cave, to keep us from finding them."

"So?" Alana shrugged. "They'll come back home eventually . . . right?"

No one answered.

What if they didn't? That question fanned Rastun's anger. If Kory and her idiot friends succeeded in scaring the Ropen out of this nest for good, they were back to square one.

The Alley Cat moved deeper into the cave. The camera showed signs that the Ropen lived here. Mounds of leaves and branches that formed nests, splotches on the floor and walls that had to be excrement, and . . .

"My God." The normally unflappable Alana pressed a hand against her chest.

Karen gasped. McClure averted his gaze for a moment. Rastun grimaced, but continued to stare at the image.

Bodies. Lots of bodies, in various stages of decomposition. Mingled with them were fish, some half-eaten, others whole.

"Damn," muttered Geek. "They're stockpiling food the way people do before a blizzard."

Ehrenberg's forehead wrinkled. "Alana. Raise the camera and check out those nests."

"You got it, Doc."

The drone's periscoping arm rose, the camera rotating left. It cleared the edge of the first nest.

"Whoa." Rastun's eyes widened.

Ehrenberg nodded. "I had a feeling this was why the Ropen made that stockpile. This food isn't for them."

The camera panned from one nest to another, revealing dozens of eggs.

FORTY

Surati walked down the dirt path, head down, the hole in her chest growing with each step. At Soehaemi's suggestion, she had been going to morning prayer more since Asnawi's death. The hope was it would help ease the pain of her loss.

It hadn't. She missed her husband more than ever.

She glanced at her youngest son, Hamdan. He kept his gaze straight ahead, fists clenched, unsmiling. His anger grew day by day. Every time another attack by the demon flyers happened, he loudly cursed the Americans, demanding to know when they would kill all the monsters.

Surati would like to know, too. She still had her other two sons out at sea – for the damned Mainaky company. She prayed to Allah to keep them safe. If anything happened to either, or both, of them, she did not think she could bear that pain so soon after Asnawi's death.

Her sister, Soehaemi, walked beside her, giving her worried glances every minute or so. Her father, Fuganto, hobbled behind them with his cane. Surati gritted her teeth. That was another thing she prayed for. That he would not go off on a rant about the demon flyers attacking more people. Every time he did, it brought her to tears. When Soehaemi told the old man to shut up, he shouted the same thing back at her. That usually resulted in long, loud arguments between the two.

Perhaps after her housework, she would go see Chief Brigadier Mohede. He would know how the Americans were doing in their search to find the demon flyers and slaughter them all.

"Hey." Hamdan stopped, head slightly raised. "Did you hear that?"

"What?" asked Soehaemi.

Brow furrowed, Surati gazed around.

"What are you babbling about, boy?" grumbled her father.

"I heard something." Hamdan looked about the still dark morning sky.

Surati started to open her mouth when her ears picked up a distant sound. Like a . . . scream?

She heard another, and another. Other people walking along the path turned to the west. The screaming grew louder.

A green light winked in the sky. Seconds later, Surati spotted another one. Her heart raced when she saw a large shadowy form above. One with long wings.

"Demon flyer!" three people around her shouted.

A wave of cold fear shot up and down Surati's body. She gaped when she saw more winged silhouettes. Four in all. No, five.

"Run!" Soehaemi hollered. A few others also echoed the word.

Surati started to turn when she noticed Hamdan standing in place, shoulders rising with deliberate breaths, glaring at the approaching monsters.

"Come on! Don't stand there." She grabbed his shoulder.

"Get off." He shrugged off her hand. "We have to fight them. We have to kill them."

"With what?" Surati's voice cracked.

Hamdan looked to her, then back to the demon flyers, flexing his jaw, unsure.

"You fool." Her father tried to shove Hamdan, but he would not budge. "Run or you'll die."

"I'll not lose you, too." Surati tugged on her son's shoulder with both hands. "Run, Hamdan. Please."

Scowling, he whirled around and sprinted down the path. Surati followed. She glanced over her shoulder. Horror consumed her.

Her father hobbled after them, going as fast as his cane and ancient legs allowed. Surati swallowed when she looked up at the Ropen, getting closer to the ground.

"Father!"

"Go!" He waved his cane at her. "Go!"

He tripped and fell.

"No!" Surati stepped toward him.

A Ropen crashed down on her father's back.

Surati screamed as the monster's jaws tore at her father's shoulder. Its head whipped left, ripping his arm from his body.

She wailed louder, tears streaming down her face.

"Mother! Mother, run!"

Surati barely felt her son pushing her forward. The image of her father being dismembered by the monster dominated her mind. This couldn't be happening. He could not be dead.

Through wet, blurry eyes, she saw walls and tables and chairs. A coffee house. She hadn't even realized her son had led her in here. Her sister. Where was her sister?

She whirled left, then right.

"It's okay." Soehaemi clutched her shoulders. "We're safe in here."

"Safe?" Surati's voice cracked. She sank to her knees, weeping. First her husband, now her father. Would the damn demon flyers kill her whole family before this day was over?

***

"Mister Rastun," the Panther's pilot called to him through the helmet's internal communications system. "Captain Teguh just radioed. He received a call from the police in Kalisangka. The village is under attack by Ropen."

Rastun gazed at the others in the helicopter's cabin. They all heard it through their ICS.

"How many?" asked Ehrenberg.

"The captain did not say an exact number. Just that there are many. He wants us to proceed there."

"Copy," said Rastun. "We'll be ready."

"I'd bet these are the Ropen from Pulau Klosot," Ehrenberg stated. "They're probably still mad after being driven out of their cave by those fireworks."

Rastun sent a glare toward Kory Hyo. So did the other FUBI members. She tried to match their gaze, but eight sets of angry eyes proved too much for her. She turned away.

"Everyone check your weapons," Rastun ordered. "Be prepared to go into a hot LZ."

"Yes, sir," the others replied.

"Pilot. What's our ETA to Kalisangka?"

"We should be ten minutes out."

"Copy. Tell Captain Teguh to get hold of Chief Brigadier Mohede," Rastun added. "We need on the ground intel before we go in."

"Yes, Mister Rastun," replied the pilot.

The check of the MINIMI did not take long. Rastun found the machine gun in perfect working order. Nothing to do now but wait.

Several minutes passed. He heard nothing from the *Grantin.* Rastun peered into the flight deck. Beyond the windshield were the lights of Kalisangka.

He let out a slow breath. Either Captain Teguh hadn't been able to raise Mohede or the policeman was a victim of the Ropen. Either way, they had no intel on how many creatures were in the village or their locations. They'd be going into a combat situation blind.

"There's a small field half-a-kilometer from the docks," said the pilot. "I'll set down there."

"Copy." Rastun looked to the others. "Get ready."

They all nodded.

He clenched his machine gun, the barrel pointed down at the deck. Everyone did the same with their weapons in case of an accidental discharge. A bullet hitting the engine above them would not be good.

The chopper started its descent. Rastun stared out the cockpit windshield, then out the window on the side door. He ran down scenarios in his head. Top priority was making contact with Mohede or anyone from his squad and getting a SITREP from them. Failing that, they'd have to assess the situation themselves, and he'd deploy his people where they –

The co-pilot shouted something urgent in Indonesian.

Rastun snapped his head toward the flight deck. The pilot cried out a curse and jerked the Panther right. Everyone grabbed something to keep from falling out of their seats. Rastun caught a glimpse of a large shadowy form passing by the windshield.

Another shout from the pilot. He banked to the left. Another Ropen silhouette appeared in front of them. Just as quickly, it vanished from view.

The sharp blow shook the helicopter. A sick, grinding noise permeated the cabin. The engine coughed and sputtered. Rastun clutched the edge of his seat. He looked above him, holding his breath.

The Panther whipped around. Screams and curses blared through his helmet's ICS. He looked to Karen across from him, dread sending his heart racing. Not like this. They couldn't buy it like this. And Emily? They couldn't leave her alone.

The chopper whirled around again, then dropped to the left. Out the side window, trees and houses sped past. He locked gazes with Karen, her eyes wide with fear.

The Panther straightened out. Maybe –

An explosion of sound hammered the air. A quake threw Rastun out of his seat.

FORTY-ONE

Rastun blinked. He was alive. No more shaking. No more deafening crashes. The Panther had come to a rest tilting about twenty degrees to the right.

He groaned and blinked again. He was not in his seat. Had to have fallen to the deck in the crash. But he didn't just feel metal around him. There were also bodies.

Rastun sat up, swinging his head left and right, fear taking hold.

"Everyone all right? Karen? Sound off, people."

"Still alive and kicking, Cap'n," said Geek.

"I'm here," McClure spoke in a strained voice. "Aw, man. I think I fucked up my shoulder."

"I'm good," announced Alana.

Rastun drew a shaky breath. He hadn't heard from –

"I'm okay," said Karen.

Relief spread through him. Karen used a seat to pull herself up.

Everyone else sounded off. Except for Kory Hyo. She lay against the door, on her stomach, letting out soft moans. Cuffed, she'd had no opportunity to brace herself before the crash.

They untangled themselves from each other. McClure gripped his right shoulder, teeth bared in agony. Ehrenberg grabbed his ankle, eyes shut tight. Sprained or broken. Alana kept her face stiff as she held her right wrist, her fingers barely moving. The MSA crew chief let out strangled cries as he held his left leg. That sort of reaction had to mean a break.

Rastun moved past the seats toward the flight deck. Sharp pain dug into his right knee. Still, he could walk. He stuck his head into the flight deck.

The nose of the chopper had crashed into a tree. The entire right side crumpled in. Mangled metal pressed against the bloody body of the co-pilot. Rastun closed his eyes and shook his head. Nothing he could do for the poor guy. He turned to the pilot. Blood streamed down the right side of his face, but his eyes were open, half-conscious.

Rastun turned back to the cabin. Yes, they were banged up, but they had a job to do.

"Doc. McClure. Alana. You're sidelined. Norgay, stay with the wounded. Everyone else, with me. We still have Ropen to fight."

"I'm fine, sir," Alana spoke through clenched teeth.

"Move your right hand."

She flexed her fingers a bit, grimacing in pain.

"You're not fine. You're out of this."

"Jack." Ehrenberg propped himself against the door. "Take Norgay with you."

"He's team medic. He needs to treat you guys."

"He's more valuable to you out there than here. I'll handle the wounded."

"You sure?"

Ehrenberg looked around the cabin. "It's not like I have far to go to do it."

Rastun exhaled slowly. "Norgay. Give the Doc your first aid kit."

"Yes, sir."

He looked to McClure and Alana. "Keep your weapons within reach, just in case the Ropen show up."

"Don't worry, we will," replied McClure.

With one last concerned look at Ehrenberg and the wounded, Rastun led the others out of the helicopter. Blood stained the top and the side of the aircraft. The blades certainly did a number on the Ropen that collided with them.

And the Ropen did a number on us.

The sun peeked over the horizon. They all scanned the dawn sky, searching for Ropen. Rastun thought he spotted a shadowy form to the north.

"Incoming! Front!" shouted Herrera.

A Ropen dove at them, its maw wide open.

Rastun hefted his MINIMI. The machine gun chattered, vibrations racing up his arms. More gunfire exploded around him. Geek's AK-47 and Herrera and Norgay's Steyr AUGs. The Ropen jerked, flipped on its side and crashed into the ground twenty feet away.

A horn beeped. A pair of headlights bounced across the field. Someone stuck a hand out the window, waving.

A decrepit old pickup stopped in front of them. Mohede's pickup. Rastun and the others approached it.

The chief brigadier slid his bulky frame out of the cab and rattled off something in Indonesian.

And we don't have Wikana here to translate.

"Okay?" Mohede pointed at them. "Okay?"

Rastun pointed at himself and nodded. He then stabbed a finger at the helicopter and shook his head.

Mohede hollered back at the pickup. Another officer hopped out and dashed to the wrecked Panther. The chief brigadier turned back to Rastun and his team, said something in his native tongue, then waved for them to follow. They piled into the bed as Mohede wheeled the truck around.

"Where's he taking us?" asked Karen.

"Probably to where the action is." Rastun's eyes flickered across the sky. No sign of any more Ropen, yet.

Mohede sped through the village. No one was out and about. No surprise with who knew how many Ropen around.

"Oh God," Karen gasped.

They passed the remains of two shredded, bloody corpses on the dirt road. Rastun ground his teeth. How many others suffered the same gruesome fate?

They came across four more bodies. Rastun grimaced when he saw an old man lying in the street, back ripped open, a cane by his side. The same cane that Fuganto used.

"Sir." Herrera pointed.

Rastun tensed, gripping his machine gun. Four Ropen besieged a coffee shop. Two on the roof, one at the left-side wall, the last sticking its head through the shattered front door.

"Herrera, Norgay. Take the ones on the roof." Rastun pointed. "I'll take the --"

The Ropen at the wall twisted its body around, eyeing the pickup. It croaked and sprinted toward them on all fours.

Rastun fired a long burst from his MINIMI. Rifles crackled around him as Mohede stomped on the brakes. Rastun took his finger off the trigger as he and the others fell toward the cab.

The Ropen spread its wings and left the ground.

"Out!" shouted Rastun.

They all jumped from the bed. Rastun hit the ground and rolled.

The Ropen slammed down on the bed. The rear of the pickup sagged under its weight. The creature wailed and leaned over the bed, its jaws descending toward Rastun.

He kicked it. The heel of his boot smashed into the lower part of his beak. Fire pierced his knee. He gritted his teeth. No time to think about pain.

Geek, Herrera, and Norgay blasted away with their rifles, barely two feet from the Ropen. Bullets tore apart its head, blood flying in all directions. It tumbled out of the bed and lay in a heap.

Mohede fired over the pickup's hood, aiming at the Ropen at the door. Scarlet holes sprouted across its back. It jerked around, trying to back out.

Geek shoved a fresh magazine into his AK-47 and fired. Rastun added his MINIMI to the barrage, while Karen photographed everything.

Rivers of blood poured over the Ropen's body. It collapsed in front of the door.

"Jack!" Karen shouted. "One of them's getting in!" She pointed at the roof.

Rastun looked just in time to see a tail wriggle through a hole in the roof and disappear.

"Shit." The dead Ropen blocked the front door. Even if it didn't, the last Ropen remained on the roof, shrieking as bullets zipped around it.

"Geek, with me. The rest of you, deal with that thing."

Rastun took off, running alongside the coffee shop. Geek was on his heels, with Karen behind him. They swung around the rear of the wood building, and Rastun spotted what he hoped would be there. A back door.

Geek swung it open and brought up his rifle. "Clear."

They moved inside. Screams echoed from the front of the shop. The trio hurried down the small hallway. Ahead of them, a group of villagers crowded against the wall. A young man threw a chair at the advancing Ropen. Was that Hamdan? Captain Adsit's kid?

The creature wailed and stalked toward them. Rastun and Geek aimed their weapons.

A man jumped into their line of fire

"Outta the way!" Geek hollered.

The man did not hear him. He grabbed a table and shoved it in front of the Ropen. The monster's jaws clamped down on the table and flung it across the shop.

Right at Rastun, Geek, and Karen.

Rastun dove behind the counter with Karen. Geek shouted a curse and dropped to the floor. The table crashed into shelves above Rastun. Glass shattered and rained onto the wooden floor, and him. Something wet and sticky splashed his face and hands. It smelled like olive oil.

He pushed himself to his feet. The Ropen was almost on top of Hamdan and the others. He turned, bringing up the MINIMI.

His boot hit something wet. He slipped and fell, his back slamming into the wall.

Something moved to his left. Karen. She had a bag of flour in her hand. She tore an opening in the side.

"Hey!" she hollered, then threw the bag.

Rastun scrambled to his feet just as the Ropen shrieked. White powder covered its head and left eye. It swung from side to side, crying out.

Geek's AK-47 cracked. The machine gun bucked in Rastun's hands as he stitched the Ropen's side with a stream of 5.56mm rounds. It let out a gargled cry and fell on its stomach.

"Everyone okay?" Geek bounded toward the villagers. Rastun and Karen followed.

A woman jumped up, hands clasped. Rastun recognized her. Surati, Adsit's widow. She repeated the same word over and over. "Thank you," maybe?

Hamdan glared at the dead Ropen. He cried out in rage, picked up a chair, and smashed it down on the dead creature. Rastun lowered his gaze, sympathizing with the kid. The Ropen had killed two members of his family. He couldn't blame Hamdan.

The villagers appeared all right. Many chattered at the same time. Rastun couldn't understand what they said, but from their facial expressions and tone, he guessed they thanked the three of them.

"Everyone here okay?" Herrera called from the door.

"All good." Rastun gave him a thumbs up. "We put this thing down before it got anyone."

"We got the last one." Herrera pointed to the roof.

"I heard shooting coming from the docks," said Norgay. "It looks like reinforcements have arrived."

They piled back into Mohede's pickup and drove to the docks. The *Grantin* sat off-shore, armed men lining the deck. Three dead Ropen floated in the water. More MSA sailors advanced toward the road, led by Bahar.

"Are your people all right, Mister Rastun?" the lieutenant asked.

"The Doc, Alana, and McClure got hurt when the chopper crashed. So did your crew chief and pilot." He bit his lip. "The co-pilot's dead. Sorry."

Bahar lowered his head for a moment. "I will send medics there. Have you killed any Ropen?"

"Five. Six, counting the one that hit our chopper."

Bahar nodded and looked around. "Perhaps this is the last we will see of these Ropen."

"Not quite, Lieutenant."

FORTY-TWO

Rastun and Karen walked into the conference room of their hotel in Singaraja on the island of Bali. His knee still hurt, but not as much as it did following the Panther crash two days ago. A deep bone bruise, according to the doctor. He'd come off of missions with worse injuries, both with the Army Rangers and the FUBI.

Ehrenberg, Geek, and Petal were already seated at the rectangular table. Petal seemed to be doing well after her concussion. Ehrenberg wore a walking boot for his fractured ankle.

The others soon filtered in, McClure with his right arm in a sling. Separated shoulder was the diagnosis. Alana also had a cast on her broken right wrist.

We got lucky. A lot of people in helicopter crashes came away with much worse injuries. Some did not come away at all.

Once everyone was seated, Ehrenberg set up the computer for the Skype call with FUBI headquarters. Lynch, Parker, and Lipeli appeared on the screen.

"Everyone doing well?" asked Lynch.

"Well, and recovering," replied Ehrenberg.

"Good. Any more Ropen sightings?"

"None since the attack on Kalisangka. The police and Maritime Security counted eighteen dead Ropen in the village. There might have been a couple that escaped, but Petal and I feel all these attacks came from the nest on Pulau Kloset. I think this part of Indonesia should be safe."

"Good." Lynch nodded. "Good work, all of you."

After a round of "Thank yous," Rastun asked, "Any more problems with protestors?"

"We still have some across the street here," Lipeli answered. "Just shouting and holding signs. There's also the usual angry social media posts about how horrible we are for killing all those Ropen that were trying to kill all those villagers. But it looks like the crazier posts calling for violence have toned down since our call with Folgosi and Minister Irama."

Rastun grinned. True, he had some doubts, but in the end the FUBI brass definitely had his back. They even goaded the UN into donating two million dollars for a new rhinoceros exhibit at the Philadelphia Zoo. He could just picture the gleeful reactions of his parents when they received that check.

"Now what about the eggs we found?" asked Petal. "Given all the food the Ropen stockpiled in that cave, they have to be close to hatching. Those babies will die if we don't do something."

The three men on the screen looked at one another, with Parker hanging his head.

Ehrenberg cranked an eyebrow. "Why do I have a feeling you're about to spring some bad news on us."

Parker drew a breath. "We talked to the Indonesian government about the eggs. Given all the lives lost in the Ropen attacks, they decided to destroy them."

"What?" Petal nearly launched out of her chair, mouth agape, looking distraught. "No. No they can't."

"This is ridiculous." Ehrenberg threw up his hands. "We can raise them in captivity away from Indonesia. They won't threaten anyone."

"That's what we told them," said Lynch. "But after so many deaths and the harm done to the fishing industry, they felt they could not justify saving the eggs."

"But we have a contract to preserve the Ropen if possible," Ehrenberg pleaded.

"And those are the key words, Randy." Parker held up a finger. "'If possible.' Our contract with the Indonesian government gives them the right to eradicate any Ropen they feel a threat to public safety and welfare."

Petal gasped. "Those eggs aren't a threat to anyone, especially if we take them somewhere else."

"There's also a political angle to this," said Parker.

Isn't there always. Rastun snorted.

The billionaire continued. "According to polls, a sizeable number of the Indonesian population view the Ropen as a threat. Along with the fishing industry, the tourism industry took an economic hit. Leaders from both sectors put a lot of pressure on the government to end these attacks. There probably won't be much public sympathy to save those eggs."

Lines dug into Rastun's face. He wondered if bribes also influenced the government's decision. Maybe Mainaky dumped some rupiah into the bank accounts of certain public officials.

"Can't we challenge them on legal grounds?" asked Ehrenberg.

"We could." Parker frowned. "But by the time we're done with all the legal haranguing, those eggs will have long since hatched and those baby Ropen will likely be dead."

Ehrenberg slumped in his seat. "So there's nothing we can do?"

Lynch shook his head. "Sorry, Randy. I don't think so. Unless you can think of a way to snag some of those eggs, the FUBI's job in Indonesia is over."

Rastun sighed after the Skype call ended. He stared hard at the table, arms folded. How fucking stupid. If the Indonesian government didn't want the Ropen around, why not just let them take the eggs off their hands?

Politicians. The word made him want to spit. The same all over the world. They did whatever it took to hold on to their power. To hell with common sense. To hell with doing the right thing. Because of that selfishness, his team would not be able to save and study one of the most unique species on the planet. That was the whole reason the Foundation for Undocumented Biological Investigation existed.

"There has to be something we can do." Petal swung her head from left to right, desperation burning in her eyes. "We can't let them destroy those eggs."

"Gonna be tough now that we don't have our ride anymore," said Geek. "Our mission's done, so the *Grantin* doesn't have to ferry us around. Even if we were still onboard, no way they'd disobey orders to bring us to Pulau Kloset."

"What about Lieutenant Bahar?" Petal leaned forward. "He was nice. He might help us."

"No," said Rastun. "Bahar's a good guy, but he's a loyal officer and won't go against orders. And honestly, after everything he's done for us, I'm not going to ask him to put his career at risk."

"This is a seaside resort town." Petal aimed a hand toward the window. "We can rent a boat to take us to Pulau Kloset."

"We'd basically be asking the owners of those boats to break the law," Karen pointed out. "When we leave, they'll still be here and might wind up getting arrested if the police find out what we did."

Petal's mouth hung open, as if trying to come up with another idea. When she didn't, she drooped her head.

"So basically," Geek began, "unless someone can pull a boat out of their ass, we're screwed. Or more accurately, those unborn baby Ropen are screwed."

Everyone sat quietly. Rastun stared out the window at the clear blue water in the hotel pool. His frustration mounted. He felt beaten. Not a feeling he was used to.

Ehrenberg lifted his head. "There might be someone who can help us."

"Who?" Rastun turned to him.

Ehrenberg winced. "I don't think you're gonna like it, Jack."

"Try me."

"No, trust me. You are *really* not going to like it."

"Doc," said Rastun. "We don't have a lot of options here. So whatever idea you have, I'll take it."

A heavy breath escaped Ehrenberg's nose. "Okay, but I did warn you."

FORTY-THREE

Ehrenberg had been right. Rastun did not like this idea . . . *at all.* In fact, he hated it.

Face twisted, he locked his eyes on the *Earth Warrior,* docked in front of him.

"You have got to be fucking kidding me," he growled.

Karen squeezed his arm. "I know. I'm not thrilled about this, either."

He said nothing, just watched Ehrenberg approach the gangplank. The cryptozoologist turned to the rest of the group. "Well, let's get going." His usual warm smile a bit forced.

They followed him onto the deck, where Marques, Paulette, Lenna, and Griffin had gathered. Neither Paulette nor Lenna smiled. From Lenna's hard expression, their very appearance seemed to offend her.

"Cesar." Ehrenberg extended his hand. "Thank you for agreeing to help us."

"Of course." He clasped his hand. "I am glad the FUBI has come around to our way of thinking and wishes to save cryptids instead of killing them." Marques tacked on that damn smirk of his.

Fuck you, you prick. Rastun glared at him. He still couldn't believe Roland Parker and Director Lynch had pulled this off. They had managed to get a plane chartered and worked out a deal with an avian sanctuary to care for the hatchlings. The UN said they could do the same, but Parker told them, "I know how bureaucracies work. By the time you arrange all that, the Indonesian Army will have blown up that cave. Plus, if any major problems crop up, the FUBI has more experience dealing with them than your people. Seems to me the best chance to save those eggs is for us to work together."

Part of Rastun marveled at Parker's negotiating skills. Another part cursed him for making them work with these SOBs.

"Come on," Paulette spoke in an unenthused tone. "We better cast off if we want to get to the island before the Indonesians."

Rastun's jaw stiffened as everyone headed to the bridge. He had hoped the UNCID assholes would wind up in a jail cell with Kory Hyo. No such luck. The Indonesian authorities had determined Marques and the others had no role in the bombing of the *Grantin* and none of them had a clue Kory had been a psycho.

That didn't make them totally innocent. Not in Rastun's mind.

"Jack."

He scowled at Marques when they reached the bridge. The motherfucker lifted his chin, a cocky half-smile on his lips, and held out his hand. "I hope there are no hard feelings."

Rastun took one step forward, then two . . . then charged Marques, grabbing him by the collar. Paulette and Lenna screamed as he slammed him against the wall.

"Fuck you, you self-righteous piece of shit!" He slammed Marques into the wall again. "All your fucking posts were the reason some nutcase attacked my mother. She had nothing to do with this. Nothing!" The wall shuddered as Marques struck it a third time.

He spotted Paulette and Lenna pulling out their phones, ready to record the assault.

"Hey!" Lenna shouted when Karen yanked the phone from her hand. "What the fuck?" Geek also took Paulette's phone. "You'll get this back when the Cap'n's had his say."

Rastun leaned in, his face inches from Marques'. The son-of-a-bitch was no longer smiling. "You wanna come at me, bring it. But you leave my family out of it. Because if you pull this shit again and someone I care about gets hurt, I will find you, and I will *fucking end you*."

He turned to Griffin. "That goes for you, too."

The actor swallowed and jumped behind Paulette.

Rastun turned back to Marques. "Is that understood?"

Jaw quivering, Marques gave a reluctant nod. "Y-Yes."

Rastun let him go and backed away. He looked around at the others. "Okay. Let's start working together."

***

The trip from Singaraja to Pulau Kloset took little over eight hours. One hour of that time had been dedicated to planning the rescue mission. Certainly not the most complicated op in Rastun's career. The *Earth Warrior* crew had some drink coolers big enough for each to contain two eggs. They'd take dinghies to the island, load the eggs, and head back to the yacht. Then they would sail to Darwin, Australia where the chartered plane would fly the eggs to the sanctuary in France. Simple enough.

Except Rastun knew it wouldn't be simple. The Indonesians had to be prepping for their own operation on Pulau Kloset. He didn't think the MSA or the Sea and Coast Guard would do this. The military would be the ones with the resources to carry it out. Maybe regular army, maybe their marine corps, maybe some special ops unit like the navy's Taifib.

They'd probably plant explosives to seal up the cave, trapping the hatchlings and preventing any surviving Ropen from returning to care for them.

As simple as that plan was, they would need time to implement it. Orders had to be drawn up, specific units chosen – after, he hoped, a lot of inter-service politicking to see who got the honor of blowing up the cave. Transportation had to be arranged, probably by helicopter. Equipment had to be drawn, reconnaissance of the target conducted, then came the planning for the insertion, execution, and extraction.

Rastun guessed between 48 to 72 hours before the Indonesians had boots on the ground. They'd already lost a day with the FUBI brass negotiating with Marques to join forces, then waiting for the *Earth Warrior* to arrive in Singaraja. He hoped it would be closer to 72 hours than 48 when the Indonesians arrived.

Or they could have some patrol boats guarding the island against people like us. If that were the case, their plan was fucked in the ass.

To his delight, the lookouts spotted no sign of patrol boats. Maybe the Indonesians didn't think anyone would go to an island Ropen were known to inhabit. Whatever the case, luck broke their way. In situations like this, you didn't question it. You accepted it.

They took two dinghies to the island, with *Earth Warrior* loitering five miles away, trying to not look suspicious in case a patrol boat or aircraft showed up. They pulled the rafts across the beach and hid them in the foliage. Even with a broken wrist, Alana had come along to operate the Flapjack drone, which would orbit Pulau Kloset looking out for Indonesian forces.

"All right," said Rastun. "Marques, Lenna, Griffin, take the coolers. Norgay, point. I'll watch our six."

"Who the fuck put you in charge?" Lenna snapped.

Rastun groaned. He didn't need this shit.

"You think because you're a man, a professional killer, you can boss everyone around?"

"And so much for working together," Geek muttered.

Rastun stepped toward Lenna. "Do you have experience with missions like this? Do you know what to do if our plan goes to shit?"

"Do not mansplain to me." Lenna stabbed a finger at him.

"Oh to hell with this." Rastun spun away from her. "We have a job to do. Saving those eggs." He glanced back at Lenna. "Which I thought is what you wanted. You want to stand here throwing a tantrum until the Indonesian marines show up, be my guest. We'll see you when we get back with the eggs."

The FUBI started toward the jungle.

"You think you can --"

"Lenna, please," said Marques. "Think about the Ropen eggs. Saving them is what matters."

Lenna scowled, but followed Marques, with Griffin joining them.

"That's the smartest thing I've ever heard that guy say," Rastun whispered to Karen.

She lightly slapped his arm. "Be nice. Remember, we're all supposed to be friends."

"More like frenemies." He winced. "Jeez, I can't believe I used that stupid word."

Karen chuckled.

Rastun checked around him, holding an Aster 7. Having had to turn the MINIMI and the Glock back over to the MSA, it was the only weapon he had. They still had to be alert in case any Ropen remained on the island.

The group started up the rise leading to the cave. Griffin stopped and raised his head. "Hey. You guys hear that?"

Rastun also lifted his head, concentrating. He picked up a distant thumping.

"Oh crap." Geek scanned the sky.

"Chopper inbound," Alana radioed. "Coming from the west, two miles out. Looks like a Panther."

Rastun scowled. So much for that 72-hour window. "Move. Go. Go. Go."

They hustled up the slope. Marques, Griffin, and Lenna had a tough time going fast while holding the coolers. Griffin fell once, but quickly recovered.

The group crested the rise. The cave lay in front of them.

"The chopper just touched down on the north beach," Alana reported.

"Copy." Rastun turned to Geek. "Get that drone in there."

"Gimmie a sec. Yeah, I know. We don't have a sec."

He plopped the little vehicle on the ground and tapped on his tablet. The Alley Cat motored up to the cave.

"I count four people in camo," said Alana. "Moving into the jungle."

"Probably a recon unit," Geek added.

Rastun nodded. They'd talked about this possibility back on *Earth Warrior*. Aerial reconnaissance wouldn't do much good with the target in a cave. The Indonesians would need recon troops, who were almost always better trained than regular grunts.

"Geek?" Urgency crept into Rastun's tone.

"Yeah. Cave's clear of Ropen."

Rastun nodded. The Alley Cat surveillance may have taken time they didn't have, but they couldn't afford to rush in and come upon a stray Ropen.

"Then let's get those eggs." Marques hurried toward the cave.

"That's why we're here." Sarcasm tinged Rastun's words.

They hustled to the cave. Marques, Lenna, and Griffin threw open the coolers. They took eggs and put them inside, resting them on the towels that covered the bottom, doing it with a combination of care and haste.

"I got 'em on thermal," said Alana. "Those soldiers are making good progress. You guys done yet?"

"Almost," replied Rastun.

"That recon team's about a hundred yards from the cave. I suggest changing 'almost' to 'done.'"

Karen lowered the last egg into the cooler. "Okay. We're good."

They closed the coolers and secured the locks. Rastun looked at the other eggs, frowning. They only got six out of a few dozen.

Better six than none.

"Move. Move. Move."

They hurried out of the cave. With the eggs in the coolers, it took two people to handle each one. Herrera and Norgay were the only ones who could cover their escape.

"Recon unit's almost at the top of the rise," said Alana. "You guys need to hide."

"In there." Rastun pointed to some nearby vegetation. They plunged through it and lay on their stomachs.

The recon squad appeared. Rifles up, alert, scanning all around them. Total pros.

Rastun watched them, chewing the inside of his cheek. He'd wait till they went into the cave, then get the hell out of Dodge and back to *Earth Warrior.*

One of the soldiers said something and pointed to the ground. The other three looked down, then raised their heads. Rastun tensed. Their gazes were aimed in their direction.

"Shit. They must have picked up our sign," whispered Geek.

Rastun ground his teeth as the Indonesians moved forward, rifles at the ready. A black mass of failure crept through him. They had talked about this possibility back on *Earth Warrior.* A firefight with Indonesian troops was out of the question. They were not enemies of the United States. Just men, like him, doing their job. Opening fire would be murder.

It had been decided if they were met by the Indonesian military, they would give themselves up. They had a better chance of the U.S.

Government arranging their release for trespassing than gunning down a bunch of soldiers.

"I'll create a distraction," whispered Marques.

Rastun scrunched his face. "What?"

"I'll distract them." He pulled out a strand of firecrackers from his pocket. "The rest of you get those eggs back to *Earth Warrior.*"

"What? You're crazy," blurted Lenna.

"It's the only way to save these eggs." Marques locked his gaze with Rastun.

Rastun nodded.

Marques lit the firecrackers, then heaved them to their left. Two of the recon troops pointed. They noticed the movement.

Sharp cracks and snaps echoed through the jungle. The Indonesians swept their rifles toward the noise.

"Aaaaah!" Marques jumped up and started running, slapping at branches as he did. "Yeah! Wooooo!"

He started down the rise. All four Indonesians chased after him.

"Crazy son-of-a-bitch." Geek shook his head.

"Let's go."

Rastun grabbed one cooler, helped by Karen. The group raced back to the south beach. Marques still whooped and hollered. Rastun heard no gunfire. Thank God those recon troops weren't trigger happy.

He looked over his shoulder. He did not like Marques, not even a little. But he had to give him credit. The asshole possessed a set of big brass ones.

They reached the dinghies, loaded the coolers in them, and took off for the *Earth Warrior.*

"Where's Cesar?" Paulette asked when she, Ehrenberg, and Petal met them at the dive platform.

"Back on the island," replied Rastun. "The Indonesians sent some recon troops to check out the cave. They almost found us, but Marques distracted them so we could get back here."

"What? You left him?" Paulette turned back to the island. "No. We have to get him."

"He's telling the truth," said Lenna. "If it wasn't for Cesar, we wouldn't have gotten away."

Paulette looked at Lenna, then back to the island.

"I'm sure he'll be okay," Ehrenberg told her. "Cesar's here on behalf of the UN. The Indonesian government won't mistreat him."

"Look." Rastun walked up to Paulette. "I know you're worried about him, but he wanted us to get these eggs to safety. When they catch him, it won't take long for them to put two and two together and realize *Earth*

Warrior was involved. Then we'll have the Navy, the Sea and Coast Guard, and Maritime Security looking for this yacht. You need to turn this thing south and get us out of Indonesian waters as fast as possible."

Paulette breathed through her nose, then nodded. "Yeah. Yeah, okay." She ran off to the bridge.

A couple of minutes later, the big yacht swung around. The engines groaned as Paulette set a course for Australia at top speed.

Rastun stared down at the three coolers. "Well, we did it."

He looked up at Lenna. The hostility usually on her face, well, lessened. She nodded to him, and he back to her. They may never like one another, but they'd managed to put aside their differences for a time. Because of that, six of the rarest animals in the world would live.

FORTY-FOUR

Five Months Later

"Are we almost there?" Emily nearly bounced in her seat.

"Soon, honey, soon," Karen told her.

"Asking the question over and over again isn't going to get us there any faster," said Rastun.

"I know. I can't help it. I'm actually going to see real dinosaurs." Emily beamed.

"Technically . . ." Rastun raised a finger. "They're flying reptiles, not dinosaurs."

Emily tsked. "Okay, Dad."

Rastun couldn't help but smile, as he had every time she called him that in the two weeks since he and Karen wed. He glanced down at her finger, the one with the sparkling diamond ring. Sometimes it still hadn't fully settled in. Karen was no longer his girlfriend, Emily no longer just her kid. He now had a wife and a step-daughter, a family all of his own.

He gently gripped Karen's hand. She squeezed back.

The chauffeured SUV wound through the country road outside Le Mans, France. It turned onto a paved, tree-lined path leading to a two-story glass structure. A sign near the front entrance read *Fourcade Institut d'Ornithologie*.

The driver opened their door, didn't smile, but nodded as the Rastuns got out. A tall, middle-aged woman with an angular face and black hair in a ponytail greeted them.

"*Monsieur* Rastun. *Mademoiselles* Rastun. I am Doctor Bilaud. Welcome to the Fourcade Institute of Ornithology." She shook hands with them.

"It's our pleasure, Doctor," said Rastun. "Thanks for the invitation."

"Can we see them now?" Emily bounced on the balls of her feet.

"Emily." Karen gave Bilaud an apologetic smile. "Sorry. She's just really excited."

"I think we all are." Rastun grinned.

"I can certainly understand. Come."

Bilaud led them down a spacious hallway, but not before giving Rastun a quick once over. The French bird expert was certainly attractive, but . . .

Sorry, Mademoiselle. This guy is happily spoken for.

They approached a door that read, "Authorized Personnel Only" in both French and English. Bilaud pulled out a key card, then turned to them. "Just so you are aware, we have another guest here today."

Rastun nodded. He imagined Bilaud and her colleagues had entertained many guests over the past few months.

She swiped the card. The light on the electronic lock turned green. Bilaud opened the door. Emily practically jumped inside.

"Oh my gosh." Her eyes went wide and her mouth hung open.

Karen clutched Rastun's arm as they stared at the scene through the window. The enclosure contained rocks, plants, a small artificial pond, and food dishes. Perched on one of the rocks was a Ropen. Not the monstrosities that had tried to kill him and Karen in Indonesia. This one was about the size of a chicken. So was the second one, which slept in a tree.

"They're so cute." Emily pressed her hands together.

Karen tilted her head. "Actually, she's right. They are kind of cute."

"Yeah." Rastun leaned in close to Karen. "Especially since they're not trying to have us for dinner."

She chuckled and gently elbowed him in the side.

"Yes, not all cryptids are terrifying."

Rastun groaned, instantly recognizing the voice. His attention was so focused on the baby Ropen he hadn't seen Bilaud's other guest.

Cesar Marques turned to him, shooting him that damned smirk. "How nice to see you again, Jack. Karen. Congratulations on your marriage."

"So the Indonesians cut you loose," said Rastun. "What a shame."

"Jack," Karen spoke out the corner of her mouth, then shifted her eyes to Emily. She had become determined to make sure her daughter did not pick up Rastun's bad habits. Not that he considered sarcasm a bad habit.

"It took some doing by the UN, but they managed to negotiate my release. Though I am no longer allowed to enter Indonesia. Much like you."

"Yup." While *Earth Warrior* had gotten out of Indonesian waters without being intercepted by the military or law enforcement, the government was none too pleased they had gone behind their back to take the Ropen eggs. Like Marques, the FUBI was barred from entering the country.

Rastun looked back at the baby Ropen. "It was worth it." His chest puffed out, pride flowing through him. Of the six eggs they'd saved, five of the babies survived. They could live in safety and give scientists a living window into a world that existed millions of years ago.

Emily snapped pictures of the reptiles, then wrote some notes on her tablet. That had been one of the conditions of pulling her out of school and bringing her along on this trip. She had to do a report on the baby Ropen. At first, she protested. Understandable. What kid wanted to do schoolwork on vacation?

"I think it's a small price to pay to see living prehistoric animals up close and personal," he had told his step-daughter. That seemed to mollify her.

Karen, too, took photos of the Ropen. This was a working vacation for them, too, since the FUBI covered their travel expenses. A kind of mini-honeymoon before their actual one in Australia a few months from now.

They quizzed Dr. Bilaud about the young Ropen. She explained they had learned much about their growth rate, food preferences, and social interaction since they hatched. They had not been able to fly yet.

"I can only imagine how much more we will learn when they become fully mature."

"What happens when they get bigger?" asked Emily.

"A special aviary is being constructed near Montpellier," Bilaud answered. "It will have plenty of room for all five Ropen to live when they reach adulthood."

"They should not have to live in captivity." Marques shook his head. "They should be allowed to live free."

"True, *Monsieur* Marques." Bilaud frowned. "But without their parents to care for them, there is no chance they could survive in the wild."

"That's the trade-off," said Rastun. "Better they live in captivity than getting blown up in that cave."

The corner of Marques' mouth twisted. He turned back to the Ropen, probably not wanting to admit Rastun was right.

"Come. Let me show you the other Ropen."

Bilaud led them back out into the hallway. Rastun made sure to walk behind Marques. Karen would probably tell him he was being way too paranoid, even for him. Whatever. They may have worked together to save those Ropen eggs, but he didn't trust the son-of-a-bitch as far as he could throw him.

"So, what is the next great cryptid hunt for the FUBI?" Marques looked over his shoulder at Rastun.

"You think I'm gonna tell you so you can follow us around and bug us?"

Marques softly chuckled. "That's all right. I'm sure it will be posted on your website soon enough."

Rastun scowled. *Joy.* "Here's a suggestion. There are plenty of cryptids in the world. How about you do your own searches, we'll do ours, and we'll all be happier for it."

"Oh, I already have a list of expeditions that will keep the UNCID busy well into next year." Marques stopped and faced him. "But I do believe that one day, our paths will cross again."

Smirking, he walked ahead of them, hands clasped behind his back.

Rastun grunted. "Yeah, I'll be looking forward to that day . . . the same way I looked forward to a root canal."

THE END

About the Author: John J. Rust is a New Jersey native who graduated from Mercer County Community College and the College of Mt. St. Vincent with degrees in broadcasting and communications. After working for New Jersey 101.5 FM, he moved to Arizona and became the sports director at KYCA radio, and does play-by-play for high school and college sports. Rust has authored 14 books, including *Sea Raptor, Reptilian, Dark Wings,* and the Fallen Eagle trilogy. You can follow John J. Rust at www.facebook.com/johnjrustauthor, on Twitter @JohnJRust, and on his Amazon page.

Praise for John J. Rust's Books:

"Superb action sequences that spanned multiple chapters and kept the action flowing, and I genuinely cared about the characters in jeopardy." – *Steve R. Yeager, author of "Raptor Apocalypse," on "Sea Raptor."*

"If you want monster-chasing adventure, this is an exciting book." – *Matt Bille, author of "The Dolmen" on "Sea Raptor."*

"Mr. Rust knows how to use twists in the story to keep the excitement high." – *Brenda Whiteside, author of the Love and Murder series, on "Sea Raptor."*

"This is a fast-paced thriller with lots of action." – *Heidi Thomas, author of "Dare to Dream," on "Sea Raptor."*

**SEVERED**PRESS

CHECK OUT OTHER GREAT DINOSAUR BOOKS

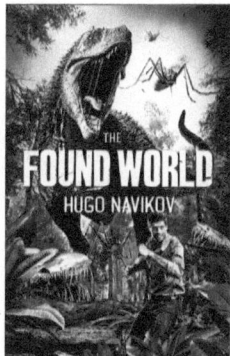

THE FOUND WORLD
by Hugo Navikov

A powerful global cabal wants adventurer Brett Russell to retrieve a superweapon stolen by the scientist who built it. To entice him to travel underneath one of the most dangerous volcanoes on Earth to find the scientist, this shadowy organization will pay him the only thing he cares about: information that will allow him to avenge his family's murder.

But before he can get paid, he and his team must enter an underground hellscape of killer plants, giant insects, terrifying dinosaurs, and an army of other predators never previously seen by man.

At the end of this journey awaits a revelation that could alter the fate of mankind ... if they can make it back from this horrifying found world.

HOUSE OF THE GODS
by Davide Mana

High above the steamy jungle of the Amazon basin, rise the flat plateaus known as the Tepui, the House of the Gods. Lost worlds of unknown beauty, a naturalistic wonder, each an ecology onto itself, shunned by the local tribes for centuries. The House of the Gods was not made for men.

But now, the crew and passengers of a small charter plane are about to find what was hidden for sixty million years.

Lost on an island in the clouds 10.000 feet above the jungle, surrounded by dinosaurs, hunted by mysterious mercenaries, the survivors of Sligo Air flight 001 will quickly learn the only rule of life on Earth: Extinction.

 SEVERED**PRESS**

CHECK OUT OTHER GREAT DINOSAUR BOOKS

PRIMORDIA
by **Greig Beck**

Ben Cartwright, former soldier, home to mourn the loss of his father stumbles upon cryptic letters from the past between the author, Arthur Conan Doyle and his great, great grandfather who vanished while exploring the Amazon jungle in 1908.

Amazingly, these letters lead Ben to believe that his ancestor's expedition was the basis for Doyle's fantastical tale of a lost world inhabited by long extinct creatures. As Ben digs some more he finds clues to the whereabouts of a lost notebook that might contain a map to a place that is home to creatures that would rewrite everything known about history, biology and evolution.

But other parties now know about the notebook, and will do anything to obtain it. For Ben and his friends, it becomes a race against time and against ruthless rivals.

In the remotest corners of Venezuela, along winding river trails known only to lost tribes, and through near impenetrable jungle, Ben and his novice team find a forbidden place more terrifying and dangerous than anything they could ever have imagined.

PANGAEA EXILES
by **Jeff Brackett**

Tried and convicted for his crimes, Sean Barrow is sent into temporal exile—banished to a time so far before recorded history that there is no chance that he, or any other criminal sent back, has any chance of altering history.

Now Sean must find a way to survive more than 200 million years in the past, in a world populated by monstrous creatures that would rend him limb from limb if they got the chance. And that's just his fellow prisoners.

The dinosaurs are almost as bad.

CHECK OUT OTHER GREAT DINOSAUR BOOKS

FLIPSIDE
by JAKE BIBLE

The year is 2046 and dinosaurs are real.

Time bubbles across the world, many as large as one hundred square miles, turn like clockwork, revealing prehistoric landscapes from the Cretaceous Period.

They reveal the Flipside.

Now, thirty years after the first Turn, the clockwork is breaking down as one of the world's powers has decided to exploit the phenomenon for their own gain, possibly destroying everything then and now in the process.

A MAN OUT OF TIME
by Christopher Laflan

Five years after the Chinese Axis detonated an unknown weapon of mass destruction off the southern coast of the United States, Special Ops Sergeant John Crider and the members of Shadow Company have finally captured what they all hope will lead to the end of the war. Unfortunately, the population within the United States is no longer sustainable. In an effort to stabilize the economy, the government enacts the Cryonics Act. One hundred years in suspended animation, all debt forgiven, and a chance at a less crowded future are too good to pass up for John and his young daughter.

Except not everything always goes as planned as Sergeant John Crider finds himself pitted against a land of prehistoric monsters genetically resurrected from the fossil record, murderous inhabitants, and a future he never wanted.

www.ingramcontent.com/pod-product-compliance
Lightning Source LLC
Chambersburg PA
CBHW031947170626
46807CB00006B/2389